GP 32/23 Fic £3

SKiNNeR

D1440192

SKiNNeR

❖

HUGH C. RAE

Richard Drew Publishing
Glasgow

First published 1965 by Anthony Blond

This edition first published 1988 by
Richard Drew Publishing Ltd
6 Clairmont Gardens
Glasgow G3 7LW
Scotland

The publisher acknowledges the financial assistance of
the Scottish Arts council in the publication of this book.

© Hugh C. Rae 1965

British Library Cataloguing in Publication Data

Rae, Hugh C. (Hugh Crawford), 1935-
Skinner.
I. Title   II. Series
823'.914[F]

ISBN 0-86267-206-6

Printed and bound in Great Britain by
Cox & Wyman Ltd.

TO MY FATHER

" 'Which is the greater,' said Sancho,
'to raise a dead man or to kill a giant?'
'The answer is plain,' replied Don Quixote;
'it is a greater thing to raise a dead man'."

CERVANTES.

Part One

AUGUST

1

Paddy

HUNG-LIKE HE stops beside me, the spadeful tilted towards the ridge, his eyes hard as mica under the cap. Then he
goes on and throws, jerking himself round in the trench so
that when he strikes again his bloody elbow digs my ribs. All
down the line the boys are stopping to look. So I stop and look
too, innocent-like. With the afternoon sun low against them
they come down the road: four of them stepping out like they
was being dragged along by dogs on tight leashes. Only
Skinner works on now, his thick arms swinging. Dirt hits the
pile above me and dribbles to a dead stop against the big hard
pasty wedges from the topsoil under the macadam. Skinner,
naked to the belt, takes off his cap and swabs the running
sweat from his arms and back, chest and belly. He puts on the
cap again tipped forward over his eyes to shade them while he
stares into the sun. He leans his weight into the spade handle,
his boots stuck in the clay, legs spread. The worn brass belt-
buckle presses into his skin just under his gut. He doesn't seem
no different from the rest of us.

I see he recognises not just Niven. I reckon he knows the
sergeant that I talked to this morning and wish I hadn't:
big beat-faced cove, fat as a calving cow, giving me all the
blarney about duty and public welfare. And the thin one with
his jacket open to show off his milk-white shirt. And the old
one who looks as if butter wouldn't melt in his mouth. As

9

they pass above us, our heads no more nor level with their
ankles, the thin one glances down at us. Skinner cocks his
head back and smiles. They move on down towards the truck
in the lay-by at the middle of the digging. Jake, getting into
his jacket, is already on his way over to where he can meet
them. When he reaches them, Niven talks quiet to him. Every
man-jack of us watching. Without turning his head to the
side, Skinner spits off his tongue through tight lips.

"What'll be up with them now?" I asks of him, wanting
him to think I know nothing of it.

"Flappin' about a muff they found up in the woods."

He shoves away the spade, fishes a bashed packet of fags
from his bum-pocket and hands one over his shoulder to me.
I take it. I strike a match and hold it to him and he lights up.
He turns back to watch them.

"Dead?" I asks.

"Screwed t'death," Skinner says, the fag jerking in his
mouth.

I say, "Holy Mary!"

Skinner says, "Maybe it was, right enough."

I don't fly up in anger. A month I've been with him and
I know him. He comes from a good family too, though you'd
never think it.

I say, "How d'you know then?"

"Fergusson told me."

He leans his buttocks on the trench wall, keeping Niven
and Jake and the policeman in his eye as they talk. Jake shifts
away now and bawls out to us to get smartly to the truck.
Skinner pinches the butt, puts it behind his ear, then heaves
himself out of the hole and picks up his jumper from
the verge. I come out on his heels. The sweat drying on me is
stiff as another skin. I unhook my jacket from the bush.
Skinner has draped his pullover across his shoulders and
knotted the sleeves round his gullet. We can go over to the
truck. A lark flies up from the field ahind the hedges, its flight

and its song all mixed together and light as peat smoke spiralling up. It's as if the hedge was nothing but a wall of small green shelves, made special to catch and hold dust. The dockens and strapping plants of dog-flourish have dust on them too. Now that the strike of spades and noise of the cutter have gone the afternoon is fine and quiet. Nobody says much as we come up to the truck. The back road curves towards Pickering behind me and runs downhill straight to Arrowmill in front. Through a hedge-gap I see the yards and cranes and the towns all jumbled together firm and grey, stumbling up the hills, right into Dunbartonshire near enough. The green is new-looking like the green of Antrim, at the nub-end of August. I'm wishing I was in Antrim now. I wish I'd never come to Scotland in the first place.

Skinner stands beside me. I can hear him breathe.

"What's goin' on then, Paddy?" Lees asks me.

I shrug. "How should I be knowin' that now."

McCaskie behind says, "The boyos'll've invaded London and'll be roundin' up recruits. Are y'with us or again us then, Paddy?"

Another one laughs: then quiets. Niven climbs on to the flat of the wagon. He fiddles with his coat collar. Skinner takes the butt from ahind his ear and lights it as Niven speaks.

"There's been rather a nasty occurrence close to us here this morning," he says, in his lady's voice, rubbing the coat collar all the while. "The gentlemen with me are police-officers and'd be obliged if you could assist them in their enquiries."

The thin officer holds up his hand and Niven comes down off the truck. Under his breath Skinner says, "Booth." I bend my ear to him but he's looking front again and don't repeat himself. The thin one speaks in a normal voice, not shouting like Niven has done. His voice is smooth as honey.

"You've all been on this gang long enough to know the lie of the land," he says. "A mile down this road from Pickering is a section of forrested land."

"The Bluebell Woods," McKechnie shouts.

"That's the place," the thin one says, his eyes flickering over to the direction of the voice. "Behind that is a stretch of fields, pastureland, reaching back about a half mile to the old ford on the river. I take it you all know the place?"

Nodding heads: at least we're all listening.

"I had a sergeant round this way earlier today asking if any of you men had witnessed anything or anyone strange along here, or even in Pickering or Arrowmill, this morning on your way to work. It might have been a man, or possibly a woman. Anything unusual at all, in fact."

There's no answer from us. He lifts his chin higher.

"Sergeant Singleton tells me one or two of you have information that might be of use to us. Will any of you with such information please come forward."

I'm not going forward, not for no policeman, that I can tell you. That fat bitch of a sergeant didn't say nothing to me about bringing along a force. I just told him what I thought and he went off and that was supposed to be an end of it. The rest of it's none of my concern nor my wanting either. A terrible bad time they can be giving you if it enters their heads.

"We'll walk round the line," Booth says, after a pause. "You can put them back to work now, thanks, Mister Niven."

Niven nods to Jake. Jake tells us to go back to work. The line is buzzing like a wasp-byke. Nobody has asked who was killed. We all know. Skinner has gone ahead of me. I watch his back as he takes off his pullover and tosses it down at the verge. He sits with his feet into the trench while I slip off my jacket.

"An' did you see anything, Paddy, with your wee green Irish eye?" he asks.

"Not me," I say. "And even supposing I had would I be one t'go running t' the police with it?"

"Booth always did give me the boke," Skinner says, "I wonder what he meant about his sergeant."

I know then that he knows. Perhaps I shouldn've pulled back from going with him to the pub at the dinner-time, breaking the habit so sudden-like: not just me but the others too. Still, I'm not scared by the likes of him, having stood up to bigger and a bloody sight better in my time. I know what they tell of him: truth too. Things missing from the hut and from the truck cabins, and his never joining up with us in the mornings, but coming over the fields like a fox, from the boulevard at Carsehorn. He can do it as quick as we can in the truck by the time we fetch into Arrowmill and Bob brings the truck through.

"Think of that now," he says, swinging his boots, duffing the side of the trench. "Poor muff goin' and gettin' out of her depth. Nasty place that an' all. Over the fence and through the hedge, with all them trees. Ay, she caught more than she thought she'd catch, I'll bet. Was it some dirty old poxy bag, or what?" he says, staring at me, but I don't come up to his bait. He goes on, "Rotten t' the bone, lurin' a young fellah off the straight an' narrow path. Then when he got a sniff of it, wheesh . . ." he passes his hand across his face, smiling, "the red mist. D'you think that's how it was then, Patrick m'boy?"

"I know nothing about it," I tell him.

"Except what you think," he says.

He spits into the pit and jumps down. He leans his arms on the side wall and squints up at me, grinning.

"They'll catch who done it," I say.

"Yeah, they're mighty efficient our little busy-men," Skinner says.

The two dicks and the sergeant are working their way down the line. Having passed the cutter the cutter starts up again. I lower myself in beside Skinner. There's little enough to do before we move up to the next stretch. The pipes'll be brought out tomorrow. I lift the spade. Skinner's in no hurry at all. He has his back to me, looking along the level of the road.

"On the other han'," he says, "it could just as easy be a nice respectable upright man like yourself. Quiet ones is the worst. Y'never know where y'are with quiet ones. Then maybe she was a quiet one herself. A real bit of a teaser, playin' it up. D'you think that could be it then, Patrick? Imagine! teased herself t'death, in a manner of speakin'."

Though his face is hid I can tell he's not smiling any more. I hear his voice and the bark of the cutter and the birds in the field ahind us and the sound of the afternoon like faraway water. I'm trying not to listen to him. Up the line Lees is shaking his head. He glances our way. The thin bogey looks up at us too, then back at Lees. Munro is crouched by them, not in the ground yet. Skinner is saying:

"I remember a bit of gimp once in Cardiff when I was down there for a spell. A real hot bint she was, tits like friggin' melons. About eighteen she must've been. She worked in the place I worked and she'd been doin' the rounds of the men, but, d'you know, not one of them bloody Welsh nancies had cocked a leg over her, 'til I says t'myself, 'Right, Arnold. Right'. She didn't get comin' the game w'me, I can tell you. Not twice anyhow. We went away out t' this place in the hills, on a Sunday."

He stops suddenly, his upper lip curled back.

"They know me. Booth knows me, an' I know Booth," he says. "They always come t'me."

I don't make comment.

"Still an' all," he says. He squares himself to the trench and leans his back against the dirt. "Yeah, somebody yowled t'that fat sergeant."

"Yowled?" I say. "What?"

"About them," he says.

His fingers brush his face gingerly and the long fresh-opened scars that rake the skin from the temple to the hollow of his jaw start to ooze blood again.

"About these: eh, Paddy?" he says.

He lifts the spade and rams the whole heart of the blade deep into the dirt wall.

"Eh, Patrick?" he says again, terrible quiet, down in the deep of his throat.

2

Booth

SINGLETON SHIFTED about from one foot to the other as if he badly needed a leak. There is something vaguely indecent about a nervous fat man. I let him dance for a moment, until I had sealed the plastic bag with the shoe in it, then I said, "Well?"

Singleton replied, "There's an Irishman on the Water Board gang tells me that one of his mates turned up this morning bearing severe facial scars, consistent with . . ."

"Never mind the deduction, Sergeant," I said. I felt the hair over my collar rise very slightly, at the premonition of pleasure. Muirhead has told me often that I've no powers of observation at all, only sensitive hair. "Did he give you a name, this Irishman?"

"Said the man's name was Skinner."

I supposed I smiled. Muirhead whipped round from where he was kneeling by the scarred patch of mud.

"You said Skinner, Sergeant?" he asked. "Did he have a first name?"

"Arnold. Arnold Skinner."

Muirhead looked at me, and I said, "Are you surprised?"

Muirhead got up like the old man he is, saying, "Well, it's his neck of the woods . . ." he waved his hand, fly-swotting. "Facial injuries don't mean a damn' thing, not with friend Skinner."

"Of course not," I said. "No doubt he'll have a minimum of five folk ready to swear on their mothers' graves that they beat him up last night."

"I expect so," Muirhead said. "Are you going over there?"

"Let's all go," I said. "Arnold will appreciate a show of strength."

"It won't worry him in the least," Muirhead said.

"What does?" I asked.

We collected Niven, the contractor, who sat up front with the driver. We had the big car, and Singleton was spilling out of the jump-seat. I asked him for details.

"I caught up with this Irishman in the hut," he told us. "The other men had gone by this time. I gather that Skinner goes down to the town at the dinner-break, has a pint or two and covers the afternoon card, if he feels like it."

Muirhead interrupted. "Did the Irishman volunteer this information?"

Singleton shook his head, "Not exactly volunteer. He'd already denied knowing anything about it. But he altered his mind and sneaked back into the hut later and filled me in about Skinner and the scars."

I said, "You didn't actually see Skinner then?"

"He'd taken a truck back to the yard. He does some casual driving on the side. He's licensed for heavy lorries."

I knew that already. Last time we'd had dealings with him he was shunting sand at the Bellemount Estate housing scheme. That time we had him for armed assault. With three previous convictions and a juvenile record as long as your arm, he landed himself five years. Singleton, who hadn't been with us that long, asked, "He's inclined to this lark then: girls I mean?"

I said, "Since puberty. Before that he only damaged property, with a bit of amateur theft on the side. But after he found out what the thing behind his fly-buttons was really

for he decided to go in for indecent assault. That's his hobby:
house-breaking's his trade."

"I remember now," Singleton said, his face lighting up
ruddily with the effort. "The Edinburgh crowd were on to
him about the little girl Forrest's disappearance."

"Right they were too," I replied. "Skinner knobbled her
for sure, but naturally they can't prove a case against him.
As Skinner pointed out, she might conceivably have run off
with an Arab slave-trader. At fifteen she just vanished off the
face of the earth."

I wondered which was kinder to relatives to vanish so completely and utterly, or to wind up as a tangible fact like the
lass in the woods. Like a wooden doll flung hard against a
wall, yet with the skin hardly broken, just bruises and
thorn scratches on her face and legs, and one deep gash across
the back of her skull under the hairline. One of her legs was
drawn up, an arm out, palm uppermost, fingers curled in.
Under the nails there might be vestiges of skin. But that's
not for me to say, yet. The forensic boys can do what they
will, though I don't need a doctor to tell me that the blow
across the back of her head killed her. She may not have been
raped. I've been surprised before now: though her position
was one of complete abandon like the vamp on the cover of
a horney magazine, but frozen in death. If I'd stooped to
draw down her skirt, Muirhead would have thought me soft.
The blood means not a thing now, but I can never fully pre-
pare myself for the totally degraded look that a female corpse
has.

We came to him at last. The same Arnold: all insolence. The
gouges are so obviously fresh, curving out of the shadow of
the cap. He looks well, flourishing under the three thousand
pounds worth of police attention that's being focused on him
right this minute. The Paddy tries so hard to look as if he's
working. Skinner hawks and spits quickly with a quick side-

jerk of his head, like a snake striking. He grins at me and says, "How're you then, Mister Booth, sir?"

"Fancy," I say, "It's Arnold Skinner. I didn't expect to meet you here."

"I was here all the time," Skinner answers. "As if you didn't know."

"Been with this job long?"

"Long enough," he answers.

"How long?"

"Goin' on a month."

"Like it?" I ask.

Skinner heaves his shoulders. His cap is raffishly set and his arms hang loosely. The anxiety in him is canalised into alertness.

"How's your old man?" I ask him.

"Strugglin' along fine," Skinner replies.

Muirhead suddenly comes to life and begins to push a little.

"I wonder if you can help us, Arno?"

"Sure, Mister Muirhead, sir," Skinner says. "What?"

"About this girl . . ."

"Ah, a girlie was it?" Skinner says.

"Yes," Muirhead says sibilantly. "A young girl."

"Mucked about, was she?" Skinner says.

"Left for dead in fact," Muirhead replies casually, but, the trick's too decrepit and too crude and Skinner betrays no surprise whatsoever. Niven already told them she was stone-cold anyhow.

"What d'you want with me, then?" Skinner enquires.

"Just the usual dreary routine stuff, Arno," I tell him, trying to sound as apologetic as possible. "You wouldn't know a thing about it, I suppose?"

"Me! Not me. Sorry, sir."

His accent constantly changes. It is fake-polished, or fake-gentlemanly, with the true inflections of an ardent concertgoer, a Festival-addict, so that no matter the content it's all impertinence.

"You weren't in Pickering last night?" I ask him.

"I haven't been in Pickering since last Thursday."

"Not last night?"

"Nope."

Muirhead says, "Just as a matter of interest where were you last night?"

"You know," Skinner says. "It's bloody peculiar why there's three of you braids buzzing round me in my little trench. Have y'run out of constables at last?"

"Come on," I say, pleasantly.

"Pictures," he says.

"I presume you don't mean the Royal Scottish Academy."

"The movies, I mean," he says.

"Which one?"

"The Rialto."

"In Glasgow," Muirhead says.

Skinner nods. "It was rubbish they were showin' though."

"Go on, Arnold," I say. "Tell us the titles."

"Okay. One was 'Corridors of Blood' and the other was one about Al Capone. You know. Al Capone. They were both lousy."

Muirhead snorts. "Like night-school, wasn't it, Skinner."

Skinner treats us to a parody of an amused grin. "Funny man."

"We can check the times of showing," I tell him. "Did you go for a jar first?"

"A jar?" Skinner repeats, wide-eyed.

I feel the inevitable irritation, and quell it. "A drink," I explain. "A refreshment."

"Nope."

"What did you do when the film show ended?" Muirhead says.

"Went home."

"No drinking at all?"

Skinner smiles. "I had a cool Kio-Ora half way through. Out of one of them cartons that crack when you stand on them. I didn't keep it. I'm sorry."

"All right," I say. "You went straight home from work, had your meal, caught a bus to the city, went to the Rialto, saw the whole show and came out about half-past ten."

"Nearer twenty-to eleven. I caught a bus from the Square straight home again. And you didn't ask me if I met anyone I knew. Well, to save your breath for you, I didn't. Not a living soul."

The rest will be fairly predictable, and we go through it as smoothly as a well-rehearsed double act on television. I know it's bluff, as does Skinner. Neither of us are amused or annoyed by it. The questions and answers are skimmed over, without weight.

I tell him, "You were seen in Pickering last night."

He states, "No, I wasn't."

"I'm afraid you were, Arnold."

"Then your bloody informant's blind."

"You were in Glasgow."

"At the pictures. The Rialto."

"Someone's bound to have noticed you there. A bus-conductor, or a cash-girl or an usherette," I say.

"And if nobody remembers, what does that prove," Skinner says. "That I wasn't there, or that they've all got bad memories for faces."

"You never knew a girl called Harriet Calder?" Muirhead asks.

"I meet a lot of girls, one way an' another," Skinner replies.

I take one of the photographs which the next of kin gave me. "This girl." I hand the photograph to him. He takes it, not gingerly and studies it. It has no startling effect on him, but he doesn't dismiss it immediately. It interests him. His eyes blink without rhythm for a moment or two. I can feel a certain greed coming from him, almost as if he longed to have the photograph for himself.

"Harriet Calder," he says. "Is that her name?"

He returns the photograph to me. I retain it in my hand, visible. It shows the girl, Harriet, seated on a deckchair on the sands at Scarborough. She wears an attractive beach suit and a wide straw sunhat, tipped well off her brow. The picture is the most recent I could lay hands on. Taken only a month ago. I have others. In them she looks much older than her years.

"Never seen her in my life," Skinner informs us.

I say, "Thanks." To Singleton, I say, "That's about all then, isn't it, Sergeant." I hope the fat man has sufficient sense to notice the deliberate feed. Muirhead has the technique quite well. Singleton glances from Skinner to me, then to Muirhead. He glances back at me. "Well, sir . . ." he says. "I was wondering if . . ." The sergeant takes a deep breath and faces Skinner. Skinner is leering now, for it's all a game to him.

"The marks on your jaw?" Singleton asks blandly.

"I ran inta a fence," Skinner answers.

"Inside the cinema?" Singleton asks.

Skinner addresses himself directly to me. He ignores Singleton completely, and Muirhead too. His voice is muted, careful but not wary. "On the way home I got off the bus at Sandspit and cut over the field. It's quicker. And there was this bit of barbed wire, some bugger'd strung up between two trees. I was lucky it wasn't an eye away."

"Spoiled your good looks rather," I say. "It would be too dark for you to know where this wire was exactly."

"Nah. I know where it is. You want me to take you there." He leans towards me. "Fix it with Jake so's I can get off now and I'll take you there."

I shake my head. "It won't be necessary, Arnold. I think the Water Board need you more than we do, for the time being."

"Take you tonight, if y'like," he offers eagerly.

I say, "Well, it would really be a bit pointless, Arnold, wouldn't it. Since you weren't in Pickering last night, and you never met Harriet Calder. Obviously you can't assist us. It must have been someone like you that was wandering around the town."

"Sure," Skinner said generously. "I've a common sort of face."

"See you again," I say.

"Right," Skinner says.

We move off a pace or two. Skinner strolls to the trench and hops down into it. The men further up the line watch us with the sort of concentration that is totally unnatural. Skinner takes up his spade now. Muirhead mutters, "Five years inside haven't changed him at all."

We walk towards the car. Singleton has gone on ahead to open the door for us. He is too heavy to make a satisfactory lackey. I turn and stare once more at Skinner who hasn't moved yet. I can see only his head above the earth, immobile, almost tranquil. Between us there is a bond of excitement. And that I hate.

"He hasn't changed, on the outside at least," I reply to Muirhead.

We climb into the car. Singleton heaves in after us and slams the door.

"Perhaps it wasn't Skinner after all," Muirhead remarks.

Muirhead is an old man, well past his prime. Shabby and almost meek. In another year we can put him safely away in mothballs. He even smells of mothballs now, faintly, of mothballs and stale pipe-smoke. I don't need him. Singleton will do, at a pinch. My voice is sharper than it should be as I say to Muirhead. "Perhaps you think she did it herself, just for the hell of it." He makes an eye at me as if I'd punched him in the gut, then sinks down into one of his moods, not even angry.

Like an old man sulking over an injury which happened in his youth. I want to get back to the station quickly. There is much to be done.

3

Muirhead

BOOTH ORDERS the driver to put his foot down. The car shoots forward away from the site. I'm tired of Booth. I'm tired of all this now. He will work all night. The beaters will cover the range of the river, hunting a weapon that won't give us so much as a clue. If only the routine could go by the board and we could wait for the lab report to tell us what the body had to say. It's odd how the victim always manages to gather a harvest of clues for us to find. She should have gone for his eyes, but she didn't appear particularly robust, though I was never much good at telling from a corpse what the person had been like in life. We have her mother's word that she was just a normal, healthy girl. The lab may contradict her. Mothers have been wrong before now.

A superb day, as close as Scotland can come to Indian summer. It seems wrong, doubly wrong, to take a human life on a night as soft as last night was, when the moths came into the kitchen in droves, batting their soft bodies against the light bowl and plastering the window pane like flakes of soiled snow. There must have been lovers in the pastures on a night as soft as last night was. Lots of them, thick as daisies on the grass under the trees. But they won't come forward. I think they think we're up to something evil, to judge by their holding back. I have no patience, now.

How does the phrase put it: A composite picture of a

criminal act is the end-product of patience and accumulation of detail.

The poor lass may not have been raped at all. The knickers are missing, of course, but he could have used them to sop up the blood, then buried them. Perhaps there's a hint of fetishism. Booth won't accept early mention of character defect, not even as conversational hypothesis. I can understand his attitude of mistrust. A crime is a crime, just the same as the Paris woman said A Rose is A Rose is A Rose. A factor cannot be a cause until it becomes a proven motive. One dead girl. The motive is desire, twisted out of shape. The end no more than the gratification of several inseparable instincts.

Suddenly Booth speaks to me. "We can drop you off at Carsehorn, if you like."

I tell him no. I tell him that the sun has given me a slight headache. He says, "Maybe you're hungry."

He fishes an apple from his jacket pocket and holds it out to me. I refuse. He then offers it to Singleton who's obviously interested and accepts it with grateful alacrity. Singleton's teeth crunch on the hard fruit and Booth seems gratified by the sergeant's appetite. He doesn't speak to me again.

There is no link between the girl and the killer: nothing between them at all but a couple of hours of mutual boredom or loneliness. If it was Skinner it wouldn't even be premeditated. Surely he must have enough knowledge of himself to realise what he was letting himself in for when he took up with her. If he did take up with her. A young girl, not pretty, but at least warm and alive, showing a shade more bosom in her summery dress than was maybe quite prudent. Only waiting a kiss and a cuddle on the stargrass under the trees. I might be wrong. She may have been an animal too, hot, chaffed and greedy for it. There are so many possible patterns.

I make a remark. "The medical report should help us."

Booth grunts. "Unless the family comes up with anything."

"They didn't have much to offer this morning. Perhaps when they get over the shock. . . ."

"We'll have to lay hands on whoever saw her in Pickering. She wasn't invisible."

Singleton wipes cider from under his lip with a large knuckle. "You'd think they'd be seen together."

"It happens—if we're lucky," Booth said. "After the press break the story we may have a witness or two. More than we can stand probably. And the usual shower of nuts."

"We'll keep other avenues open, in the meantime," I say.

"Of course," Booth retorts. "I know what I'm doing."

"No one's criticising," I tell him. "But I think it's wrong to have an *idée fixe* about Skinner."

"We can do without the Latin," Booth says. "I'm bloody positive that Skinner's responsible for doing the girl, but I'm not going to garrotte him with my own bare hands. Not that boy. He knows his rights. He's not the type to stand for any messing around. Not once we stop amusing him and begin with serious pressure."

"He'll go all outraged," I say. "I remember the performance."

Booth kneads his eyelids with finger and thumb, and sinks back into the soft upholstery. He must hate Skinner. It's almost unethical the very way he stares at him out of the hooded lids, as if he'd be willing to scatter twenty years of law enforcement to the winds just for the pleasure of sinking a knife into Skinner's belly. The lean, scraped face, and the cold, cold eyes of Booth, which go one better than making a man feel guilty by making him feel despised. He smiles like an alligator.

I continue, "We can't tie him in with anything we have at the moment."

Singleton says, "Unless your friend Skinner's got the dolly's panties tacked up behind his wardrobe door, like a war souvenir."

Booth laughs curtly then slides into his comfortable moroseness again. He will be thinking of how many stones he can turn over. I've no stomach for the labour now. God, I wish this headache would go away. I should never have invented it.

Singleton cranks down the window and shoves his apple core out into the wind. Sucked back it smears a streak of juice upon the polished glass. Booth doesn't bother to chide him. Booth is almost asleep. The car swings neatly into the Main Street and we go on up it at our customary exhibitionistic lick.

4
Nora

A LOVELY piece of meat: smells as if it cost a fortune, but
it wasn't near as dear as I'd expected. Arnold'll love it with a
couple of eggs on top and a tin of peas. He'll pat his belly,
giving me a wink and a nod. If I don't want him waddling
like Gertie's husband I'll need to be keeping my eye on him.
He's not like his Da. There's always been enough lean on
Joseph. If Arnold doesn't heed my words though, he'll be a
right tub in five years. It tells on a boy, when he gets out of
his twenties. Still what with him shovelling all day in the
fresh air he has to have something nourishing to fill his
stomach of a night. He's looking better than I've seen him
since he came out of that place. It was that place shot him
up from being a boy to being a man, but not in the way a
mother likes to see it happen to her son.

The woman told me it was his upbringing had done it to
him. I didn't hardly understand what she meant, but I'm not
to blame myself for the trouble Arnold was in. How could
it be me, I mean. She was wrong: her that never had a man
or sons of her own. I know all about their training and all
the rest of it, doing this for them and that for them. They
couldn't even keep him there, never mind sort him. Every
minute he was in that place and I lifted the phone or saw the
black car coming into the street, or the two bobbies at the
gate, I'd know it wasn't me had made him turn out as he was

doing, but them. Just the very look of them places they put
him in was enough: not even as decent as a jail but all black
stone and men in sports-jackets with pencils in their pockets.
Thursdays and Sundays going up the path through the
grounds towards the black school building I got the same bout
of the horrors I had that day in the cemetery when I was tidy-
ing Mammy's grave a year after she'd passed on.

Rosemary's back with the bread and scones from the dairy.
She hangs up her coat in the hall like a good girl. The kitchen
smells good with the cooking meat. I hope she got the loaf
sliced as I told her to, or Arnold and him'll tear it to bits as
if they'd never saw food before. She comes in.

"There's your change, Mam," she says.

She got the loaf sliced like I told her to. The fat makes a
clear puddle on top of the blood in the hollow of the steak.

"Phoof," Rosemary says. She never did like the smell of meat,
even as a baby. That'll be why she's thin as she is, and forever
feeling the cold even in the summer days. She steps up to the
sink edge and pushes open the top of the window to let the
smell out. Joseph'll be able to niff it now as soon as he comes
round the corner.

"Did you not see your father, Rosemary?" I ask her.

"No," she says.

She rattles a plate from the cabinet and opens the bread
poke and takes out butter from the cooler and the hollow-
handled knife and spreads the slices.

"Don't be skimping it now," I tell her, though there was
a time not so long since when I had to insist on the opposite.
I fetch the peas from the cupboard and open the tin with the
gadget Arnold bought and screwed to the wall for me. I tip
the wet green heap of peas into the pot and set it on the gas.
Rosemary is awful quiet.

"And what's wrong with you, Miss?" I ask her. "Did you
have to take the tawse to one of your pets today?"

She stays quiet, buttering the fresh white slices of bread.

I put the handle of the pot to the wall, and spoon fat into the pan. It hisses and spits. Rosemary is quiet. She picks up the plate and puts the bread on it and carries it ben the room. It's warm in the kitchen here right enough, and her time of the month always did make her sorry for herself. She comes back.

"What's given you the sour face?" I ask her again.

"Nothing," she says.

Having secrets is Arnold's trick, not like our Rosemary at all. If some man's bothering her and Arnold finds out, he'll sort him good and proper. That'll be why she's keeping her mouth shut, in case Arnold finds out. The air is heavy. I stir the peas, and the meat's near done. If the pair of them waste half the night in Kerrigan's and this dinner spoils I'll give them licks when they do come in.

She goes into the living-room again with teabread from the bin. She doesn't come back so quick. I leave the stove and go into the living-room. She's sitting in the armchair reading the paper, her legs drawn up under her, the paper on the arm of the chair. I see big headlines but I haven't time to bother, with the dinner on the go. When I ask her to set the table she looks up and nods her head. There's something far back in her eyes, but how am I to know what she's got in her mind if she won't tell me. It's something you can never do, if you're a right and proper mother to them, and that's make them give up their thoughts to you, if they don't want to. I leave her, knowing she'll do what I've asked her to. I'm on my way through the hall when the door opens. I don't need to look round to tell that it's Joseph. His boots clank on the loose scraper, and he kicks the door shut behind him.

"Smells rare," he shouts, while he takes off his cap. He enters the kitchen and throws his bag on the chair.

"Time you were painting that chair again," I tell him.

"Get your crippled son on the job," he says. "I've had my share of doing things round this house."

He pushes past me and nips my rump to make me shift

over and let him into the sink. I take the towel from the string above the stove and fling it where he'll find it when he gropes for it, his face all soapy from the basin. He washes himself loudly enough for the neighbours to hear, splashing everything. I slip the big plates out of his way. I'm not having him taste the steak with carbolic. He hasn't turned down the collar of his jacket and suds skim the seam of it.

"You're a right mucky devil," I tell him.

Through the towel, blowing, he tells me what to do with myself. He keeps two suggestions, one for me and Rosemary and one for Arnold. He's still got enough sense never to get them mixed up.

The meat is near cooked. I take the tray of baked potatoes out of the oven and put it up on the high grill to keep warm.

"Are you ready for this?" I say.

"Am I no' just," he says. "Did you want t'wait for Arnold then?"

"Will he be long?"

"How in hell's name should I know?"

"Rosemary's through there. See if she's set the table."

He nods and goes on through. Out of the kitchenette window I can see about half a yard of the road between the gables of the houses and our front hedge. I watch out for him coming. Through the house I can hear Joseph and her talking, then the clink of the plates.

Rosemary says something, then Joseph says something. Rosemary speaks again.

I see Arnold's head over the hedge, moving fast.

Joseph barks loud enough for me to hear, "You'd better not say that again in my house, girl."

I go through the hall, and stand at the living-room door and ask, "Say what?"

Rosemary's setting the table, got as far as the cutlery she has. She takes the bread and teabread from the top of the sideboard and puts them down. She doesn't look at me. Her face is flushed, and her mouth has that hard pursed look she gets when she's trying to be angry instead of crying. I say to him, "What have you been telling her now?"

He pokes through the envelopes to see what letters have come in the post. A note from Sadie and the gas bill is all he finds. He puts them under the candlestick again.

"I never said nothing to upset her," he says. "She's got some daft notion in her head about . . ."

Arnold comes in through the front door. Joseph clamps his jaw tight, sits down in the armchair and lifts the paper. Arnold goes through the hall past me straight into the kitchenette to the pan and hangs his nose over the smell.

"I hope y'didn't waste it with flour," he says.

I come through the hall again as he says this. Behind me Rosemary goes upstairs and the bathroom door closes.

"I was cooking meat before you were thought of," I tell him. He glances round at me. I see the marks on his face. Inside me my heart leaps up, pressing against my shoulder. I go to the sink and for no reason look out at the sunshine.

"Have you been fighting again?" I say.

He stands behind me and curls his arms round my waist.

"Not on your life," he says. "It was a bloody hunk of barbed wire: that was all I was fightin' with. Mind you, if I'd've got my hands on the bugger who put it there, there'd've been bloodshed okay."

I turn round and put my hand on his chin, lift his head up to the light. The cuts are narrow and deep. He's washed them and dabbed them with something. I remember finding the iodine bottle out of the box. If I'd got up to give him his breakfast this morning I'd've seen it then. The cuts've been bleeding a bit. Then I don't know it didn't happen to him at his work.

"Last night," he says. "I was late comin' home. I came over the field."

"Is it sore?"

"Nah." He shakes his head, and I let his chin go. "I heal quick, so you always said anyhow."

"Get through then," I say. "Your Da's been waiting for a while for his dinner."

"Do'm good."

"Get through with you," I say.

He goes in to the living-room. I serve, and take the plates through. Arnold is at the table, already eating a slice of the buttered bread.

"Where's Rose?" he says.

"Upstairs," I say. "Give her a shout."

As I go through to fetch the plates, I hear Arnold bawling from the living-room door, "Grub's on the table, Skinny. Come an' get it."

I come through again and put the dinners down, and go back to brew the tea. Arnold and Joseph are already eating. I infuse the tea and come back with the pot on the mat under the cosy, and stop to shout for Rosemary myself. I don't know what's ailing her. I shout and tell her to come down. She opens the bathroom door and I hear her going in to her own room. I go in to the living-room and put down the teapot on the table and sit down. The meat's cooled just a bit too much already, but it's tender enough. I should've had some onions with it, either that or gone ahead with the eggs as I'd intended. Still, Arnold's tucking in to it with appetite enough.

In spite of all the times I've told him Joseph has his paper plastered over the sugar-bowl and the sauce bottle. He eats. Not a manner I like, a lazy man's way, holding the fork in one hand after cube-ing up his food first as if it was for a babby. It's no use talking. Papers are dirty things and shouldn't be brought to a table. Still, it's his house, and a man should be able to do what he wants in his own house. That's one thing Mammy always used to say. She let my Daddy have his head even in the matter of the drink, right up to the day he was killed.

Rosemary runs downstairs, comes into the room and is in her chair. She's washed her face and done her hair up right with a ribbon, but she still has that flushed feverish look that I don't like at all. I'll need to keep an eye on her. If it's some man annoying her: at the school. I didn't go scrimping and saving for three years just for her to get into trouble with some man who'll look down his nose at her after it's too late. I can't tell her a single thing now, it looks like.

"Were you on anythin' the day?" Joseph asks him.

Arnold swallows before he speaks. "Nope. I didn't get a chance t'go down. The busies were fleein' about."

"Ay," Joseph says. "I had the feelin' they might be."

"What for, Arnold?" I ask him.

I can't take the potato at all just now. It sticks at the back of my throat. "Was it you?"

"No, what?" he says.

Joseph says, "A girl was found murdered in the woods at Pickering. It's in the paper."

"Yeah, Booth was up, and Muirhead," Arnold says, eating away. "Askin' questions."

"Did they get anyone then?" Joseph says.

Arnold shakes his head. He puts down the knife and leaning back slides his dirty plate on to the sideboard.

"They came an' asked me," he says.

He takes a coffee bun from the plate and bites into it. "Pour the tea, Rosemary."

She's picking at her food, but then she never did fancy meat much. She pours the tea for us all. Joseph folds up his paper.

He says, "So they asked you then, did they. I'm not surprised really."

"If anythin' goes on round here, they expect me t'be in on it," Arnold says. "Just because I had that bad time early on, when you was moving round the country."

"Ach," Joseph says. "Busies are aye the same."

Rosemary rises, lifts her plate and mine and her father's and takes them into the kitchen.

"I don't think Rosemary likes to hear about it," I tell them.

Arnold looks up at her as she comes into the room with the hotwater-jug.

"Is that what's botherin' you then?" he says.

"Yes, Arnold," she says.

"It's just . . . life," Arnold says.

He shrugs his shoulders and sips his tea, blewing on it first with the cup to his lips. Joseph gets up and takes his tea over to the fireplace, putting the cup down on the bottom ledge of the mantelpiece. He takes my cigarettes from behind the clock, lights one and sinks down into his chair like an old man. He hasn't taken off his shoes so I know he'll be going out again soon.

"What were they after?" Joseph asks. "Did they have somethin' t'follow?"

"They were runnin' round like headless chickens," Arnold replies. "Did you not want us t'talk about it then?" he asks, smiling at Rosemary.

"Did they ask for you in particular?" Rosemary says. She's watching him close now. I don't like this feeling between them, as if she thought he had: as if she thought he wasn't going to tell us what they said. It's not his fault they won't let him alone.

"Booth made a bee-line for me, because he knows if anyone can tell him anything round there, it'll be me. It's hard for busies t'get anythin' concrete out of that bunch of peasants. Christ, if y'dropped dead in the middle of the hut not one of them buggers'd notice 'til it came your turn t'make the tea."

"What did he want with you—specifically?" Rosemary asks.

"Showed me the dame's picture—the same one as's in the papers," Arnold says. "He wanted t'know if I'd seen her about the place, or anything."

"Y'didn't though," Joseph says. "You wouldn't've been the one t'tell them if y'had."

"Ay, I would," Arnold says.

I know he would now. He gets on well enough with that man Booth, in spite of what Booth did to him. Arnold's like that. He'll never hold a grudge against anyone. He knows what he done was wrong, but it's all in the past. If he could only meet some nice girl, and get himself married and settled down, I'd be happy.

"I'm not against them, Da," he says. "But I didn't."

"That was all?" I ask.

Arnold nods. "Well, naturally, as you'd expect they quizzed me about the marks on m'gob. But I told them what happened and they went away."

"Just as easily as that," Rosemary says.

"Yeah," Arnold says. "They went away. They'll catch who done it. Ought t'bloody nut the bastard too when they find him."

"Don't say that, Arnold," Rosemary says.

Arnold gets up suddenly.

"T'hell," he says. "Ever since you went t'a fancy school and learned how t'be a teacher, you've turned wet."

He takes his comb out of his pocket.

"If you can't even stand t'listen t'me speak then I'll go somewhere that m'company'll be more appreciated."

He isn't angry with her. He's just telling her, the same as Joseph told me about letting him live how he liked in his own house.

Joseph says, "I'll walk up with you. If that's where you're bound for?"

Arnold combs his hair in front of the mirror.

"That's the place," he says. "We'll pick up the latest there. Sam'll maybe know if there's any suspects on the slate yet."

"Put on your other jacket," I tell Joseph. He looks a right sight beside Arnold.

"What for: t'spill beer on?" he says.

Arnold says, "You're not spillin' anythin' I'm payin' for."
They go out together and slam the door.

Rosemary sits at the table with a cup in her hands looking
at it as if she was reading the leaves.

"You shouldn't be talking to him like that, Rosemary," I
tell her.

"No," she says, without looking at me. "I shouldn't, should
I."

I pour another cup from the pot. It's the first fresh cup of
tea I've had since breakfast this morning after they were all
away. I take it over to the fireplace and sit in my chair. I see
the paper lying where Joseph left it. I don't know if I want to
really. I lift it and look at the headline. It says: Dead Girl
Found Near Lovers' Lane.

There's a picture of the soul too. I pity her Mammy tonight. I know a bit of what she's feeling, but I knew that
Arnold was coming back.

Poor woman: it's not a thing I'd wish on anyone. A dread-
ful thing to happen right enough, especially slap on our own
doorstep.

5

Joseph

I SAYS, "You don't want to worry about your sister."

And he says, "Nah, she's not the girl she was before you gave her an education."

I says, "She'll be married and away from us before you know it."

And he says, "She's acting queer enough to have found herself a man."

He turns it like a question, so I tell him I don't know if she has or not. He tells me he reckons it'd be a good idea for her to get herself married and settle down. He says something about Nora wanting to be a Grandma, and looks at me then away. I tell him I don't care one way or the other whether I get to be a Grandpa or not. I'm in no hurry at all for that sort of honour. We walk on through the long sunshine under the bridge and out on to the Brig Road. The walls of the cable works, painted in the Spring there, catch the sun full on, like a picture of France. The cows in the field are all lying down, except one that's standing with its face over the fence gobbling long grass from the verge. I hear doos in the trees making soft noises and the traffic over on the Boulevard. It's a place to live this all right, what with the breweries and the steelworks all mixed up and fields and houses and the tall chimneys together. I didn't know where I was at for the

first while: but it's a place to live, just like any other. And
farming's a good life.

It shows what they're thinking. Even Sanny hinted at it.
I'd have took it from none of the rest of them, but even swearing at that old bastard's like pouring water on a duck's arse.
Rosemary is of the same opinion as them, underneath. That was
what she meant and why should I pretend it was anything
different. Once they put the mark on a man it surely sticks.
I didn't put the mark on him: though I'll share the blame
if it comes to that ever. If only she hadn't said that to Nora
about him. I know Nora'll not forget it. Still Arnold was
never one for rubbing our faces in it. I'll say that much for
him. When he did that series of jobs, I knew it right away.
He had no calling to lie to me. It's one of them things that
exist between him and me that you don't get between a man
and a woman, nor even between a son and his Mam, in spite
of what they say. There's not many can tell their old man all
they've done wrong either, no matter what, and trust him to
stick by them with it all the way through. And he won't
hear a word against me. I've seen him take it from Booth
about himself, as much as the rotten bugger could dish out,
and just swallow it all, but when it came to starting on me,
no, Arno wasn't standing for that.

It wasn't fair on Nora either. I know she fretted about having us both inside at the same time. I'll have to bear the bur-
den of him, just to keep it off her. I always did after my way,
and neither the two of them can argue against me on that
score. Still, it's over now: the taking. It never was an old man's
game anyhow, say what you like. He can gang his ain gait
without me poking my neb in. I'll do what I can for him. But
it's his own life to lead; though, God knows, I'll stand by him
if the needs arise.

I says, "Did Booth give you a roughing up then?"

And he says, "I told you all that."

I says, "I thought it was maybe just a story for their benefit."

And he says, "You know Booth better'n me."

"He's right up on your back then?"

He says, "If it wasn't my back, it'd be some other bugger's."

We walk on, not hurrying any, without talking for a while.

"If they come round to the house," he says all of a sudden, "it'll maybe set Mam off again."

"Do you think they will?" I asks.

"Public enemy number one," he says, tapping his lapel.

"At least they'll not be able to hook you in and give you the ride round from shop to shop," I says.

He grins: "Christ, give's a chance, Da. I'm only three months out. Fun's fun."

"You've seen McNally though. I didn't know...."

He says quickly, "My nose is clean."

"I didn't mean that," I says, "but I want you to keep an eye on that McNally. And that bitch Ruby an' all."

"Ach, Ruby's all right," he says.

I'd like to ask him for a couple of straight answers, but I don't want him to think I'm sticking my neb in. She was a tidy-bit of wench, if her photo's anything to go by. He sees my looking at him.

"I wasn't in on it," he says.

"I never thought you were: a thing like that," I tell him.

"I can get jags aplenty without goin' in for that stuff," he says.

I say nothing, because he has said those words to me before, the night Booth was down on him about the Stone girl's complaint. Maybe there is something that makes him want to have them that funny way. I've had experience of it too, but there was aye a streak in me that denied it, said no to it: always the block to stop me when it came right down to it. Though I wouldn't have minded trying it—once. That's part of the beauty of getting on in years, it's all behind you, all the messes you're not going to get yourself into again, all the harping for what you know you can't risk having. Ach, they'll bawl their frigging heads off at him and that'll be the end of it.

He's not afraid as I was at his age. He's got a bit of iron in him that I didn't have. It's something to do though, worth more than all the tuppenny-ha'penny jobs. It's a man's right to take what he wants, if he knows what he wants and realises that if he takes it at the price, it'll be nothing but take, take, take from then on all the way down the line. They don't know how it swells up until it takes the place of even being frightened of it, or mindful of them. Some of us still aren't bloody beggars. It sounds like cold thunder in you, just cold thunder.

They'll have me too, if it comes to the bit. Spread us all out and trample on us. That's what Rosemary's scared for, in case they fling her out of her precious school. She's afraid for herself, like all women. I don't mind if I lose the farming job. Jobs on the land is ten a penny. I'm not afraid for myself. If he had to, then he had to, and all I can do is try to let him know I understand it better than he'll give me credit for.

There's not many have the privilege of going on past themselves.

"Don't let them worry you, son," I says.

"Well, we've nothing to worry about, have we?" he says. "At least not with me. They imagine I'm just another stupid punk. They mark me down as bein' the same as you were. . . ."

I says, "You're not though. I'll be the first to admit that."

And he says, "Give me a while t'get back on my feet and I'll show you."

"That's right then," I says. "You don't let them frig you round like they done me."

As we come to the yard at Kerrigan's, he puts his hand on my elbow and stops me before we can go through the doors.

"I'm up on them all now," he says. "Right up, head an' shoulders with the rest of them."

He pushes me gently towards the doors, and we go in to the warmth together.

6

Booth

S O W E C A N just about tear up the lab report. We found the girl friend Harriet was supposed to have an appointment in Pickering with, but that did no good. The so-called friend had gone off with a boy instead. Simplification does not set in. The Press can go on yapping about early arrest and print all the speculative junk they like. I know they won't have an early arrest.

If only the corpse had told us something. It seems almost unfair that the girl herself couldn't accomplish the automatic act of self-defence. And the weapon is still missing. I can assume from the total lack of evidence, that Skinner had plenty of time.

Blood had come from a scalp wound, coagulation helped by the mass of her hair. Death fifteen to twenty minutes after the blow. Interestingly meaningless bruises around her throat. She was probably conscious when the fatal blow fell. According to simple geometry she'd been beaten while lying face down on the grass. Muirhead can place all sorts of obscene constructions on that, if he likes. The body had not been moved, though it seems she was chased through the wood. Yet the damage to the brush wasn't nearly extensive enough to suggest that she was panic-stricken. Anyhow Skinner would have caught her much earlier than he did. She was three hundred and forty yards from the road. The shoes she'd been wearing stood neatly side by side against the base of a tree, eighteen feet from the body towards the lane. The single discernible footprint five and one half yards from the corpse, was her own.

She was not a virgin, was not pregnant and had not been engaged in sexual intercourse on the night of her death. No rape. Slight bruising in the hollow of her groin had been caused by the pressure of a thumb. She had eaten nothing since her evening meal four hours before. Nor had she taken drink.

The handbag, the underwear and the weapon are missing. Frogmen working the river in the region, up as far as the Pickering viaduct, found nothing.

The girl-friend, Marion Walters, had arranged to meet Harriet at The Noah's Ark café at half-past nine. Marion Walters hadn't turned up. She'd gone dancing in Paisley with a newly-acquired beau. But Harriet hadn't been seen in Pickering, not positively, though three people vaguely recalled seeing a girl in the vicinity of the Market Cross around that time. Almost certainly she hadn't lingered at The Noah's Ark café. The proprietor claims he would have noticed her if she had hung about outside. He knew her well enough by sight.

The only break came from three boys who'd been sky-larking about the ruins of an old paper-mill about a mile out of town. They'd noticed a girl, almost certainly Harriet, at something like twenty-past nine. Time means very little to young boys, but they seemed sure. She was going towards the river, to the tow-path. The boys left shortly after and we have no way of knowing if she returned by the mill to keep her date with Marion at the café (and she would have been late in any case) or if, for some unknown reason, she continued up river to the iron bridge. The fact that no road leads from the bridge across the meadows to the lane, doesn't mean that she didn't take that route. She could have crossed the fields, which were dry after the drought. Taking the evidence of the boys as valid, she didn't meet Skinner until she reached the path by the river.

If Skinner sat out the whole show in the Rialto then he did not kill her. The field at Pickering is too far for him to have reached there by eleven, the latest time at which Harriet could have died.

Though not a virgin, I can't quite picture Harriet Calder as immoral enough, or stupid enough, to meander over fields at gloaming with a total stranger. She knew him. She knew Skinner. And somewhere, at some time, they were seen together.

I worked the warrant to remove clothing from Skinner's house. With ten days grace of course, Skinner had got shot of anything incriminating. The panties weren't tacked behind the bedroom door.

He worked up a fine show of outraged innocence. The woman, and old Joe, protested too: the latter with his customary vehemence, dragging in the class-thing, shouting about "Us dirty fascists rubbing a poor honest farmer's nose in the dung." (Which I'd love to have done.) For the entertainment of the neighbours at the gate, Arnold gave out with his favourite beef; his debt to society being paid in full, chanting his piece about how a dog's bad name is at cross purposes with all the shit he'd had rammed down his throat in prison. "Is this your bloody rehabilitation," he shouted. I told him it was. The clothing was clean.

The Irishman was the first, and he looks like being the last, to really open his trap and tell us what he thought of Skinner. And that's odd, for the Irishman couldn't stick it out. Two days after we took his statement, he took off like a baby rabbit and as far as I know is now peering out of the sod in County Kildare or whatever wilderness he went back to. Skinner did that: the power of his reputation, or the weight of his threats.

I've had nothing from the underside. They don't like it any more than we do. It breaks up the smooth flow of trade.

Besides there's an element involved which offends their lax moral code. They detest a rogue in their midst. The sex-killer is alone. He hunts by himself. He has nothing to sell, and nothing to run away from. At all times, his crime goes with him. All the lags can tell you is if any of the madness shows through, like bones bursting the canvas of a rotten sack. They know, these criminals, that I'm not combating a scuffler, or a payroller, but the unpredictable, invincible malaise which has finally taken Skinner over, making him heedless of his neck. Perhaps Skinner and I have a common enemy, perhaps even a single purpose. To exterminate the familiar that hides in his head and feeds, from time to time, on the poor bastard's addled brain.

7

Paddy

THE ROAD comes up ahead, rushing at us. His hands hardly seem to be touching the wheel at all. He just grips it when it leaps, and it leaps too often for me to be happy. The springless lorry holds down at the back with them damn pipes and the cabin as light as a feather shakes us up like two beans in a bottle. He foots the brake pedal for a second as the bloody contraption jars over the rise, to shoot us round wide to the side wall of the viaduct. He's spoken barely a word to me since we left the yard.

The long straight stretch, dipping twice in a couple of miles, rolls out right to the railway bridge now. At least he has it in top. If he can't hold it then he can't hold it. He sits back against big McLuskie's stained pillow as if he was driving along easy in a dog-cart or something. If he can't hold it then there's little enough I'll know before it goes over. If he's waiting for me to beg him to stop then he'll wait a while. It's one of his games, this hurting people.

Sweat glues my shirt to my back as the damn wheels shudder against the verge and run dunting over it and along it, long ragged twigs off the hedge slashing the fender. He cuts off and draws across to the middle of the road again. I feel as if we was being sucked down it, then shot up not to come down this time but to go straight in to the air, the tread biting on nothing at all, 'til we turn heavy and lazy like a big bird bulleted on the wing, and crash full tilt into the fields: everything bursting wide, us bursting, with the big round roll and bound of them pipes all over us.

I got one hand on the windscreen, the other round the frame of the seat under me. He tries to urge the truck forward again, as if it was a bloody horse and not an engine and four wheels at all. I pray to Jesus he can judge the bridge corner: a bad one, snicking in a tight zig-zag with the span in the middle, half hid from the turn too, on this side, by the high wall. He wants me to plead with him, so's he can crow after.

"Paddy," he shouts over the noise.

I don't pay him any heed, even when he turns his head and looks at me, and me watching the road expecting to see some of the others coming back or a car or a van or a woman with a pram or something. The wheel kicks up at him and he fights it down again with his fore-arms.

"Patrick," he shouts.

"What is it?" I say.

"Why did you have t'go an' tell them?"

"What!" I say.

"The busies: about me," he says.

"Who did that?" I shout.

"You did, you sneaky Irish bastard," he shouts, grinning with the corner of his mouth.

"I never did," I say.

"It's a big wide world, Paddy," he says. "See more of it before your time comes."

"See more of what?" I say.

"Look," he tells me, nodding ahead.

"There's nothing coming," I tell him.

"D'you never stop t'think of all the nasty things can happen to a man workin' round here," he says.

"Never," I say.

"Gettin' run over by one of them wagons, standin' too close to a pick when it's on the fall back. . . ."

"I've a habit of being a careful sort," I tell him.

"Pitching out a lorry at a speed like this," he goes on. "It can happen to the best of us."

"So it can now," I say.

"What did y'beef t'the busies for?" he says.

"I never beefed t'anybody," I say.

"Booth told me it was you," he says.

"You're a bloody liar, Skinner," I tell him.

"Some bloody black whore beefed t'the sergeant," he says.

"Who'd go an' do that now?" I say.

"You did, Paddy."

"An' what if it was me?" I say.

I take my hand off the window and leave it loose by my side ready to block him if I have to.

"You shouldn't've done that," Skinner says.

The lorry snatches at the top of the dip. The load pushes us right into the dust and the tyres don't contact for the first two yards over the brow: then we're past it and climbing again without slowing at all. The pipes behind us go groaning and clanking against the ropes, all through themselves.

"You did that girl," I say to him.

"Sure," he says. "But neither you nor Booth's goin' to be able t'do a thing about it. Because I'm too smart for you all."

"How do you know I'll not tell him?" I ask.

"He knows fine well it was me," Skinner says. "Why d'you think he was down on me as fast as he was. He's a friggin' toad, Booth is, but he knows enough t'be sure that if I'm round he don't have t'look far for the man he's after. I've led him some dances before this, an' I'll lead'm some dances again, for a long time yet.'

"What did you kill her for then?" I ask him.

"Try it some time for yourself, Patrick," he says. "Then you'll know what's in it."

"They'll catch up with you," I say.

"Catch up! How in hell d'you make that out? They've

nothin' t'catch up with, for I'm not runnin' anywhere, see?"

Then we take the second dip. He hasn't slowed at all, and we hurl over it, coming to ground with a crack that'd break your bones. Even above the roar of the engine I'm near deafened by the noise the pipes make, like the echo of tambourines trailing away behind us. Just at the crest before we fork down I catch a squint at the bridge about a half mile on, then it goes behind the trees and I see only trees, and the fence sort of warped and blurred.

"Did you know the girl?" I ask.

But he's not telling, either that or he doesn't hear me.

I close my eyes, and open them again, blinking to clear my vision. The inside of the cabin is rank, and I can smell my own fear, a bit like the smell of sweat. We're running into the sun now. It lies flat and direct, glazing the dirty glass, so that Skinner has to take one hand from the wheel and hold his arm crooked over his forehead, grasping the wheel low on its arc near his belly. A killer's hands keep me alive. He gives me a quick look, enjoying my fright.

"Shittin' away there, Paddy," he says.

I tell him to shut his mouth. He opens his mouth and I can feel him laughing though I hear no sound. His tongue is pink and soft and his teeth white. The oil on his hair mingled with sweat had made a sort of greasy stain along his brows, so that they glisten bright-like when he takes his arm away.

"Wait 'til y'see this," he shouts, pointing the lorry as we come out of the final long curve to the bridge, pointing the lorry straight at the wall out of which the bridge breaks right.

He stabs the pedal, hauling on the wheel, feeding it round fully from hand to hand with his elbows jutting high. I see the wall straighten and whirl away, streaming beside me for a second as he takes us down the middle of the span; then the next wall mounting up left, scrubby trees toppling over it and faded blue sky above and ahind. The hands braking us, pulling the thing round and away across to the opposite side. It seems like the lorry isn't turning at all really, not as you know a lorry to turn, but sheering away at a tangent like a panicky animal. The clattering of the load and grate of the wheels on the rough edge as the bridge meets the track again say that we're through it. The road lights up where the bar of shadow of the banking stops and the sun falls full on it; plunging down into the light.

"See," he says.

Far ahead's the scab of the trench and the flare off the sheet-metal hut, and the other trucks drawn up. A crane to the left of us turns slow like something coming round to look at us, over the half-built wall of flats.

Skinner begins to brake the truck down gradual.

"Think about it, you black Irish bastard," he says, hard now.

I nod my head.

When I take my hand off the edge of the seat, it's shaking like with the ague. The shaking works all through me, and I curl my boots under my calves to stop my heels drumming on the floor.

Jake stands in the middle of the road, stiffly wagging his arms like a traffic policeman. The lorry crawls in, stops, starts again through a three-cornered turn and stops facing the un-loading bay. Skinner sits back and takes a fag out of his pocket. He lights it.

Jake comes round and opens the side door.

"Christ, you didn't waste any time, Skinner," he says.

Skinner says, "Are y'bitchin' about it then?"

Jake shakes his head.

I open the door on my side and swing down and go round the front of the lorry. Skinner stands with one hand against the radiator, leaning, the fag in his mouth. Jake has his back to us, shouting to the men at the hut to come over and shift off the pipes.

Skinner looks at me, his head held back and the cap tipped over his eyes in the way he favours.

"Sling your hook, Patrick," he says under his breath. "I'm tellin' you."

He doesn't see it coming, so he doesn't have no chance of meeting it with his thigh. It feels as if my arm sinks knife-like up to the elbow in his gut. The fag and a dribble of spit fly out of his mouth as he doubles forward, his eyeballs starting to roll and his body squirming round my feet.

I hit him again on the throat with the blade of my hand and three or four times down the heart-side in the time it takes him to fall. The front of the lorry holds him up for me and I could have hit him quite a bit more while he was still open and sliding if Jake hadn't grabbed me. They're running over from all quarters. I watch him double slowly, peeling away from the grill. His cap falls off and he follows it, like a clownman trying to catch it again on his head before it drops to the ground. I stop myself using the knee on his face. He rolls over, face into the dirt, one hand flung out, the other holding his guts together.

"For Jesus Sake!" Jake says. "What d'you go'n do that for?"

I don't look at him. We stand together looking down at Skinner at our feet. Fergusson kneels beside him.

Then I'm going towards the hut, with Jake coming after me. I go through all the men looking and into the dimness of the hut, and take my bag from the hook and my coat.

I say to Jake, "I want my cards."

He puts his hands on his hips, blocking my way to the door. He says nothing while I look at him, then he nods his head.

"All right then, Paddy," he says. "We'll go up to the office and get them."

"Now," I say.

After a minute, he says, "Now."

We go out again and over to the ganger's van. Munro comes

and says something about Skinner to Jake and Jake waves his arm. Skinner is still lying there, his cap under his head and his face to the sky. Someone's taken his boots off.

I climb into the van and Jake gets in ahind the wheel. When we draw out to manoeuvre for the Pickering road, I see Fergusson and Munro at feet and head carting the bastard over to the tap.

Jake shakes his head and laughs.

"By Christ, Paddy," he says, "you really laid him out."

He glances at me out of the corner of his eye.

"Whatever your reasons was, you really laid him out."

I don't say anything. I just want to get my cards and get shot of the place. I'm not obliged to tell him nothing, nothing at all.

Part Two

OCTOBER

1

Ruby

THE STEEL buttons on his blazer shine as if he was winking them at me through the smoke. He waves his hand and, holding the jug up in one fist, starts to come over. Then he stops, points at me and at the bar, asking me what I'll have. I make a mouth, but he doesn't get it right first time and I repeat the performance. He understands, nods and smiles and pushes back to the counter still holding his jug up carefully.

His hair's near as thick as mine, and near as long, though he keeps it neat, waved back with scented grease, shiny too. Only his eyes never seem to shine : like scuffed leather buttons.

Some bitch has been at him, that's a certainty. The claw-marks haven't quite faded away. Some scrawny slut he's banged against the wall, dragging her talons across his cheek to make him think he's thrilling the steam out of her like smoke out a funnel. I suppose it's the mouth makes him so heathenish, or the way his legs bend like a jockey's. I can picture him in a pair of Nazi jackboots and riding breech things, jodhpurs. The shiny leather plastered round his calves. Good for clamping his legs round my waist while he brought my rosebuds up without his tongue entering into it, full bags nesting in my navel like two eggs. He's strong too, the same Arno : not like bloody comrade McNally there, with his dirty bones sticking into me and the wee sacks of grey fat hanging under his ribs like rolls of sour dough. He knows nothing either, humping on and in and humping away to light himself a fag. Not worth the living with. And I wouldn't be living with him either, but a woman's got to have someone to look out for her, and keep a roof over her head. I never did fancy the streets much, not now that I'm getting on a bit; and not with my feet. Even that night after the job at the jewellers in Kirkavon he was too bloody lazy to arch his backside off the bed. He considers himself a great thinker, does Mike. Thinking all the time about the next job he's going to pull, fretting about it. He tells me he gets quite wore out thinking about it. Lazy big lump of sow-dung. Look at him over there with Arno, laying it all off as if it was the Bank of bloody England he had his eye on and not some cardboard bungalow up in Rendall that you could sneeze your way into without being spotted.

I wonder if Skinner's thinking about the girl. He'll have to be thinking of something just to keep himself awake listening to my old man drivelling on for everyone to hear. Not that Arno's exactly the strong silent type. But at least when Arno talks it's worth hearing, which is more than can be said for Mike McNally.

If I could work him round to it right maybe he'd tell me all about it. I mean all about everything. Mike says it's true. I can believe it of him, in a way, but I doubt if it really was him. People you know never do things like that. If it turned out to be him, he could tell me it all, while he did the same to me. He wouldn't need to go the whole hog, of course. I'd let him hold a pillow over me, breathing and prodding, like underwater. I can still remember that lovely sailor in Portsmouth all those years back at the beginning of the war. Spoiled me good and proper, he did, strapping ankles and wrists with his leather belt. I kept on ripping his arms with my nails until he squeezed the cap over my face. It came over me in black and red waves, all the while his hands were feeling me. I'll say this for him, he treated me well. A

real rose, he said I was, and admired my ruby lips. A perfect
gentleman—away from the mattress, my sailor, not like
Mister George Black, my bloody hubby. Still that was the reason I let George marry me, so I can't complain now if it didn't
pan out. There are too many damn gentlemen in this world
like George: gentlemen because they haven't the guts to be
anything else. George called me a rose too: his flower, and,
by God, fluttered round me like a virgin butterfly, frightened
I was going to wither under him. His Mammy must've
been a right straight-laced old cow. He was just like a boy
wanting to pore over me with the light on, brushing me with
his hand occasionally to keep the dust off. The night the
bomb blew the lamps he held a candle over me as if he was
an undertaker laying out a corpse. I can see him to this day
in his A.R.P. Warden's bib and Wellington boots going over
me slowly, the candle held aloft, then when a blob of hot
wax dropped on my belly and I let out a yelp he was down
on his knees near crying with repentance. Ay, it drained all
the spunk out of him too, and he went off to soothe himself
playing darts in the shelter, leaving me to get dressed and
trudge down to the coalhole with the cantankerous old bitch
from across the landing.

I wonder where George ever got to. One thing, he never
married her. He can't have or I'd have heard whispers
from him asking me for a divorce. After I pawned the ring,
he packed up and took wee Sally to his mother's place in New-
castle. It was him that did it, not the poor wee lamb, in spite
of what I told McNally at the time about me being sick of
looking after a bairn. It near broke my heart in two, taking
her to the school, then going away to phone George at the
factory to tell him he'd better collect her himself because
I was getting out for good. Crying on the phone too, he was.
But he never came to try and coax me back, though he knew
fine well where I was and who with. He was too busy crying
out of pity for himself.

It was a good year with McNally that first one, when he was labouring on the farm out at Pickering. He would come home at night burned and hard, pretending to girn for me all the time he was eating, pretending to butter my backside with his knife while I served him. And when he'd done eating he'd fling me on to the bed. About as old as Arno is now Mike was then, and I was still young for all I'd been around a bit and carried a bairn.

Arno leans across my shoulder and puts the glass down in front of me on the mat.

"Gin an' bitter orange," he says. "An' how's it goin' with you, Ruby?"

I give him a toast.

"Jogging along, Arno, and yourself?"

He sinks half the pint.

"Can't complain."

"I heard you had bother with the busies last month?"

"A . . . misunderstandin'," he says, grinning.

I can tell by Mike's face that he's narked at me for asking Arno straight out. To hell with him though. Arno doesn't mind. We're all friends here. I say, "Who was it?"

"Booth," he says.

He swings out a chair and sits on it, leaning his arms on the back, the flat ale slopping over the glass, 'til he tilts it back and drinks again.

"A right bad bugger," I say. "He'd have nothing on you, of course?"

"Arno's not here t'have you chewing his ear," Mike says.

"Away," Arno says. "Let the woman talk, Mike. That's their pleasure in life."

"I was just saying that Booth's not exactly the best kind of blueboy to deal with," I say.

Arno nods emphatically. "A bastard."

Mike rubs his nose with the edge of his hand, which is a

sure sign for those as knows him well that he goes to say something he thinks is daring.

"Was it . . . was it the Calder girl then?" he says.

"Fine well you know it was the Calder girl," Arno says.

"How did he tie you in with that then?" Mike says. Now that I've brought it up, Mike's not wasting his chances.

"Christ knows," Arno says. "Maybe he thinks I'm the type."

"But you're in the clear now, anyway?" Mike says, managing not to sound too worried.

"Clear as I'll ever be," Arno says.

He finishes his beer and pushes the jug over to Mike who, after giving himself a minute to try and think of a way out of it, goes over to the counter for refills.

I shout and tell him I like gin and bitter orange. No sense in not having it when it's going. Arno's got his eye on me. I wish I could read him like I can read Mike. If I thought he had that sort of thing in his mind, I'd give him some encouragement, but then again I don't want him to be running away with the idea I'm a soft mark, or one of his quickies. The marks on his face show white against his tanned skin.

"Well, I'm glad you're out of it," I say. "And out of the place an' all. I missed you when you were in there."

He gives me a cigarette and leans over with the light. He looks at my face and not down my blouse like the others do.

"Three years is a long time right enough," he says. "Still. it's a risk you've got t'take if you want to get anywhere."

"Next time it'll be longer?"

"A friggin' sight longer," he says.

"If you don't mind me asking," I say. "Have you got anything lined up?"

He turns his head to me, and I see him looking at Mike over at the bar.

"I won't say a word to him, y'know," I say.

He comes back, as if he hadn't been listening to me at all.

"What! No, I'm workin' on the water board just now, up at Pickering. That's how Booth got on t'me in the first place. Just because I was in the neighbourhood, trying t'do an honest day's labour—now there's a confession for you if you like: me workin' like a bloody peasant—anyhow some friggin swine told Booth about me bein' there, and havin' marks on my face, and that was how he came t'be down at the house."

"What bit of fancy stuff gave you the lovin' tokens, then?" I say.

"Lovin' tokens," he says, grinning like a young boy. "Them's barbed wire marks."

He tells me some story about walking into a fence in the dark, which I don't believe and he doesn't expect me to believe. Then he starts talking fast about Booth's coming to the house and how much it upset his Mam with him only being out of the nick for three months and all about how much trouble he's had because of it up at the Pickering site. He has his worries too, I suppose. I always think he's fit to take care of himself, fitter than many another, but I suppose he has his worries. If it wasn't him that killed the Calder girl, then the bogies have a sin to answer for. It's all you can expect from them, persecution. My Mike's just been lucky. Four times they've had him and three of those times he's got off scot free. Then they had him in for three months because he punched some drunk in the face in the Armour Bar. He was rotten with drink himself at the time too. That's the way it goes. You make a living one way and they pull it out from under you another. Now if Arno hadn't been inside himself then, we could've had some fun.

"You must come up t'the house some night, Arno," I say, watching Mike pick up the beer and start back.

"D'you still bake them rolls, and them brown scones?" he says.

"I will if I know you're coming," I promise him.

"Comin'; who's comin' where?" Mike asks. He puts the drinks down careful and goes back for mine.

"What about him?" Arno says. "Has he anythin' special on the books just now?"

I nod. "I'd better not let on though. I think he'll want to work round to it in his own way."

Arno shrugs. "He can suit himself. If it's good an' safe I might be interested. But I'm not playin' for funny any more."

"You never did anyhow," I say.

"Too bloody often I did. Just doin' a job on the spur because I was hard up. No more of that lark," he says. "I haven't got another five years t'waste."

"Ay, it's a thought, when they've had you up already," I tell him.

Mike gives me my glass. We all drink. Mike sits down beside me and starts eating the packet of crisps he's brought with the drink. I reach over and help myself to some of the big ones. "What was that you were sayin', Arno?" Mike asks.

"I was sayin' it's a hopeless caper just doin' jobs when it comes up your hump."

"Planning: I've always advocated it m'self," Mike says.

"More than just settin' up a break-in somewhere," Arno says.

"Ay, I know what you mean," Mike says. "But y've got t'be careful these days. I mean you know as well as me that if y'pull a job which brings in a couple of hundred quid the busies won't bother their shirts much, but if you get off with a couple of thousand then they'll set the dogs on y'good an' proper. I mean a lot of wee jobs pay better in the long run than the big hit when you've got t'lay low for a year nor more after it."

"You did all right out of that jewellers," Arno says.

Mike's jaws grind to a stop like a machine run out of petrol.

"What jewellers?" he says.

"Ach, come off it now," Arno says and slaps him on the shoulder. "I know the whole story."

"Did you tell him?" Mike snaps at me.

"Ruby didn't have t'tell me," Arno says. "Everybody knows it was you."

"Do they now," Mike says. I can see that he doesn't know whether to be glad or sorry that everybody knows it was him.

"That's the bloody trouble with this town," Arno says. "Y'can't keep nothin' t'yourself."

"Well, it's all in the past now anyhow," Mike says.

"So it is," Arno says. He sucks at his glass, leans forward, "But what's in the future, Mike. Will y'tell me that?"

Mike glances to right and left, hunches his shoulders forward. If ever a man managed to show he'd something secret on his mind, then it's my old man.

"Y'know that big spread of bungalows up an' down the hill at Newtonard?" he says.

Arno says, "Ay."

Mike goes on at a quiet rush, "Well, I've got one or two picked out there. Good stuff in them too. None of this cheap junk, clothes and watches. None of that muck at all."

"Hard cash," Arno says, pushing out his under lip.

"An' some stones. I've got a new place to get rid of stones," Mike says. "So it's just a case of hangin' off until the places is clear, then hittin' them."

Arno says, "How many places?"

"Two," Mike says.

"Y'mean you've got two in mind. You're not just goin' up there on spec?" Arno says.

"Naw, I've got two, near each other an' all. Could do them both at the one time."

"When'll they be empty?"

Mike says, "I can't tell y'yet. I'm just waitin' for information."

"Is this another'f your dreams, Mike?" Arno says.

"Was the jewellers a dream then?" Mike says. "I ask you, was the jewellers a dream?"

Arno waves his hand impatiently. "A'right, then," he says. "So you've a couple'f places lined up."

"How about yourself?" Mike says.

"Nothin'," Arno tells him. "I'm open for offers."

Mike glances at me. I know he's got it in his mind to ask Arno, he told me as much, but he's not wanting Arno to come in and run the whole show. It's already too late not to ask him, so I nod my head, looking at my gin.

"There's these two," Mike says.

"Will it be worth it, though?" Arno says. "It's a'right for you, but if I get hooked again. . . ."

"Not a bloody chance," Mike says. "An'it'll be worth it."

"Where d'you get your news?" Arno says.

Mike says, "That's my business."

Arno sits back, holding the jug in both hands, swirling the beer around in it. He sniffs, grins a bit, says, "D'you not trust me then, McNally?"

Mike says, "It's not that, Arno: it's just that . . ."

"Y'don't trust anybody," Arno says. "Ay, you're quite right an' all."

"Are y'in with us?" Mike says.

"I'll think about it," Arno says.

Mike nods.

"Who all's in on it anyway?" Arno says. "Just you'n me?"

"An' her," Mike says.

"Ruby," Arno says. The thought of me being in on it too doesn't seem to fill him with any joy.

"Ay, me," I tell him. "Who d'you think's been holding the bag for the last five years."

"You, was it," Arno says. "I thought maybe you'd found somebody else."

"Nobody else," Mike says. "Just me an' her."

"That's fine then," Arno says. "I'll think about it."

"Don't strain yourself," Mike says. "We don't need you along, y'know."

"Just doin' me a favour, eh?" Arno says.

"That's right," Mike says. "A favour, for old times sake."

"Suits me," Arno says. "I'll let y'know."

Howie comes in. At least suddenly he's there, shifting over from the counter with his half pint jug and the big smile on his face.

"Here's your friend, Arno," I say.

Arno looks round, sees Howie, looks back at me and winks. Mike has a face like thunder. Howie and my old man never rub each other right. Anyhow it'll not be Mike that Howie wants t'see but Arno. It's always Arno. All the time Skinner was inside, all you could get out of Howie was Arno this and Arno that. If Howie'd been a woman he'd have laid down and spread his legs for him long ago. Still, he's young enough to learn. What'll he be, about twenty-two or three. God, his wife's not twenty yet, and her with two bairns and all. At least that's one way of making sure he knows where she is of a night. He's got his natty shirt on tonight and the blue suit, and his eyes are shining as if he'd polished them special just because he knew Arnold was going to be here.

"What does this bugger want?" Mike says, not troubling to whisper.

"He'll be wanting to see me," Arno says.

Howie comes over and puts his hand on Arno's shoulder. In the light, proper voice he says, "By Christ, Arnold, it's good to see you again."

"Sit down, Howie," Arno says. "What are y'drinkin'?"

"I'm fixed thanks," Howie says. He smiles at me and Mike. Mike doesn't say anything. Arnold hauls forward a chair and Howie sits down.

"And how was it inside then, Arnold?" Howie asks eagerly.

"I don't think I'll tell you," Arno says, grinning at me and Mike. "Then it'll be a nice surprise when your own time comes."

"What?" Howie says; he draws his brows together. "What do you mean, Arnold?"

Mike laughs, coughing, then laughing again. Howie doesn't know the score. He's not daft enough to think it's not him we're laughing at, but he'd rather be laughed at by Arnold than buttered up by anyone else: poor daft young bastard. He'll learn. Mike gets up, tilts his jug and pours the rest of the beer back over his throat.

" 'Mon, Ruby," he says.

"Are y'goin' already?" Arno says. "The night's young."

Mike puts his hand across his belly and rifts a bit.

"Bloody beer they sell in here," he says. Then he does that thing with his mouth that makes him look like a horse. "Makes y'randy though." He grabs me round the waist and half covers my breast with one hand under the coat. I lean right into him, off balance on my high heels. "Does it make you randy too, dear, eh?" he says.

Arno's looking at him and at me steadily. I wonder if he's wishing it was him. I wonder if he knows (fine well he knows) that McNally's nothing but a big bag of wind and piss. Randy. He hasn't been properly randy for the last five years.

"See y'around then," Arno says, without getting up.

"Ay; y'can let me know," McNally says.

I just get a chance to give Arno a smile and a wink, before the clumsy big oaf pulls me away home to watch the telly. Randy! God, that'll be the day. When I turn at the door, with Mike's arm still round me, I see Arnold and the boy Howie talking together as if they really had something to say.

2

Howie

I KNEW he was getting out about now, but they wouldn't tell me just when. None of them like me of course. I can't fathom out why, not actually having done anything like. Just working day in and day out. But it's okay for them, without a family. Now if I had his nerve, it'd be all right. It's just a question of starting on the right foot.

"Still running the railway, Howie?" he asks me.

"Still at it," I tell him.

"Lost your ambition?" he asks me.

"No," I tell him.

"You're in the best place," he tells me.

"I know," I answer. "But it needs a big outside organisation. Some of the blokes do it regular."

"What's the staffing like down there now?"

"We've moved," I tell him. "We're in a new office in Swiggart Street. Makes no difference really."

"How about dicks?"

"Well, there is a regular and a night patrol and you have to keep an eye out for the bosses, but others do it."

"What d'you handle?"

"Everything: clothes, radios, T.V. sets."

"Small stuff?"

"Sometimes. Cameras and watches," I tell him.

"Could you lay something on then?"

68

"I'd need outside help to get rid of it," I tell him.

"That could be arranged," he answers.

"Well, I'll need to see."

"Still scared, Howie?" he says.

"I am not," I tell him. Now is the time I've got to ask him if I'm going to ask him at all. It came along much faster than I thought it would.

"You haven't quit, or anything?" I say.

"Christ, what for?" he answers.

"I just thought, what with you being in and doing a bit and all," I say.

"Balls," he answers. "What's on your mind?"

"I've got a place lined up."

"A railway property?" he asks.

"No, a private house."

He makes a long face. I thought it would be up his alley. It was always houses and shops he did before. I hope he hasn't lost his nerve or anything.

"You're sittin' on a pile of friggin' jack a mile high an' you want t'do an outside job. You're a mad bastard, Howie. Green as a cabbage."

"It's a good one," I tell him.

"I'm not interested," he says.

"Please, Arno," I tell him. "I've been waiting for you to get out. It's right up your alley."

He sighs. He pushes his glass over at me. "Your shout, lad," he says.

I go over for another two pints. I pay, and go back through the thin crowd at the counter. Two men have sat down at the table next to ours. One of them's got a long nose. He keeps looking at Arnold as if he knows him. When I come to the table and put the drinks down I know he's sizing me up too.

"Can we go outside?" I say, giving him the beer.

"What for?" Arno says.

"I want to talk to you."

He has noticed the two men as well. They seem awful interested in us. In half an hour it'll be closing time anyhow.

"Drink up then," Arnold says. We drink the beer fast.

When we get outside the air is cool. It's almost dark, with a spit of rain, or maybe just dew, but it's a fine pleasant night otherwise. I can smell the fish and chip shop from halfway down the block. The street isn't all that busy: the pictures aren't out yet, and the dancing's gone in. It's an in between time.

"Which way?" I ask him.

He turns to his left and starts to stroll along towards the park. I walk beside him.

"This marvellous job of yours," he says, suddenly. "How much is in it?"

"About five or six hundred quid," I tell him.

He glances round at me and raises his eyebrows. "In cash?"

"Maybe more," I say. "I can't tell exactly."

"You mean some clown keeps this much in the house?"

"Just at certain times in the year," I tell him. "Are you interested?"

"I might be," he says. "Tell me anyhow, since you've been savin' it up all this while."

Some kids come at us suddenly out of the park gates, girls in shorts and blazers with tennis rackets. One of the boys is on a bike. They're laughing and shouting and don't look at us, but I don't say anything until we go past them, past the gates and round into the quiet by the railings.

"They're not bothered with you," Arno says. "Are y'goin' t'tell me or not?"

"Well it's one of them bigger detached houses up in Abbotshead. In the Abbotshead Road."

"I know them," he says.

"The bloke's a joiner."

"Come on now," Arnold says. "A joiner don't have that much ready cash."

"He has a business," I explain. "Anyway, he pays out himself every Friday noon, but he draws the money from the bank in the morning then."

"So what," Arnold says. "I thought this was a breaking job. Scufflin's not in my line."

"Sometimes though he takes the money out and keeps it in the house, overnight."

"That's bloody nice of him," Arnold says. "How d'you find out?"

"Never mind. I'll swear it's the truth."

I don't want to tell him in case it comes back that Larry had anything to do with it. I mean, it's not that they could do anything to Larry, 'cause Larry didn't know that I knew someone who'd be interested. I mean Larry doesn't hardly know me.

"Jesus Christ," Arnold says. "Are you goin' t'tell me, or d'we forget the whole thing?"

"What do you want to know for?"

He stops, grabs the railings round the spikes, and bends his head in against them. I think he's going to be sick, until I hear him laughing, thick and quiet into his chest. Then he lifts his head and says into the bushes. "Howie, you don't think I'm goin' t'stick my neck out an' risk pullin' a big job like this's unless I can depend on the information. I mean, d'you think I'm bloody nuts or somethin'?"

"I know, I know," I tell him. "But the gen's okay. I'll swear it is."

He turns right round and leans into me as if he was really drunk.

"Tell me," he says.

"My wife's cousin's man works in the bank that give him the cash."

"Right," Arnold says. "Now we know where we stand."

"Are you game then?"

"This ... this banker bloke, did he tell you because he thought ...?"

"I was there when he told my wife. He was bitching because he thought Matheson was being stupid keeping all that money in the house."

"Right," Arno says. "D'you know anything else?"

"Like what?"

"About the house?"

"I've had a look at it. I reckon you could get in no bother. It's got a lot of trees round it for one thing."

"Does he keep the stuff in a safe?" Arno asks.

"I don't know. Larry says he doesn't think so, but I just don't know that."

"Matheson's the name: what's the address?" he asks.

"Seventeen Abbotshead Road," I tell him. "Are you going for a look?"

After a bit he tells me, "Nah, it's not my line either."

"Aw, come on, Arno," I say. "I can't do it without you. You know that. How about taking a look at the house anyhow."

"No go," Arnold says. "But I'll keep it in mind. McNally ..."

"God, I don't want to bring McNally into it," I tell him. "I want to do this with just you and me. Six hundred quid. Three hundred each. It's a year's living near enough."

"Too risky," he says, and I can tell by his tone that this is final.

He turns across the pavement from the park and goes over to the lane up by the garage that leads back into the top of the High Street. Now I've got him this far, even though he won't help me, I'll maybe just carry on. He might feel he owes me something anyhow.

"There's something else, Arnold," I tell him. "I want a gun."

He's lighting a cigarette and looks up at me through the cup of his hands.

"What d'you want a gun for, Howie?" he asks me.

"I just do. Can you get me one? I mean, have you got one or anything?"

"This isn't a job for a gun," he tells me.

"Never mind the job, I just want to have a gun. Any kind of gun."

He spits into the air. "Planning on blasting your barnacle?"

"What?"

"Killing your wife," he says, sneering at me quite openly now. I don't care.

"No, I just want to have one handy."

"Look, you don't just go keepin' guns lyin' round the house," he says.

"How much'll it cost me?"

We're coming up into the High Street again. The shop lights throw down big patches of yellow on to the pavement, and there are a lot of couples about.

"A tenner, maybe more," he says.

"Okay," I say. "I'll give you a tenner if you can get me one."

"It might be more," he says.

"That's okay. Where'll I see you?"

"I'll see you round, in one of the pubs," he says.

"When, then?"

"I'll let you know when I get it. D'you want me to bring it round t'your house?"

"No," I tell him. "My wife doesn't like people comin' t'the house, not now we've got the kids to get t'sleep."

"Kids," he says. "How many've y'got, Howie?"

"Two," I tell him. "A boy and a girl."

"Very nice," he says. "I'll let y'know about the gun."

3

Ogden

I MET him for the first and last time in the early part of October. I know it was the early part of October because I was home on leave, embarkation leave at that. A couple of weeks after I seen him, I was off to Malaya for a two-year tour, so that's how I know when it was. Another way I have of knowing: that was the last time I was ever in the Alexandria Club, and met Sydney Faith face to face. Sydney was dead before I got out of the Army.

I knew when I went that night I only had so much money to spend. It wasn't all that much either, come to think of it. What the hell, I thought to myself, here you are being dragged off to the back of bloody beyond, to some stinking jungle, you may as well get rid of the bloody money before you go. Then, I thought maybe my luck would be in after all because it was going to be my last bash at it for two whole years. But Mrs. Luck wasn't in. Still, I liked the place and I liked playing cards enough not to worry if I happened to be losing for a spell. I only had about three or four quid left, and I still maintain that Faith knew this and that was why he brought him over to me.

I was playing at the far table, through the billiard hall behind the curtain, like in a cowboy picture. There were three others and me. I only knew one of them, Campbell his name was, a well-off sort, lawyer or doctor or something. The other two were the kind you never ask about, not even their names, so I don't know who they were. Anyhow right in the middle of a good round when Campbell was fattening up the pot and I was holding a high prile, Faith comes up behind me with this bloke. I'd seen him too, once or twice, and I thought it must've been at the Club but I wasn't sure. I knew they were there and I remember thinking that I didn't want to play a five-hand even though I was sure by that time I had the strongest cards. They were behind me and it was me they was watching. You get to be able to feel things like that after a while. I waited on Campbell to call me for a Show and when he did, right enough, my Three beat his Three, so I won the pot. I felt better then, and turned and said to the bloke with Faith, "Are you keen to join us?"

"Fair enough," the bloke said. He nodded to the two johnnies whose names I didn't know.

Campbell said to Faith, "Send up a fresh pack, Sydney, will you?"

Sydney went away and sent Rafferty over with a fresh pack of cards. We started to play again. The change of pack broke the rhythm and I started to lose again. I was losing all round, but not much to the new bloke. You would hardly know he was there. He put out his Ante and held his cards close but that was about all. When he went in on a hand, everyone else cleared off and left it to him. He must've raked in a good bit that way, but he didn't really play, if you know what I mean. Then, with Campbell dealing, I picked a good pair, sat on it to the draw with Campbell and the new bloke at me, I held Kings and a stray Ace. I had dealt another Ace and a Rag. I went on. Now I know I shouldn't have gone on but Campbell after sizing up the situation with a raise folded out and the new bloke and me were left at it. I thought: you've been getting away with murder, fellah, meaning him, and I thought I'd have a do at him with what I had left just to see if he had been pulling the wool. I might've won on skelps after all. It turned out he had a good prile. That was goodbye to me. I was cleaned out. I got up and said finish, and that I'd see them in a couple of years, then the new bloke got up too and said he'd had enough, did anyone mind if he chucked it. Well, as it was my money he had, none of them put up any complaint, even though it was leaving the game short-handed. I went out through the corridor to the bog, and he came with me. He came right into the bog with me, and while I stood pissing away and feeling like a mug for having blown the whole lot in a couple of hours, he comes out and says to me, "I hear you're in the Army, is that a fact?"

"Right enough," I say.

"Y'hard up?"

I shot him a look, wondering what his game was. I didn't have to wait long. I reckon Sydney Faith must've told him that I was all right. Anyhow the next thing is he comes right out, bold as brass and asks me if I've got a gun I'd like to sell him. Now nobody knew about that bloody gun, I'll swear to that on a stack of Bibles. Christ, if my father had found it he've flayed the hide off me just for bringing it into the house. I got it off a Corporal when I was billeted near Shrewsbury. He was an M.P. too, and I don't know what the hell he was doing with it just lying about or where he got it from but he came up to me in the NAAFI one night just when I'd finished winning a Tombola jackpot and asked me if I was interested in firearms. I said no, then I changed my mind because I thought it might be nice to have one just as a keepsake and guns aren't the sort of things you can really pick up all that easy, unless you go out of your way to look for them. I've had my chance at one or two since, but I never bothered. Anyhow, I told the Corporal okay and he met me in the old bogs at the back of the band-room and we did a deal. I only gave him a couple of quid for it, maybe three, I can't remember right as I'd been boozing a bit. My first week's leave after that I brought it home, because I didn't want to have it lying around the camp what with inspections and all that bullshit. I wrapped it up—there was about a dozen bullets with it too, though they looked pretty dud to me—and put the whole lot away inside an old jig-saw box among the junk on top of the wardrobe in my room, at home. I didn't even tell my brother Robby about it, because he's just the sort of irresponsible nit who'd take it out the back-green to shoot sparrows with. So this bloke in the bog at the Alexandria Club had a lucky break: I did have a gun and bullets for it (somehow I reckoned he'd want one he could fire) and I didn't have any cash. I'd lost interest in the weapon anyhow what with going away to Malaya for three years and all.

"What if I have?" I said. "What's it got t'do with you?"

"I'm lookin' for one," he said.

"Are you now," I said. "What for?"

He took out a packet of cigarettes before he answered and offered me one. I took one and while he was lighting it for me, he said, "We've an old Spaniel bitch at home, rotten with all sorts of things and stinkin', I want to get rid of her."

"You can get rid of her for thruppence," I said, "just by 'phoning the people to come and take her away and put her to sleep, can't you?"

He waved the hand with the cigarette in it.

"My Mam'd never have that," he said. "She's awful attached to the beast."

"So you're going to put a bullet between its eyes instead."

"Ay," he said. "I thought I'd take it out some day and do it, then tell'r it'd got lost."

"You could always poison it," I said.

"Look," he said. "Have y'got a gun for sale or not, an' if y'have how much d'want for it?"

"Okay," I said. "I've got a gun, and some shells for it."

"I'll give y'a quid for it," he said. "If it's in good nick."

"A quid! Away and chase yourself," I told him. I knew of course that we were going to haggle and that he knew I was going to sell him it anyhow: but neither he nor me knew just how much it was worth or how much we would settle the deal at. He hadn't even seen it at this point. Still, it was one of those things that just happen on the spur of the moment and I did want the bloody gun out the house before I went away.

"Come on out'f here an' I'll stand y'a drink," he said.

I was in no position to turn down free booze. We went round the corner to the Sunderland and had a half and a pint each. He paid. When he paid for the second round too, I knew he wanted the gun pretty badly. It worried me a bit because guns aren't the sort of thing that a man'll want for any sort of honest purpose, but I mean I wasn't mixed up in anything really shady myself, just because I was selling it. Just having it was against the law, after all, and he looked all right. He didn't look the sort that was going to rush away with it and mow down his wife, or stick up a bank or anything drastic, like that. We talked about this and that, about me being in the Army and going to Malaya. He told me he was in the Civil Service and that he'd been a fighter pilot in the war, and other things, this and that, before we got back to the subject of the gun.

"Ten quid," I said. "It's worth it, believe me."

"A fiver," he said.

"Eight quid," I said.

"Split it," he said. "Make it six."

"Make it six ten and you can buy another round off the ten bob," I said. That was only fair.

"Right y'are then," he said. "When can I get it?"

"We'll go round just now, if you like," I said, because I didn't really want to have to see him again, though he was a nice enough fellah, you know. I had a girl lined up for the next day anyhow and I thought the cash might come in handy. I was glad I'd met him in a way because I didn't fancy borrowing off my Mammy again.

"Where is it?" he said.

"You know the Kelvin Bridge?"

He nodded.

"Well, it's near there. We'll take the subway."

When we were on the Underground he told me more about himself, but it was nothing you could really believe, you know; nothing sort of current. When we got off and were coming up the stairs, he suddenly asked me if I'd read about some girl that'd been found dead over on the other side of the city. I told him I hadn't, because I'd been in Essex for the last three months. Then he said that he'd helped the police a bit in their enquiries.

"How?" I said.

"I'm pretty familiar with the district, y'see," he said. "I've helped them before with cases over in Carsehorn."

"Is that anything to do with why you want the gun?" I asked him.

He gave me a sort of secret smile. "You can take it as near enough," he said, then, "I can't tell you any more, but I've got m'self in a hell'f a hole over this dead girl, and I just want t'make sure I can protect m'self an'm' family."

"You're married then?" I said.

"My Mam and m'sister," he said. He laughed and shook his head. "It's funny y'know when you're working with the police as close as I am, there's damn' all they can do to protect you. I mean if this person knew I was in with the cops, my life wouldn't be worth a button. So that's why I've got t'look out for myself."

"I see," I said. "Well, I don't care much really. I just want rid of the thing."

I left him at the close-mouth and went upstairs and let myself in with my key. I'd have taken him up but I thought it would be easier to get the gun away without my Mammy

or my Daddy seeing it if I went alone. I went through into
the kitchen, and told them that I was just back to collect some
gramophone records, then I got two big bits of paper and
some string from the top of the lobby press and went into my
own room. I took the jig-saw box down from the top of the
wardrobe and took the gun and the poke of bullets out. I'd
kept the gun wrapped up in a thin bit of oily rag and it seemed
to be working okay. I wrapped it and the bullets in one of the
bits of paper and tied it with string and put it in my coat
pocket. I grabbed a sheaf of E.Ps. from the cabinet and
wrapped them up, went back and told my Mammy I was going
round to a mate's house and wouldn't be late: then I went out.
It was no bother at all really.

He was waiting at the close. We slipped into the back for
a minute while he took the gun out and looked at it and
worked the action once or twice. He took out one of the bullets
and put it in the magazine and lifted it up into the chamber.
I thought for a horrible minute he was going to shoot it, but
he cleared it again and put the bullet back with the others.
He parcelled it and put the lot in his pocket.

"I filed the markings all off it," I told him.

"I saw that," he said. "That's fine then."

He had the six pounds in a roll in his hand and he gave it
to me and waited while, by the light from the ground floor
window, I made sure it was okay.

"Have y'time for another drink?" I asked him.

"Nope," he said. "Maybe another day. I'll have t'get away
home now. I don't like leavin' them on their own—if y'see
what I mean?"

"Sure," I said. We shook hands. That's the part that grinds
on me most: the way he stuck out his hand and I shook it.
He went out of the close and turned off in the direction of
the Subway. I know it sounds queer now, but I'd no idea
who he was. I didn't even find out his name. As far as I was
concerned he was just a bloke I met in a pub, and anyhow

a week later I was thousands of miles away, right out
of the country. I never thought much more about it, at the
time.

4
Ruby

I'M SITTING in alone waiting for my old man to come back from God knows where. The telly was on but I had the sound turned right down because it was one of them Shakespeare plays or something and all I could hear was words pouring out of the box until it didn't mean a thing to me any more. The clock in the bedroom was tick-ticking away like a time-bomb, grating on my nerves. I'd have gone right off to sleep sitting there on the chair if it hadn't been for the clock tick-ticking in the bedroom. I just got up to put it off when I heard the knock on the door. I knew right off it wouldn't be Mike, first because he's got a key, and second because you can hear him coming from the minute he enters the close. This is about half-ten at night. I goes out into the lobby, putting on the kitchen light first, then I puts the big chain across the door and latches it, then I opens the door a chink.

Skinner's standing there, like a young boy, hands in his pockets and his head hung.

"It's yourself then, Arno," I say.

"Is Mike in?" he asks. "I came to see him."

"He'll be back in a minute," I say.

I fiddle the chain loose and open the door wide.

"You'd better come on in."

He comes into the lobby and closes the door behind him,

and we go on into the kitchen. I tell him to sit down in the armchair by the grate.

"I can offer you a snifter, if y'like," I say.

"Nah, thanks, Ruby," he says. "I've had enough for the night."

His face is sort of flushed, not bad, but with two spots of colour high on his cheeks, like as if they'd been rouged on. I go over to the stove behind the pantry door and light the gas and put the kettle on. "Tea, then?" I say.

"Ay, all right," he says. He settles down into the chair. I take the cake tin from the shelf and sort out the fresher cakes on to a plate and go over to the sideboard for the cheese and the cream-crackers.

"Is it something special?" I say.

"Well, it's a job," he tells me. "Will Mike be long, d'y'think?"

"Should've been in ten minutes ago, but I don't know where the hell he's got to."

The cheese is fresh enough and the crackers haven't got soft yet, so I put out a lot of them on the plate.

"How about the job Mike spoke of," I ask him. "D'y'fancy it?"

"I told you, Ruby," he says. "I'm pickin' an' choosin' careful just now."

I go over and switch off the telly. I lean over the back of the couch to see if he'll try looking down the valley under my dress. I took my bra off a while back and I'm not that old yet for a man to want to turn his eyes away. He looks all right, then goes on speaking, still with his eyes on me. I stare at his face, pretending not to notice. I don't want him to get the impression that I'm forward or anything, or that I'm actually inviting him to come on and take liberties.

"You know that job, the one that Mike wanted me in on: well, I've a hunch the best man y'could take with you'd be Howie."

"Christ, no," I say. "Don't try to tell Mike that. He hates the wee runt's guts."

This doesn't put Arno off. I can see he's been thinking hard about it. But I don't know what's going on in his head, expecting Mike to take a gringo like Howie along.

"Still," Arno says. "It's not this time I'm thinkin' of. Y'see Howie's not as green as he's cabbage lookin'."

"How do you mean?"

"I mean he's kept his ears open an' he's lined up a good thing."

"How good a thing?"

"Bloody good," Arno says. "Five or six hundred quid in cash, there for the taking."

I push myself off the couch and go back to the stove. I talk round the edge of the door to him while I make the tea.

"Who do we have to knobble?" I say.

"It's a straight break-in," Arno says. He laughs a bit. "I've even been up and checked over the house for you. Nothin' for you an' Mike t'do but break in, grab the cash and beetle-off again."

"All right then," I say. "We can do that without Howie bein' any the wiser."

"Think," Arno says. He taps his forehead with his finger like someone out of a play on the telly. "Think, woman. If you do it without Howie, then you're givin' him a fine chance t'squeal on you. I mean he's as green as they come with a yellow streak in him as big as the boulevard, but he might just not fancy bein' cut out of it."

"Mike'll give him something." I say: but I doubt it really. I know what Mike's liable to give him and it won't be money.

"Howie's not after pennies, just," Arno explains. "Howie wants in, and he's not the kind'll go right in on his own."

"Ay, but will he settle for us?" I say.

"He'll settle for you, if I bloody tell'm to," Arno says.

"I won't argue with you there," I say.

I put the teapot under the cosy and come out with it and the milk bottle and put them on the coffee table in front of the fire.

"What's the job like anyhow?" I ask.

"Toffee," Arno says. "I'm not tellin' you any more, if you'll pardon me Ruby."

I pour out his tea. He's lying back in the chair with his feet up on the hob, quite at home now. His soles steam with the heat and he looks happy enough. Once I get the tea into him, if Mike's not back, we'll see. I sit down opposite him and cross my legs.

"Right," I say. "But why cut him in on a good thing like our job first?"

Arno heaves up and reaches for his cup and drinks it fast, without sugar.

"So's he'll trust you, for one thing, an' so's you'll have something on him too, an' so's he'll know the ropes."

"Mike won't have anything to do with Howie," I retell him. "He hates his guts."

Arno sits back comfortably with the tea and a cake in his hand, a big pineapple cake which he demolishes in a couple of bites.

"D'you know where Howie works then?" Arno asks me.

"How should I know that now?" I say. "I could see the point in me being interested in him if he was as much man as you are, but . . ." I don't think Arno even picked me up on that, he just goes on talking. He's getting to be as bad as Mike. Christ!

"He works in the railway yard. Parcels Office. The unloading shed."

"What the hell's that got to do with it," I say. They'd drive you grey these men would, with their twisted plots.

"The bloody Railway yard," Arno says. "A bloody goldmine."

"Why hasn't he thought of that before?" I say.

"He needs coaxed. All the poor joker lacks is the confidence. He's been stuffed with this crud about crime doesn't pay," Arno says. "An' he sees me and Mike an' you and Spenser and Mahaffey and Rab and Jeff all at it and gettin' on fine . . ."

"Wonder what he thought about you gettin' those years inside?" I say.

"He thought that was the berries, t'tell you the truth," Arno says.

"Stupid bastard," I say.

Arno takes another cake and I watch it go the same way as the first one; two mouthfuls, he doesn't even stop to draw his breath before he's talking again. If I could shut him up for a couple of minutes just 'til I get started, what with Mike due back at any time, this is the best moment to strike, when the iron's rare and hot. I can at least put the idea into his head and if he's the man he looks, then he'll be back to find out if I really meant it, even if we can't get on with anything right this very minute.

"He half fancies a stretch himself," Arno says. "Maybe it's just t'get away from that wife an' kid, kids, of his. Anyhow me gettin' a bit behind bars didn't put him off. He was waitin' for me—ay, y'saw that for yourself—waitin' for me t'get out. He's had the bloody job on ice for two years. Two years!"

"Tell it to Mike," I say. "He's the man you'll have to convince."

"It's a grand set'f leads, I'm tellin' you."

He takes out his cigarette packet.

"What about yourself?" I say. "How come you're so anxious to hand jobs away free."

"I'm layin' low," Arno says, winking. "I've got somethin' real big brewin' up an' I can't afford t'take chance for peanuts."

"Must be some job," I say, not believing him for a second, "if you call six hundred quid peanuts."

He winks at me again, cheeky. "The biggest."

He hands me the cigarette across the table. I take it and lean over for him to light it for me. The dress-top yawns as if I'd opened it myself. I put my hand on his knee. I expect to hear my old man thumping up the close any minute. This is the way I like it.

"The biggest what, Arno?" I say.

He doesn't say anything, but sits staring at me with his hand still out and the crisp of the matchend still in it, my body forward to him. His eyes have come to life. They look moist now and hard and not flat. He stares at my breasts and the line of my throat. When I hold my chin up it looks full and not fat and the stretching takes the lines out. I put the lip of my tongue between my lips.

Without moving, he says, "Cut it out, Ruby."

"Cut what out?" I say. "Move the table."

"Ach, cut it out, will you?" he says again. "I'm not the kind's does tricks with m'friends missus."

"I'm not his missus, Arno," I say. "I'm just his friend too."

"Don't give m'that patter," Arno says. "As far's I'm concerned you're his bloody missus."

"You don't have to be scared he'll come in," I tell him. "I've got the chain on the door."

"Cut it out."

I push the table back and get down on my knees in front of him and wriggle over the carpet until I'm sitting between his knees.

"Just friendly-like, Arno," I tell him.

"You a bloody nympho or something?" he says.

"I'm just interested in you," I tell him. "Right since you've been around this house."

"Well, I'm not ..." he starts to say, then he stops when I touch him.

In the bedroom I can hear the clock tick, and the rumble of the trams from the street at the end of ours. I keep listening too for Mike, but that's the fun of it, isn't it, being all keyed

up waiting for the show to burst. I know exactly what's worrying him, he's scared I'm going to make a fuss when it comes
down to it, or that if he gets carried away with himself he'll
not be able to stop himself doing what he wants. He must
like me right enough to be afraid of making me scream. I
thought his kind would've known right away that a woman
like me didn't mind being made to yell now and again, in the
course of events. There should be this feeling between his
kind and me, but he knows now, I think. I think he knows
now just what I'm trying to do.

"I'd've thought that after five years . . ."

"I've been out for quite a while, Ruby," he says.

I lean my elbows on his thighs and put my chin on his belly.
I can feel the buttons pressing against my chin. He's lying
right back now, his face dark and his gullet bulging as if he
was trying to hold something back. I know the signs.

"If you've a lady friend lined up," I say, "you've no need
to fear I'll go running an' tell her . . . or Mike."

"I can get women when I want'm," he says, hardly opening his mouth to let the words out. "I don't like bein' . . ."

"Don't like this then?" I say. I keep listening for Mike, to
hear his footsteps coming up out of the rumble of the trams.

I look down from Arno's face to his belly and that's when
he does it, so that I don't even have a chance to anticipate
it coming. Just a blur and scarlet streamers first, until the pain
gets going into my head. I must fall against him, clutching
my face into his trousers to save it when he cuffs me again.
I see him rising up enormous and my legs get all twisted up
under me as he stoves me back on to the rug, and drops down
on me, kneading me, so that it's agony with his knees hard
sticking into my ribs and the hand scything back and forth,
back and forth like a pendulum across my nakedness. It feels
like being scalded with chip fat after a while and I think I'm
kicking at his back with my legs, trying to get him round the
throat with my crossed ankles to stop him, but I don't know.

It's all sliding away from me, as if I was being tilted back into the carpet. I grab at his hand and bite it and the solidness of it in my mouth, wrenching my teeth and buckling my tongue, holds me the right side of knowing what he's doing to me: but it's all just hitting and hitting long past where I thought it would be, until I hear myself screaming against the dirty lump of his hand, the sounds being driven down into my chest and swelling like the sort of whisky-sick you can't bring up. Then he takes his hand away and I feel him touching me, as I try and try to keep this side of knowing the good from the bad. And he just brushes me with his fingers then stops. I close my eyes and can't see, while my breasts and my ribs and my legs run with a sort of shaking heat. It's like I can still feel his hand inside my mouth. I turn over towards the fender and roll up and put my arms round the empty chair and try to get up on to it, really half-waiting for what he'll do next to me now that I can do nothing to him and he has me turned over and all open. I can't see anything but splashes of light from the lamp and from the grate and the dirty chair covering, then I fall against the arm and my head begins to clear enough to make him out, standing by the table putting the spilled cups and the bottle up again with one hand and holding the last iced cake in his hand eating it. His hand is all shaky as he brings the slab of cake up to his mouth and chews a bite off. His clothes are open down the front, and he's shaking, and his eyes are not long now but round as if he'd been half blinded by a flash of something or by looking into the sun, wide open and red.

"Arno," I say.

"What d'you want?" I think he says.

"Bottle's in the lobby press."

He stuffs the cake into his gob and goes out and comes back with the Haig's. He pours some into a cup and gives it to me. I get round into the chair properly and take it. The stuff cuts through me, after I can get enough of it down to let me swallow properly, and I begin to feel the pain drawing in on itself. My heart's banging hard still and I'm breathing as if I'd run a hundred miles. He stands behind the coffee table holding the bottle but not drinking from it, not buttoned yet, shaking.

"Mike," I say. I don't want to hear them steps coming now, because there's nothing I can do to collect myself in time to pass it off and sit there, calm, pouring tea.

Skinner looks at me. He puts the bottle down on the table, and moves behind me. I hear the door opening and listen for the outside door, but it doesn't rattle and I hear him coming back, quiet as a cat. I can't help myself coiling up like a spring, covering my belly with my arms. He stands at the door. I look over my shoulder at him. He puts out his right hand in a fist and tosses my panties at me. In a soft tight ball they fall across my arm.

"I'll be seein' you, Ruby," he says, and walks out. The outside door clacks behind him and I can just hear his shoes scuffle on the stairs.

After I finish the whisky I manage to get up. I feel worse than I did ever before in my life, as if I'd been truncheoned by the busies with their rubber hoses and leather clubs. I get to the sink and open the curtains. There's nothing in the street down below but three or four people staggering up from the fish'n chip shop on the corner. I run the tap and start to wash my face with the cloth and cold water to get the tear marks off and to cool it. In the shaving mirror I can see myself, the sore redness striped across my chest and breasts. I still haven't stopped shaking, though the liquor's helped. I go into the bedroom and take the bath out from under the bed and throw the bundle of washing back and bring the bath into the kitchen. I start running the cold water into it through the green tube that fixes to the tap. Through the window when I look I see Mike coming. I button myself up to the throat as he crosses the street and vanishes into the close under the big

ledge. I can't hear his steps. Then he comes out again, with
Arno. They walk across from the front of our building to the
other side of the road. Through the curtain I watch them
strolling over towards the fish'n chip shop. Old Mike stops
under the lamp and looks up towards the house. I see Arno
taking him by the arm and pointing up the street to the lit
shop. After a minute they go up the street.

I stop the water and drag the bath to the front of the fire.
I get down the big mirror from the wall in the alcove and
put it on the chair. Everything I do sends aches through me.
and I don't have very long probably, to get myself straightened
out before my old man comes walking in. I prop the mirror
up with a cushion so that I can inspect the damage while I
wash. I hope he has the sense to keep Mike out for a while,
and not to come back here with him. I'm not in the mood to
see any more of Arno just now: not for a while at any rate.

5

McNally

I T H A D a bit of a stink about it, whichever way I looked at it. Him standing there waiting in the close-mouth for me, just to tell me he had a sudden urge for a hot fish-supper. I was beginning to wonder if Ruby'd anything to do with it. She can fair ding a man's lug when she's a mind to. I'd taken it into my head to give him the go-by for a while anyhow, to march right up there and see for myself if there'd been any hanky-panky going on behind my back. Though as far as I know she's never gone on the razzle since she took up with me. She's got a righty sparky nature and I'm honest enough to admit that it's not all the honey-love it used to be between the two of us. But I've never caught her at it, or even the rumour of it. There's nothing to Skinner either. He's all right really, if he'd just keep his clanger shut and take a bit of advice now and again. His proposition, for instance, about me giving that twit Howie his schooling in the ways of the world, was hardly the sort of suggestion even Skinner'd put forward in all seriousness and expect me to accept with a smile on my face. Not that I couldn't see he had it all well worked out, and the pile of stuff the boy Howie was sitting on wasn't hardly the sort of capital gain a man in my position could ignore. It doesn't grow on trees, and things are not over easy these days, for a craftsman who'll not stoop to just breenging into a pub or a bookies with a stocking wrapped round his chops and a shooter in his mitt. That's all very well and nice for the kids just out of school with a bit of devilment in them they want to let off and a yen for a quick way to easy living: but I know my place. It's never been said to my face that I ever tackled something I didn't know was going to go a mile. A bit of forethought and a nice easy approach've kept me away from disinfectant and gullion so far, and I've no wish to make my fortune by doing a stint on the rock-pile. Just living fair eats away the money though, eats it away from under your hand. Rent and high rates and fags and a drop now and again, and the insurance on the house and on me—still that's about the least I could do for the old bag—nothing that the average man hasn't a right to expect; only I don't have to get out my bed at half-seven every bloody morning in the year come wind, frost or shine, and slave my guts out with some whelky snot half my age in a collar and tie driving me to an early grave with his threats of the sack. I've the same as any blue-blooded gent, the choice to wake up in bed of a day and think to himself what he's going to be at: to rise as he likes, eat when he likes, tickle the missus when he likes, stay in by the fire or go out in the sunshine, and that's enough to see me through happy. But I've got to keep them coming, line them up ahead and work them out and do them safe! Just going to the Buroo to collect my unemployment benefit every week isn't going to keep a roof over my head and pay for the telly. Besides a man's got to do something, even if it is only like a hobby to me. It's all in the way you think about a thing, I always say.

We stood there for a while with the chips. I'd rather have been away home to my bed to tell the truth, for I'd had a hard night's snooker with the lads and the lights in the hall always did go for my eyes. Still he was there, and he had something on his mind and as we all know by this time, when Arnold Skinner's got a bug biting him there's nothing the rest of us mortals can do but button up and hear him out. I still wasn't too happy about what him and Ruby'd been up to, what with him developing this appetite for a bag of chips. I doubt if Ruby's his style though. I've never seen him with a woman over twenty in his life, except Edith and her two mates and that's just a function of nature, as you might say, without any pleasure in it either for them or him. But, I'd hardly really seen him in years, and there's no telling how prison affects a man. Five years storing it up might not have made him so fussy as to what he was messing with. And, in spite of the fact I trust her, I don't think I'd really like to put temptation in the shape of young ardent Arno in her way. She likes a wee twinge of danger to spice her life, does Ruby, and she knows as well as the rest of us that Arno can be dangerous if you let him slip the leash too much.

It was hell of a cold, and my head was gyping again and I didn't want the bloody chips either because the vinegar always pains my gums since I had my teeth drawn for falsers, but there he was, bright and lively as a mongrel pup, set up to tell me that the best thing I could do for myself would be to hitch up with Howie. Howie, Christ!

"I'm telling you, Mike, he's all right," Arno said as soon as we got outside the shop. "He's stacked with ideas that just need developed in the right way. I mean t'say, everybody 'round here knows who's the best man t'make a good idea work."

"Don't give me none of the butter, Arno," I said.

"God's truth," he said. "It's no fancy snow job, Mike. Here I am tryin' to give you a slice of friggin' pie, an' all I get out y's bitchin' and moanin'."

"I don't see what you should be handing him over to me for," I said truthful-like. He's all right is Arnold but he's not the bloody fairy-queen.

"I've told you once, I'm tryin' t'keep my neb clean so's I can get on an' map out a big one."

"But you're keeping that one under your hat," I said.

He wagged his hands at me, spilling the chips into the gutter.

"Ach hell, Mike," he says. "This one's not your style at all, and besides I'm only in on it by invite."

"Ay, right," I said. "So you expect me to get Howie off your back, is that it?"

He stopped for a minute before he decided that I wasn't the sort of joker you can fob off with a bunch of lies. "That's it," he said. "But there's a lot in it for you. I mean I'm making you a gift of the whole thing, all the deals."

"But he knows nothing," I said. "What . . ."

"Take him with y' and let the bugger hold the torch t'keep him happy. That's all you'll have to do. I'm tellin' you," Arno said.

"This job he's got tucked up his jumper, is it safe?"

"Dead safe. I'll guarantee it."

"But you won't tell me?"

"No," Arno said. "I can't do that. But you take him out with you first an' I'll bet he's at you t'join'm on it before you're half way home."

"He works in the railway yard, doesn't he?" I asked.

"He does," Arno said. "Prize pig, Mike: yours for the askin'."

I was too wore out to spend half the night arguing with Arno. My head was buzzing like a top, and my feet were cold. The vinegar off the bloody chips I'd scoffed was burning my mouth like acid. So I told him yes, I told him I'd take his precious Howie off his hands for a while, provided of course that Howie'd do it with me. I still had the feeling that what Howie really wanted was to get in on something with Skinner, just because it was Skinner, though what the hell ever made Arno so special to an irk like Howie is beyond me. So anyhow, just because I wasn't sure Howie'd wash it anyhow, I told Arno he could go ahead and broach the subject of a bit of collaboration with no strings attached. We fixed it to meet with Howie the next Friday in Kerrigan's Bar out at Carsehorn, then I left Arno and went across the road to my bed.

6

Howie

I MUST say it came as a shock to see him. I thought he'd just walk off and forget about it. But it was a pleasant sort of shock, especially when he pats his coat pocket and winks at me to let me know he has the gun.

It was coming down in buckets outside too and he looked wet enough to have been there for a couple of hours, standing across the street under the shelter of the wall, when I came out of the gate at the end of the back shift, about half-past-eight. He'd put himself under the lamp so's I wouldn't miss him, and I broke off from the rest of the shift and went over to him. It was while I was on the way over that he patted his pocket and tipped me a wink. We walked on out of the bunch and turned left under the bridges until there wasn't anybody about, then I said, "You got it?"

"I told y'I would," he says.

"How much do I owe you then?" I said.

"Fifteen quid."

It was more than I'd bargained for, but I didn't let Arnold realise this.

"Have you shells for it?" I said.

He says, "About a dozen. I'll throw them in for free."

"Can I have it now?" I said.

He says, "If you've got the cash."

"Well, I can give you ten now and the rest on Friday, if that'll do."

He gave me another surprise, by saying, "Sure, that suits me fine."

We turned into the Station by the side entrance, ascended the ramp into the catacombs that fork off to the Low Level platforms. At that time of night it was as deserted as a graveyard. It was possible to hear anyone coming from a mile off given the echo of the tiles and the curve of the walls. We stopped on the inside of the curve and he took a parcel from his pocket and handed it to me. I unwrapped it. It was a nice gun, much better than I'd expected. I didn't know it was going to be so easy to lay hands on a quality gun. The number had been filed off, but I could see by the way the scores on the metal had died that Arnold hadn't done it himself. It seemed safe enough to take it just there and then. It fitted my hand snug-like, and felt good and heavy. I wrapped the shells up again and put them in my top pocket, but I didn't wrap the gun. I tucked it into my deep coat pocket where I could hold it in my hand without anyone seeing while I walked along. Arnold was standing by me, grinning while I looked at it, and when I put it in my pocket he gave a sort of laugh.

"Nice piece of weapon, i'n't it?" he said.

"Lovely," I said. I put my hand round the butt in my pocket and my finger through the trigger guard. "Lovely."

"Yeah, I wouldn't've minded hangin' on to it myself," he says. "It's a while since I've seen one as good. Mind you it's not exactly cheap, an' I'll tell you this, friend, I'm not soakin' you for much more'n a marginal profit. Cost me thirteen."

"That's good of you then, Arnold," I said. I didn't know whether to offer him something extra come Friday or not. I took out my wallet and counted out the ten pounds. It left me only a quid to get along with for the rest of the week, but it was worth it to me just to have the thing. We started to walk up the tunnel again towards the platforms.

" 'Member the other business you spoke about?" he says.

"The job," I said.

"Well, I took the liberty of havin' a squint at the place," he says.

"What do you make of it then?" I asked.

"Looks like a piece of toffee," he says.

"Do you fancy a bash at it some Friday, then?" I said.

"Come on an' I'll stand y'a pint," he says. "Unless you've got other things t'do?"

We had mounted the steps to the station and were walking down towards the book-stall by this time. It was about twenty to nine. I knew Jean'd be expecting me in off the 8.50 and would have a meal ready for me, but I felt that Arnold had a lot on his mind and it wasn't the sort of chance I was willing to pass up just because of a dinner wasted. We went through the station and round to the Bergen Bar just off the Square. I was never fond of the place, with its arty-farty hangings from Norway and Sweden. Everything about it was fake except the dames behind the bar: they were just the usual. We went into the lounge, where it was quiet enough for us to find a table to ourselves. A bunch of R.A.F. boys were having a spree down by the door and four stockbrokers sat drinking steadily down the long wall, but none of them were within earshot. The beer was thin and wersh, and I didn't like it.

Arnold says, "Yeah, well, about the job. I reckon it's a good one. If you're gen's right then it'll be easy money."

"Will you do it then?" I asked.

He swallowed off some of the beer before he said, "It's not for me at the minute."

"Christ," I said. "Why not?"

He leaned over the low table, and spoke into my face. "I've got a big one comin' up," he says. "An' I can't afford t'take any risks at all just now."

"After the big one?" I said. "It'll keep, you know."

He glanced down at the four gents and, still watching them, said in a voice I could hardly hear.

"I'll maybe not be round these parts for a long while after the big one."

"That's not . . ." I started to say, then I stopped as the man came over to gather the empties from the table next to ours. Arnold and me drank our beer until he went away, then Arnold says, "If it comes off for me, it'll be a taste of the big time, y'see. I'll be away abroad before y'can wink."

"Where to, Arnold?" I said.

He shrugged. "America maybe. There's a land of golden opportunity for y'if y'like. I think I'd do well t'pay a visit. Or Spain maybe."

"When this big job coming off then?" I said: not because I wanted to know more than I should, but I wanted to learn how he operated and the only chance I was going to get was before he did it and ran to hide-out in the U.S.A. or wherever he had the notion for.

"Very soon," he said. "It'll set the whole country by its ear, take it from me. It'll shake Mister Booth t'the core when he finds out I've flown the coop. Them tuppenny-ha'penny cops'll not be able t'muscle in on this. Nah, this'll be one for the Yard, take it from me. They'll never get us for it either, not with it bein' nothing but the professionals that's workin' it. Still an' all, it'll leave you high an' dry, won't it, an' that's what I'm here t'talk t'you about."

"I appreciate that, Arnold," I said.

He took a cigarette out of my packet and lit it and sat back in the cramped seat. I had the vague notion he was going to propose something like what he did.

"Now," he says. "You've got a good head on your shoulders, an' you've got a fair piece of work lined up in that Matheson place, but y'll not be able t'pull it off by yourself. Y'know that?"

"Sure," I said. "That's why I've been waiting for you."

"Well, I'm out," Arnold says. "So you'll have t'find some-one else, and that's where I can help you."

"I'm not that keen, to do it with someone else," I told him straight.

"There's better men than me in this town," he said. "For this kinda thing anyway. Take McNally f'instance: d'you know McNally?"

"We don't get on very well," I said.

"Never mind about that. I'm not askin' y't'love the man, just t'give him the chance of helpin' y'out. He's a wily one the same McNally."

"Just forget it, Arnold. I think . . ." He cut me off again.

"Now I've mentioned it t'McNally. I didn't tell'm much, but just enough t'make'm realise that you're not as dumb as people think."

"Thanks for that anyway," I said sarcastic-like.

"Well, y'can't blame them really. They don't know you well enough. Y'can change that with a couple of good jobs."

"I suppose so," I said.

I didn't like the idea of telling McNally my business: then finding out he'd gone and done it on his own, and got off with the whole lump for himself.

"Now, I know what you're thinkin'," Arnold says. "You're thinkin' he'll just step in an' carve you right out: well, he won't do that. He's not a bad bloke McNally. He's never been nailed yet by the busies, for pinchin' anyhow."

"He won't work with me," I said, flatly.

"Ach, but that's where you're wrong. Old McNally's gettin' on a bit. He's not so spry as he was, an' he'll be havin' a hard time pickin' up the right kinda place. It's no' just a ques-tion of runnin' into a house an' breakin' down the door and grabbin' what y'can get an' gettin' out again. It's got t'be worthwhile."

"The Matheson place would be worthwhile."

"I know. I told Mike that, an' he says he'll go in with you, provided . . ."

"Provided what?" I said.

"Provided y'take on a job or two with him beforehand."

"What sort of jobs," I said. "Scuffling?"

"I thought maybe that's what y'had in mind when y'wanted a gun so bad," Arnold says innocently.

"I just wanted a gun to have around," I said. "I'm not as keen as all that to go out and knobble anybody."

"Fine," Arnold says, with a grin. "McNally's never laid a finger on anybody in his whole life, except t'use's mitts in self-defence when he was drunk. Take my advice an' go in with him. Help'm out a couple of times and then he'll help you out with the Matheson place. Think'f the spare cash. He'll give y'n even split."

I didn't like McNally or that wife of his, but all the things that Arnold said struck me as being true. I mean McNally'd been getting away with it for years and that was what I wanted to do too: just what McNally was doing, to pull an occasional job and earn enough extra cash to buy a nice house somewhere in the country with a garden for the kids and maybe a car for weekends and not get caught. Nobody wants to get caught of course, but I had to total it all up and work it all out and decide that if I was going to do it at all, I had to be sure I'd more than a passing-fair chance of getting off scot-free every time. I didn't want Jean to have to live with an ex-con, or the kids to have a daddy that was always inside, but no more did I want them to have to grow up with nothing but a stinking street to play in, always wearing cheap clothes and never getting taken anywhere nice. I had too much of it from my old man, and I told myself I'd get something better for my kids than he got for me. But what can you do on a neat twelve quid a week: sit back and pray to God every Friday night that you'll be the one in a million to make a killing on Littlewoods? No. Get a better job? How can you do that, with trained men walking the streets, and me with nothing except six years in the railway behind me, and nothing but another forty-five to look forward to, knowing that if I just hung on long enough and nobody takes a spite at me and I didn't get caught coming out of the gate with a pocketful of bashed strawberries or a split melon under my coat then by the time it's too late for it to be any use to my kids they'll give me some position and a wage an inch or two above the starvation-line. No. I'd been toying with the idea for a long enough time: ever since I'd met Arnold in the pub before he got stuck with the assault charge. He knew the score too, and he was man enough to risk it. So, even though it was a bit different for me with Jean and the children to think about, I was surely more than man enough to do the same.

I drank the rest of my beer. I could hear the R.A.F. lads laughing away. It was a grand life for them, good money, but they had to stand a lot of crud being slung at them by officers and the like, a lot of crud that'd make any self-respecting man wriggle in his shoes. And what really was different between myself and the four gents sitting at the table looking sort of alert and sad, drinking brandy out of fat glasses, glancing at their gold wrist-watches occasionally, thinking it was time to go home in their flash cars to the big fine house in Bearsden or Maxwell Park or Newlands, just what was really different between them and me? Nothing that you'd notice if one of them and one of me was stripped down naked and stood in a field. If it was McNally or nothing, then I reckoned it'd better be McNally. I told Arnold I'd be pleased to have him fix it up.

7

Ruby

ACTUALLY, THE whole thing was a bit of a giggle, if
you look at it the right way. I've never dared say as much to
Mike, of course, because he still can't see the funny side of it.
He still takes fits of rampaging up and down cursing Howie
blind, though it doesn't seem to me as if it'll stop him going
ahead with the break-in at the Matheson place. The shamoozle
was about as much my fault as poor Howie's to tell the truth
—and Mike knows it, but then I can defend myself a good bit
better than the youngster. It gave us all a terrible fright at
the time, but once we were safe away and no harm done, if
you don't count the dog (which didn't seem to belong to anyone anyhow) I couldn't help laughing. Him and Howie sitting
there in the front seat, green about the gills the both of them;
Howie trembling like a jelly, still holding the damn gun in
his hand, keeking at it now and again as if it was live and
might decide to go off again at any bleeding minute.

I wasn't there when Skinner and Howie and Mike met for
their big pow-wow. My old man's mind was pretty well made
up then that he was going to give the youngster a chance.
What Arno said to make him agree I don't know, but right
enough the Matheson place sounded promising and it might
just have been the thought of getting away with half of six
or seven hundred quid that inveigled Mike into burying the
hatchet with Howie. Whatever it was, Howie was in with us

when we got the word down from the old woman—Edith's
mother-in-law's sister she is—who charred for the Kissocks at
Newtonard. She told us that the couple would be away from
Friday morning until the middle of the next week. Kissock
was the couple's name, and they were elderly enough to be
well off. Mike tried to get the old woman to leave the latch
off the back door, but she'd have none of it, told him in no
uncertain terms that if he wanted to break into the bungalow,
then it was his business and not hers and she wasn't running
no risk of losing her livelihood just to suit a man she'd only
met twice in her life. Even Edith didn't want to have anything to do with it, but we didn't have to bother over much.
Like I've said, you could've taken off a whole wall without
anyone hearing you, ay, and put it back when you'd done.
The bungalow was one of those flung-up jobs, pretty and
modern, but about as strong as a plastic tent. Mike had been
to size it up the week before we pulled it. He said it was easy,
and if Mike came out and admitted that it was easy, by Jesus,
it was easy all right.

He told Howie to dig up a car or a van. In a wee high voice,
Howie said, "Steal one?", and Mike told him savagely, "Well
I don't mean bloody buy one." You could see Howie's chops
falling down on to his collar. I got him aside a while later and
told him where to look and what to do once he found one with
the door open. He seemed to get a better grip on himself then.
He's not a bad sort, is Howie: game enough really when you
push him the right way.

We were hoping the other bungalow, only five minutes walk
from Kissocks', might be possible on the same night and
planned to take it in before we did the main job. There were
another two houses as well that Mike thought might be fair
game. He went up to Newtonard after teatime on the night to
have a good scout around but when he came back he wasn't
any too happy about the prospects of doing more than one.
Still, he'd seen the Kissocks leaving by taxi with their cases,

so we knew for sure they'd be well out of the way. Only once have we ever got inside a house and still found people there, and we got out with as much as we could carry too before they woke up (never woke up 'til the next morning none of them) so it proves you really can do without having to crack a skull or two. But, like Mike, I prefer to hang off until it's a clear run, until you have the whole night with the folks well out of the road, and take your time.

Mike wasn't too sure about Howie having the nerve to steal a car and he had a place lined up to try if Howie didn't turn up. We could've done it on the hoof and saved any chance of an identification but it's always better to have transport handy in case anything unforeseen happens, or you hit such a load of stuff that you just can't carry it. Besides it's a hell of a long walk back from Newtonard, near seven miles, when you're carting a case or parcels, and there's always the chance that a nosey busy'll jump out of the bushes and ask to see what you're carrying.

We got the late train out to Willmington and walked back over the hill to the Community Centre at the side of the Willmington fly-over, where the new flats are. We stood at the bus stop there. It was about half-past eleven by this time and I was worried because I knew there was no buses passing at that time of night and I thought someone would see us, but Mike told me it was all right. We were supposed to meet Howie with the car at half-past the hour. Mike had told him to get a decent vehicle if he could, and I clued him up on the best places, telling him to make sure that he took one from the South side or even from out of the city altogether, say, Dumbarton or Clydebank, and not to use the ferries to bring it over. It was about ten past the half-hour when he finally showed up, driving at a hell of a lick down from the direction of Cloptonfield. He was in a bit of a funk, but after we got in and he started up again, he seemed to settle down. He had the gloves on like I told him and all his clobber stuffed in a paper bag on the seat beside him. He was breathing so heavy you'd have thought he'd pushed the car all the way from wherever it was he'd hooked it.

"Nice smooth vehicle," Mike said. It was a Singer Gazelle, green, quite new. The tank meter showed over half full. "Any bother getting it?"

Howie shook his head, took a big deep breath, and told us, "No bother at all really."

"Where d'you get it then?" Mike asked him.

"Stirling," Howie said.

"Stirling! What the Holy Jesus did you go all the way to Stirling for one for when the whole of Glasgow's littered with them. You took a chance driving all the way back from Stirling in a hot car."

"Safe enough surely," Howie said, jutting out his chin to show us the right spirit of neck-nor-nothing. "I took the diesel at teatime when the train was mobbed, and I walked out of the town a bit until I came to a pub then I hung around outside until four lads came along in this buggy, parked it at the kerb and went inside. They left the door open and the keys. I didn't think it'd be just that simple."

"Y'were lucky that's all," Mike said. "But y'bloody make work for yourself, traipsing away out to Stirling."

"Well," Howie said, "I thought it'd be safer, since it'll take the cops a while to circulate a description."

"Maybe so," Mike said sourly, but I could tell he didn't mind. I think it tickled him to find that Howie and he both had this thing about going a long, long way to rub out casual errors. I remember thinking at the time that the association might be good for us all.

We drove along the back way to Newtonard to a quiet street in the heart of the residential zone. Howie and I got out there and went into a phone box. Mike went off with the car to park it somewhere where it wouldn't be too obvious, nor too obviously hidden, while Howie and I took turns each at phoning up the numbers Mike had given us and saying our little piece. I liked that bit, because it was a sort of thrill waiting while the automatic operator kept on ringing and ringing at a number and we stood there hoping it would bring no answer. Mike had made a list of five addresses he fancied. When we did get an answer we'd put a hanky across the mouthpiece and say something daft, like, "Hullo, Effie, this is Sheila," or "Is that the Newtonard Cottage Hospital: I'm phoning about my wife," or just "Wrong Number". We didn't have much luck; the first four on the list all got answers, so that the only one not to reply was Kissocks' and we knew about them already. We'd only just finished when Mike comes strolling along with his briefcase under his arm and the rolled umbrella swinging, for all the world like a blasted stockbroker. Howie nips out and tells him that it's no go with the spec houses. I let the Kissocks' number ring for another three minutes to make sure, then I came out and we strolled about a hundred yards and cut off into a lane that runs along the back of the Terrace where the bungalow is. We could see people in the kitchenettes here and there as we walked along but none of them seemed to notice us. The lane was dark, one half of it lined with the backs of garages of the other houses. The Kissock house had a fairly wide garden with only a low fence at the back, so we climbed the fence and skirted the side of a garden trellis to the back door. The house to the right was still lit, at least the bathroom, but we didn't make the slightest noise and before we got more than halfway across the garden that light went out too. There was a sort of porch affair round the back door but the glass opened all right and we stood inside it, while Mike got busy on the lock of the back door. It was one of those big green monsters with a key about the size of a sewing-machine. I whispered to Mike then to try the windows first, but he just shifted me back with his elbow and kept going in the dark with the thick metal slat he'd brought. He can do wonders with that thing and in a couple of minutes he got the lock shifted back and we were inside. They didn't even have any chains or bolts on the kitchen door, though the front was dripping with the contraptions. It was a nice kitchen. I wish I had one like it, but there was nothing in it for us. Howie was hanging on to me, holding my hand and all, as we went through into the other rooms.

Mike muttered about looking for a bureau and told me and Howie to try the bedrooms. They were easy enough to find: first two doors off the kitchen. One was hardly furnished at all, just a bed, and a wardrobe which was empty, and a side-board which was empty too except for a lot of electrical tools of the small kind, and a drawerful of games like Monopoly, cribbage boards and cards. There was nothing there for us either. But the other bedroom looked promising. I got Howie to shine the torch for me, telling him to keep it pointed low. I started going through the drawers, beginning with the wee ones on top. She had some nice stuff all right. I tossed the jewellery on to the bed, quite a bit of it, good old-fashioned gold settings too. The other drawers had just clothes. I took some stockings and underwear, but the rest of it wasn't my size. Down at the bottom she had one of those drawers that women like her keep; a white Bible, letters, old Christmas cards and photographs. I looked at them. She wasn't a bad-looking bird in her early days, if that was her in the photos. I put that lot back and left it. I went to the wardrobe. Howie hisses at me, "Hey, Ruby. How long are we goin' t'be here?"

"I don't know," I tell him. "As long as it takes. We've got 'til Tuesday."

"Ruby," he said. "I'll need t'find the bathroom."

"Well, for God Sake, go and find it. What do you want me to do, take down your trousers for you."

"Where is it?" he said. "Where is it?"

"Go and look for it, Howie," I tell him. "If you can't find it, pee in the sink."

He slouched off through the door, taking the torch with him. I was just going to bawl after him to tell him to leave the torch when I saw Mike out in the hallway with a drawer in his arms, and a smile on his face.

"What have you got then?" I asked him. "Any cash?"

He put the drawer down on the bed and shone the torch on it. I saw a full bottle of Cutty Sark.

"We'll have some of that now," I said, hoisting it up and opening it.

"Take it easy, Ruby," he said.

"Do you want a dram?" I said.

"Ay, give's a sook," he said. "Then come an' see what else I've got."

I took some out of the bottle. It was rare stuff. I'd been feeling sort of light and floaty before—being in someone else's house where I'm not supposed to be, usually has that effect—but the whisky really tuned me up. I got up on the bed, on the silk counterpane, and tucked my legs under me. Mike held the torch up again and pointed it into the drawer. "Dirty old bastard," he said.

It was full of pictures, girls tied up naked, bulging their bottoms and breasts out at the cameraman, and girls and men, all tangled together, lots of other poses too.

"He's about sixty and all," I said. It's amazing what you find in other people's houses. I mean you wouldn't think the sort of man who kept a nice house in a nice district like Kissock would be hoarding filthy pictures in the bureau drawer. "A good life she must've had."

"That's not all," Mike said. "Take a squint at this." It was a packet of special rubbers.

"I wonder who he's boffing then," I said. "Maybe we should get Edith to contact him on the Q.T."

"Ay," Mike said. He scoffed off a slug of the Cutty Sark and passed it to me. I was looking at the pictures. They were

as good as any I'd ever seen, and they must've cost him a
packet. I knew people who'd buy them.

"We'll take them along," I said.

"Nah, nah," Mike said. He started to laugh, and I could
smell the reek of whisky off him. "Nah, nah, Ruby. I've a
better idea. We'll spread them out in here. That'll shake the
dirty old beast more'n the breakin'll do."

I saw it then, and started to laugh too. I couldn't stop myself. I could imagine the old josser's face when his missus
came storming in and found them. I could see her face too,
when it came out that they were her dear hubby's.

"Where?" Mike was saying. "Where'll we put them. In the
lavvy?"

I rolled over on the bed and stuffed my face into the
pillows. I was laughing so much I'd have wakened the whole
neighbourhood in a minute. I knew where to put them all
right.

"Put them down in that drawer there, at the bottom of the
old dear's dressing-table, along with her other momentoes," I
told Mike.

Mike got down on his knees and rummaged through the
drawer. I could see the torch shaking with his laughter, and
holding his lip in his teeth. He put a sheaf of the dirty pictures in the drawer, under the other stuff at the bottom, then
he closed the drawer up right again. He was snorting and panting with laughing by now and he put the torch on the carpet
and rolled over like a big hound his arms over his mouth. I
was well away too, thinking about her being glad and maybe
remarking how nice and decent the burglars had been to leave
her heart's treasures untouched. And then her face when she
found the pictures. I'd love to have been there. I think I
downed some more of the Cutty Sark, then Howie came in.

"Christ," he said in a sort of strangled voice. "Will you
shut up. What the hell y'trying t'do, waken the whole burgh
up?"

Mike rolled over and put his hand on Howie's leg, still laughing with a sound like an old pair of bellows.

"Calm down, son," Mike said. "There's nothin' t'panic about."

"What's the joke anyhow?" Howie says.

"Nothing," I tell him. "Want a drink? Nothing but the best."

He hardly looked at me when he said no. He wanted to get away. They all do, or most of them, and that's their big failing. Rush in and rush out and miss the fun of the thing, and probably some interesting profit besides.

"Have a guzzle. Go on," said Mike to Howie, as he got to his feet.

"I don't want one," said Howie. "Let's get what we came for and clear out."

Mike sobered up enough then. "Have y'found anything interesting?"

Howie shook his head.

"He's been to the lavebo," I told Mike. "What do you expect him to find in there?"

I knew what Mike would say, and he did. I was laughing again before he had the word properly out of his mouth. Howie was getting desperate. I couldn't help it. When Howie came over to the bed, in that furious jerky way of his, and tried to pull me off, and take the bottle away from me, I managed to turn so that his hand went between my legs. I shut them on him. I think I said something like, "I know what you're after." Then Mike came over and pulled him away. The whisky was all over the place by this time. I could smell it rising off the pillows and the silk quilt. Mike took me under the arms and hoisted me on to the floor. The bulb of his torch seemed to get bigger and smaller, bigger and smaller, bigger and smaller. I heard Mike saying, "Come on, Ruby, sober up now. Sober up." I stood up, holding on to the table, and dropped the bottle on to the bed. I focused on Mike standing there like somebody's tossed-off overcoat hung up in the dark, until things righted themselves.

"There's an electric shaver in the toilet," Howie said. "Do we take it?"

"Ay, take it," Mike said. He still had his arm round me and except for giggling, I was all right. "I've got a couple of watches and this jewellery here."

"No money?" Howie said.

"Not a bloody red cent," Mike said. "We'll go an' look in the other rooms again, just t'make sure."

I held on to him while my legs took shape again, then we went through the lobby and into the other rooms. Mike shone the torch. I saw he'd just about taken the bureau to pieces and there was a lot of papers strewn about. He'd been through the cupboards too and turned out the ornaments and moved the pictures. Howie picked something off a coffee-table and shone his lamp on it. It was a big Ronson. "Take it, if y'like it," Mike told him. Howie put the lighter in his pocket along with the razor he'd got from the bathroom. We went into the hallway and turned out the cupboard there, but it was just the usual junk in it, brushes and stuff, that we had no use for. Mike went back into the bedroom and cleared my collection off the bed. He returned with some of it dripping from his hand and shoved it at Howie, saying, "Here. Stuff this in your bag."

"No damn cash, at all," Howie said. "Come on let's get out of here."

I looked into the other lounge and saw that Mike had combed it out already. It was lean pickings this time. I put my head back into the hall and saw they'd gone into the kitchen. I heard Mike growling at me to come on. We stood in the kitchen, while he opened the back door and spied out through the glass porch. There was a bit of cold moon over the houses at the back and I could see the grass patch of the lawn as if it had been a pond or a loch. There was no lights at all on the houses out back.

"I left the car at the other end'f the lane there," Mike said. "Me first. An' close the doors behind y'Howie. Maybe nobody'll notice we've paid a visit 'til the Kissocks get back."

Howie was all tensed up, as he had been ever since we met him, only it seemed to be getting worse. I could feel him as I brushed past to go out the door; he was stiff with fright, like an ironing board folded half out. Mike had gone out to stand scout 'til I came, then we went up the path to the grass. Howie closed the doors and I thought he was right behind me when Mike and me went over the grass. Then suddenly I heard him saying something and a dog starting to bark and bark, deep baying and panting. Mike and me turned at the one time, crouching. It was a black dog and it had come out of the lee of the house to hurl itself at Howie. I heard Mike say, "Christ," then saw Howie jumping over the flowerbed and running towards us, the beast jumping at his legs and round the front of him, yapping its head off. The light in the house next door went on and made a track as bright as day across us. "Come on quick," Mike said to me, grabbing my arm and hauling me towards the gate in the back fence. More lights were going on I think. Then I heard the sound and turned in time to see Howie lying on his back on the grass in the centre of the lights with the dog like a black fur coat spread all over him. I didn't know what the sound was because it was muffled, and I didn't know what had happened until Mike shoved me through the gate into the lane and stood back holding the gate open. Howie came belting through into the lane and paused. He held his hand up. I saw the gun and the wet black blood and heard him say in a sick voice through the rasping breath, "I shot it: I shot it."

We got down the lane in double quick time, and Howie had the car door open before Mike and me could even reach him. He would have been in behind the wheel if Mike hadn't

pushed him over. "I'll drive, you ..." Mike said. Howie
slumped over and sat low with his head against the door. I
scrambled in the back. Mike started the car and we were away
up the hill backwards, into a reverse turn and streaking
forward this time past the hospital before I knew what was
what.

"Y'fair loused that one up," Mike said. "Where d'you get
the bloody gun anyhow?"

Howie sucked in a breath. "It's mine: I didn't mean t'use
it on the creature, but it'd have had me by the throat if I
hadn't."

"Okay, okay, okay," Mike said, and I could see them both
in the mirror at that moment and I couldn't help laughing.
Neither of them bothered with me and I just sat there laughing to myself until we got to the end of our street.

"Right," Mike said. "Out, Ruby. Take the stuff up an'
dump it. I'll get rid of the car."

"What am I goin' t'do?" Howie said.

"Go home," Mike said.

"I've to go right to my work," Howie said. "I'm on the day
shift: start at four."

Mike hadn't cut the engine and we sat at the end of the
street for a minute until Mike said. "Give's your coat. Is
there blood on anything else?"

"Up my sleeve," Howie said, sorry for himself.

"Bad?" Mike asked him, then said, "I can't help it. You'll
just need t'wear the thing. I'll hide the coat."

They let me out, Howie's coat tucked inside my coat, then
they drove off to ditch the car. As soon as I got in the house
and salted the stuff away under the floorboards in the lobby
press, I went through and made myself a cup of coffee with
a couple of spoonfuls of rum in it. Just to steady myself. After
that I sat down in the chair and had a right good laugh.
It was funny right enough, Howie and his big bloody dog.
That and the Kissocks' faces when they found the photos in

the remembrance drawer. Maybe we didn't make much out of it, but at least it'd cheered me up. Better than a night at the Metropole it was, far better.

8

Howie

ARNOLD WAS terribly decent about the whole thing. I took the gun to him right away the next night, trailing him round the pubs up Carsehorn way until I run him to earth in The Miners' Arms. I had a drink with him, his old man and a couple of other lads I only knew by sight. I still had the pickings McNally'd given me, the shaver, the Ronson, a watch and some beads and a brooch, in a big plastic bag taped to the inside of the cistern at home. Logically I realised that the police wouldn't be liable to come sniffing at my door, because they didn't know me from Adam, not being endowed with a record or anything, but there was always a stray chance some rat would blow the gaff and I wanted to be sure I was clean. The thing that really worried me was the shooting of the dog. I had to do it. It had me by the trouser leg and all; no doubt in my mind it'd been off with a mouthful of identifiable leg if I hadn't pulled the trigger on it. But that left a bullet, and bullets are the easiest things in the world for the cops to trace what with all the scientific gimmicks there are today, once they dug it out of the poor beast's brainbox. I like dogs too: and it was only being friendly I think, but I'd never have got away from it if I hadn't done what I did. At least I proved to myself that I had the presence of mind to go ahead and say damn it all and pull the bloody trigger, when all McNally could do was run away and the stupid crow Ruby laughing

herself silly. Imagine: and it all plain sailing up 'til then too.
I see the animal hasn't been identified either, not according to
the *Evening Times*.

After Arnold's old man goes away with his two friends,
Arnold asks me about it. I tell him, missing out some bits here
and there.

"So you drilled a poor dumb defenceless creature in cold
blood, did y'Howie?" he says.

"I'd no other choice," I tell him. "We were out and away
too if it hadn't come and kicked up a rumpus fit to wake the
dead."

"Ay, ay," he says. "Poor defenceless beast."

"Defenceless," I say. "In another couple of minutes it'd've
been horsing off with my leg in its teeth."

"Y'panicked," he says.

"I did not," I say. "It was the dog or us."

"What did McNally have t'say about it?"

"Nothing much," I tell him. "But that bitch Ruby was
laughing her head off all the time."

"I'll bet she was an' all," Arnold says. "I don't know yet
why McNally drags her along with him. She's nothin' but a
friggin' menace any way y'look at it."

"It was hardly worth it either," I tell him.

"How: did y'not get much out of it?"

"A few gash things, shaver, lighter, you know."

"No hard cash at all?"

"Not a bloody penny."

"Funny," Arnold says, pursing his mouth. "Not like
McNally to pull a place that's arse-bare."

"Well, that's what he said, and I saw nothing myself."

Arnold sits back, then leans forward again.

"What d'you want me t'do: get rid of the stuff for you.
It'll not be worth much," he says.

"I want you to get rid of the gun for me: take it back," I
tell him.

He did nothing to tell me I'd said anything he didn't expect, just grinned his grin and drank some of his ale, sliding his eyes in my direction over the thick rim of the glass. Then he put the glass down with a clack on the table-top, and says in a slow thick sort of voice,

"So you've got tired of it already, then?"

"No," I tell him. "I just don't want t'have it lying around the house."

"Because you plugged the dog with it?"

"That's half of it," I tell him.

"An'y'expect me t'take it back now? What the hell'm I goin' t'do left holdin' a hot gun? Fling it in the Clyde, Howie."

"I thought . . ." I starts to say.

He says, "You thought I'd maybe give you the ten quid back, well, I'm buggered if I'll do that. I told y'it was dear in the first place, and m'chances of gettin' a tenner for a hot property are minus nil. Naw, naw, Howie," he says. "Y'can frig off with it."

"I'm not wanting the ten quid back," I explain. "I just thought that you'd maybe take the bloody gun and wipe off the fiver I'm still owing."

"And the Matheson job," he says. "Has McNally scrubbed it off the slate?"

"I think it's still on," I tell him.

"You'll be needin' a weapon for that then," he says.

I shake my head. "No more guns," I tell him. "Something could happen that I don't want to happen."

"Squeamish, Howie?" he says.

"Will you take it, Arnold?" I say. "I'll give you the gun and you keep the ten quid into the bargain. Otherwise I'll just pitch it into the Clyde and nobody'll gain out of it."

"Ay," he says. "I'll take it."

"And the fiver still owing?"

"Forget it," he says. "I reckon I'll manage to palm the thing off on some mug for a coupla quick quid profit."

"That suits me then," I says. "Any word of your big job?"

"Nah," he says. "It'll come any day now though."

"Well," I tell him. "I hope you make it."

"I'll make it okay," he says. "You worry about yourself."

Then we went into the gents. I slipped him the parcel with the gun and the bullets. After I'd thanked him, I went home a good bit lighter at heart. And Arnold went off with the gun.

Part Three

DECEMBER

1

McNally

THE BEAUTY of getting yourself woke up early on a rotten wet morning is that you can lie in your pit and watch the rain pouring down the windows thinking about all the poor irks slaving off to work in it. It makes it better knowing, like I do, that there's a lion's share of six hundred and twenty pounds stashed away safe and sound under the lino in the lobby. The peak of living, this is. I can think about it and mull it over, and have a quiet little ball all to myself till Ruby gets back with the fags and the papers and brews us a cup of tea.

Considering the drooking I got, I feel in pretty good shape: tip-top in fact. The whole process was simple and for once young Howie was right. It's incredible that folks can be so stupid as to leave a brief-case stuffed full of notes standing on the table while they nick off to the pictures. Except for the rain, it was a grand night's work: well, hardly work, hardly work at all, just a half hour's unpolluted risk. Howie stood outside the house from teatime, keeping back in the shelter of the bushes until they come out at the back of seven and got in their car, the whole damn' family, kids, nursemaid an' all, and buzzed off, then he came and got me from the car and we walked round and up the front drive as bold as brass, stove in a plate of glass in the lavvy window, opened the sneck, hopped in, lifted the bag and beat it. Not even half an hour, ten minutes and it was all over, and we had six hundred-odd quid to slice up between us. It didn't ought to be allowed: making things that easy. So now I can relax, and enjoy myself, with nothing to do and all day to do it, until I works out in my mind just how I'm going to cash in on the Railway without getting Howie the sack or myself all tied up with expensive distribution. There'll be a way.

The rain comes down off the gutters like a blasted stream, and it's as grey as a whore's knickers in here. I light the bedside lamp, and have a cigarette. Arnold'll be cursing himself that he never stuck with Howie for this one. Howie's all right. Bloody near wrecked me the time before though, having to scarper out of the Kissocks' like a fox with the pack on its tail, but nothing come of it. At least there's that to be said, and I did get off with seventy quid clean as a whistle, which was just about what young Howie owed me for running my neck into a noose, and getting Ruby and me jugged on the very spot. If he'd known about that seventy quid he'd have been fuming mad, but what he don't know won't kill him, and it's all water under the bridge now. I'd've given the whole jing-bang for a keek at the old dear's puss when she opened her drawer and copped a squint at them dirty pictures though. Filthy old queer, with his bonded blondes, Kissock must be. I thought Ruby was going to collapse on me though. I'll have to keep my eye on her, she's getting a bit too cocky to be as safe as I like. With the Railway thing, if I can think of a way, she'll have to keep out, or take a back seat, because I can't afford to fumble this one or the busies'll throw the whole book at me for every bloody thing that's been snitched out of the yard for the last five years. A cop's a cop but I'm blinded if I'll get handed a stack of charges on fiddles I'd nothing to do with. No doubt Arnold'll be around today, if he's got wind that we pulled something last night: what the hell! I'd feel better if he kept his nose out of here though, 'cause you don't need more than half an eye to see that the busies

are interested in him, and I've not got the slightest intention
of getting hauled up as an accomplice to any of his dark deeds.
I've got enough of my own to keep me warm, without adding
his in too.

The door opening, and Ruby coming in. Through the door
I see her standing in the kitchen with the long oilskin dripping on to the carpet, and the headsquare plastered to her hair.
She never looks so good in the morning. I want a cup of tea,
woman, for God Sake, stop nittering about and get on with
it, and get the grate lit before I get up. She hoists up the string
bag on to the table and takes out the poke of rolls, the milk
bottles, the fags, and the newspapers. As she takes off her
coat she reads the front page of the *Record*, on the table in
front of her.

"Look inside, dear," I shout to her. "Or chuck the lot in
here an' I'll have a shuftie while you're putting the kettle on.
Okay?"

She looks up at me. The hair's stuck down on her forehead
and her hands are wet. She gives the paper a shake to fold it
out and picks up the rest of them and comes through the kitchen to me. She's got that weird hard look on her clock.

"You're soaking wet, woman," I tell her. "Don't drip on
me."

She puts the papers down on the bed in front of me, and
goes away back into the kitchen, saying, "Well, you didn't
make the front page anyhow, Samson," then sticking her
head around the jamb to watch me while I get busy reading
the stuff under the headline, says, "Not unless it was you and
the boy that did it."

"Christ," I say. "It's bloody rotten."

"Isn't it," she says. I get propped up and go on reading all
about it from one paper to the next, while Ruby makes the
tea. I've nearly finished by the time she brings it through.
She's got it on a tray, the warm rolls and the jam and the
butter, teapot, the lot. She's peeled down to her slip and climbs

into the bed beside me, with her freezing feet planted against my legs. "Shift over, y'hulking brute," she says. "I'm chittering." I give her the warm half of the bed, to get clear of her feet.

"Wonder who done it?" she says, couping out the tea.

"Some young bastard," I say. Actually it doesn't make much difference to me. I mean, it's happening all the time and even though you're in the middle of it, if you want to put it that way to yourself, it doesn't matter a monkey's: but it's not pleasant, just the same way as it's not pleasant to hear of the niggers in Africa raping the whites, or a couple of newlyweds getting ground to pulp under a bus, or a bairn being found drowned in the canal. "Wonder how much he did it for?"

"About thirty-five or forty quid," she says. "Christmas takings."

"Three of them. He must've got the wind up about the kiddy, or he'd never have had to do that to it," I say. "Still they don't make any connection between the Matheson's and this mess, which is one thing we've got to be thankful for."

"There's that," she says. She gives me a cup of tea and I drink it. "Do you not think we should get the stuff out of the house for the time being though?" she asks.

I can see her point. I supposed we should. "Where to?" I say.

"Edith would hide it," Ruby says. "We could give her a pound or two."

"They'll be combing the whole place," I say. "Okay. You can take it round this afternoon."

"How about Howie?" she says. "He'll have the breeze up good an' proper."

"That's his look-out," I say. "I'll tip him off to get rid of the paper for a week or two, but, Christ, if they cotton on to him, they'll be a hell of a sight smarter than I take them for."

That's it settled. Edith can keep the money for us for a month or so, and that'll be us clear just in case. It's after a do like this that you get all the conscientious wallahs in the Force breathing down your neck, and half the constabulary over the border from Glasgow just to give a hand. Ruby butters a roll for me.

"Do you know what Howie did with that gun—the one he bumped off the dog with at Kissocks' place?" she asks me.

"I just hope he got rid of it, that's all that worries me," I say.

"He gave it back to Arnold Skinner," she says.

The penny drops.

"So what?" I say. I'm not in the mood for idle talk with Ruby. I don't want to know what the hell's going on in her mind about that wee runt, not with it pouring outside and me with half of six hundred quid here and not a care in the world. She knows me well enough by this time to steer clear of the subject.

"Nothing," she says. "I was just thinking."

"Okay," I say. "But think quietly, will you. Whatever it is, I'm not interested. I just don't want to know about it."

She leans back and sips her tea, comfortable and warming up nicely now, and I know she's not going to say any more about it, which is fine with me. The less you know about murder, the better it is all round. That's what I always say.

2

Muirhead

THE CORRIDOR was over-heated, and the backs of my legs ached, as I walked down to McAlister's room. I could tell myself that I was walking slowly simply because of the dull pain in the joints, which I had known would result from my drenching, but in truth I was reluctant to face the boss at that time of day. As I approached, the door of McAlister's office opened and Walter and Thompson came out, both young and enormous and with that fresh-as-paint appearance in their uniforms. Thompson was replacing his ballpoint into the upper pocket of his tunic and carried a folder under his arm in a manner which informed me that he had just been given McAlister's confidence and that he was prepared to guard the responsibility jealously. Walter must have been at the conference too, for they were discussing it together as they started up corridor towards me, stopped speaking as they came past, and said good-morning.

"Is he in at the moment?" I asked, more to discomfit them than because I really wished an answer.

"Ay, he's in," Walter said, and they went off towards the control room in silence.

I had my hand on the doorknob, when Booth rounded the corner from the entrance. He had his raincoat on and it was sleek with water. His tricky little hat, which he held in his hand, was running like a boiled cabbage.

"Jessie says he wants me?" he muttered. "You too?"

"Me too," I said, then with a gesture, "After you."

I knocked lightly. McAlister called for us to enter.

He was seated at his desk, holding the new pipe awkwardly to his lips. It was not lit. His lips and teeth caught the stem briefly as he looked at us, then he drew it away and held it cocked in his fist while he creaked back in his chair and told us to have a seat. His face was large and coarse, but I noticed that the unsightly exema which blistered his jowls and neck in summer had all but died away. The stiff white collar caught the long hairs below the line at which he could safely shave. He had taken off his glasses and they lay crossed like a large insect on top of the khaki manila folder with which he had covered the papers on his desk. Booth sat down on the deep seat to the left of the desk, leaving the small uncomfortable stool-like chair directly in front for me.

"Bob, John," McAlister said.

We told him our good-mornings politely. The atmosphere of strained familiarity never quite succeeded in covering up his desire to keep us, as Inspectors, at a safe distance, as if the nature of our work was a contagious disease which he, as a Chief, had no wish to risk catching. The wires of interior politics between Division and Division which had jerked him from Glasgow and landed him two rungs up the ladder in Carsehorn, were none of my business but it was impossible to ignore the fact that he was conscious of them, and suffered guilt about them, far out of proportion to the real issue involved.

"I should take my coat off, if I were you," he said. "Bob. You might be here for quite a bit."

Obediently Booth slid out of his coat and hung it, still wet, over the back of the chair.

"First question," McAlister said. "Any progress?"

I glanced at Booth, who pursed his lips until they resembled those of a Hottentot woman at the height of sexual elegance, and shook his head.

"Nothing, sir," he said. "The place was clean as a bone. We know what the gun was, as I expect you've already been told. That was all in the report."

"That's it then, is it," McAlister said, placing his palm deliberately on the folder.

"That's it, so far," Booth said. "Unless you've had anything further."

"I haven't," I said.

"Not really much, is it, I mean," McAlister said.

"I'm afraid not, sir," Booth said.

"It's a battle, isn't it," McAlister said, toying with his pipe again indecisively. He looked up at Booth, not at me at all, as if he discounted my existence.

"The Glasgow mob want to come in," he said.

"I don't think ... it would be ... the best thing," Booth said. His lids had come down again, coldly. "Not yet."

"They seem to think ..."

"Paige and Strachan?" Booth said.

"Most likely," McAlister said. "They seem to think it's about time we ... bolstered our forces. I mean, with the girl Calder's death not cleared up and now this thing. The Press are screaming blue murder."

"Let them," Booth said.

"You haven't established a connection yet," I said, before Booth could start.

"All the more reason," McAlister said. "If we've two killers on the loose in the County now."

"You know as well as I do that we've done everything we can so far," Booth said. "I'd rather not have Paige and Strachan in on this ... not yet anyhow."

"I might have no choice," McAlister said. "I mean, it might be better to ask for it, than to wait until we're given it, don't you think?"

"No," Booth said. "I don't hold with the idea. I think the timing's all to cock, if you'll excuse my saying so, sir."

"I realise how anxious you must be to continue along your own line," McAlister said. "But what's the use of it if we can't lay our hands on him and put him out of harm's way. It'll just go on, you know, Bob, and we can't afford to let it happen again."

"There's no direct connection," I said again. McAlister looked at me.

"Striking while the iron's hot is half the battle," he said.

"I questioned him, this morning," Booth said. "He's openly scathing about our chances, which is always a sure sign."

"You and he seem to have learned each other's foibles pretty well," McAlister said.

"Yes—sir," Booth said. "I was taught that as part of the game."

"It may very well be 'part of the game', as you put it, but it doesn't alter the fact that while you and he are sparring round looking for holds, Glasgow are breathing down my neck to put a stop to it. I mean, one more, just one more of this nature and we've got a proper little crime-wave on our hands."

"We've always had," Booth said. "It's just coming to the surface now."

"Will you be able to nail him?"

Booth hesitated. "Not unless he goes mad and starts spending the money. The house was bare."

"And there's that unsatisfactory alibi," McAlister said.

"He has a dozen bods in the pub ready to swear he was there all night," Booth said. "But we know he paid a rather prolonged trip to the lavatory around half-past eight. I don't know if you're familiar with the bog at Kerrigan's?"

McAlister shook his head.

Booth continued drily, "Well, it has two exits, one into the public bar and the other leading directly out to the road through the yard at the car park. Now it's perfectly feasible that Skinner could have gone straight through the bog and out into the car park. If he found a car open and used it, it would take him only three or four minutes to drive to the shop."

"How long if he walked?" McAlister said.

"A minimum of ten, going across the field past the Broken-hill farm and into Lauderton Road from there, then he could have cut across the waste ground and approached the shop from the rear. The whole of the west side of both Lauderton and Ashton Roads have been demolished; lying waste preparatory to rebuilding. Walking, he could have done it in ten minutes easily."

"How long was he in the . . . lavatory?" McAlister said.

"No one's quite sure. His father, who's an unreliable old bastard anyhow, says not more than ten minutes, but no one else can really say."

"Singleton's checked this out, by the way," I added. "The times are accurate."

"I see," McAlister said. "It's not much is it, really? The same story as before. He as good as admits he did it—you'd go that far, would you, Bob?"

"Hell, yes," Booth replied.

"But he wasn't seen by anyone, either leaving or returning to the pub, and as far as you've traced out he wasn't seen around the area of the shop either. Yet the old ladies are found dead. Just like that. Skinner is either completely blameless, else he's a very lucky or skilful operator," McAlister said.

"He's an opportunist. I think I've told you that before. He doesn't really plan things out, but he's always ready to snatch the opportunity: which is all very well when there's only property involved, but . . ."

"Life and limb, that's a vastly different matter," McAlister said.

"He'll get more and more confident," Booth said. "It's in his nature to run us very close."

"Perhaps, we should bring in Strachan then," McAlister said. "Fresh slant on . . ."

"Look, sir, Strachan's a good man, but not . . . there's absolutely nothing he could do that we haven't done."

McAlister sighed. "This business has cost us a great deal of money, and I'd like to nab this fellow as soon as possible."

"We all want that," Booth said, explosively. "Christ, I'd give my left arm to stick him properly, but we can't be too hasty about it."

"If he's not apprehended, he might kill again," McAlister said, with a sort of solid logic.

"I want to get him and hang him," Booth said vehemently. "The Calder girl couldn't do that for us, but now he's done for himself. Multiple homicide, robbery and death by the use of a firearm."

"If it was Skinner," I said.

"You damn' well know it was," Booth growled.

"I think it's likely," I said. "I think he's beginning to run amok, and that it's just the sort of thing he would pull— right up to the point of shooting the child too, as a sort of culminating thrill."

"Or to avoid identification," Booth said. "But the whole thing's split down the middle. I mean, here he is, the sort of psychopathic little worm who'll throttle any poor girl he happens to meet under the right circumstances, when the mood's on him, suddenly creeping out of the pub (which was alibi aforethought) on the off-chance that he'll find the shop quiet enough to rob on the spot."

"Perhaps he only meant to break in," McAlister said.

"What for?" Booth said. "Sweets: paper-hats. No, sir, he meant to kill. The gain was only to salve his . . ."

"Not conscience," I said. "You don't believe that he's got one."

"Intelligence," Booth said. "Reason."

McAlister sighed again hugely. "This is all very well, but it doesn't get us anywhere. I think you should have Strachan and Paige in now, and begin again as if you'd never heard of Skinner. I mean it seems to me that it might just as well have been any other wandering brigand with a gun in his pocket: some nasty little tearaway who got the wind up while he was trying the game on the old woman."

"And would he have shot the child too?" I said.

"In fear, probably," McAlister said. "Find the gun, for a start."

"We're doing our best," I said.

"Find the gun, and find the money," McAlister said. "And then we'll begin to worry about Skinner again. That's why Paige and Strachan . . ."

"Look, sir," Booth said, getting to his feet. "If I reach a stone wall, I'll come and ask for assistance, but in the meantime . . ."

McAlister was suddenly roused. "I can't afford to let a ridiculous . . . well, personal pride, professional dignity get in the way when I'm trying to shoulder the responsibility for a rash of killings in the County. It's not good enough to let this man go on slaying innocent people right left and centre while you sit back and wait for him to make a mistake."

"I'm sorry you think I'm sitting back," Booth said. He draped his raincoat carefully over his arm and stuck his hat on his head. "It's up to you."

"All right," McAlister said. "All right, I'll hold off for a day or two, but you've got to be more positive."

I got up too, and said, "Is that all then, sir?"

"Yes," McAlister said.

Booth and I went out.

Booth kicked the office door with his heel and it closed loudly. He walked a few steps down the corridor and flung his coat over the top of the radiator grid under the window. The window was grey with steam and the rain on the outside of the glass was like a contour map. Booth put his hand flat

on it and brought it away, staring intently at his palm-print
and watching it until it hazed and blurred and sank gradually
back into the blanket of moisture. He turned and rested his
elbows on the heater. He was looking at me but not seeing me,
and in his eyes I could read what he was thinking: I could
see what he saw.

The shop, small and bright and clean. The window was always stuffed with interesting things, in the manner of a
mirror which reflected not just the calendar month but some
sort of ancient and almost mythic survival of the great fes-
tivals; the February hearts, the ghoulish masks of Hallowe'en,
the straw brimmed hats of high summer and wooden spades,
tin pails and postcards, the November fireworks. Now, at
Christmastide, the riot of cards scattered between the mock-
net stockings plump with twists of sweets and Hong Kong
toys, the dolls and gollies and teddy-bears, the ducks that
quacked and wagged their wooden bills when dragged along
on string; across the deep tunnel of the window paper lamps
and streamers, coloured bulbs and baubles, a paper Santa Claus
and a full-bodied cardboard bell. The tobacco case, cleared and
neatly stocked again, was like an altar there behind the
counter, a giant mosiac of compendiums and books and wrap-
ping tissue. The children love a shop like that, cluttered, cheap
and rich for them. The two old women shifted back and forth
behind the counter frame like pouter pigeons. This place was
their nest, nice and snug and safe. No doubt it made enough
to meet their needs, enough even to sustain the notion that
they would one day soon relinquish it and retire. But they
never would. It had long since ceased to be an enterprise and
had become a way of life. They worked there six and a half
days in every week, and every week in every year, and the
shop itself was their security, a wood and tin castle armoured
with dented enamelled boards which touted Black Cat,
Nestlés, Robertson's Jam, Brasso or Sunbrite bleach. The shop,
a hut, held on like an isolated trading post in a half acre of

vacant ground, ringed round by the rubble and dust of the demolished tenements, while approaching nearer every month from the river road the new high flats' foundations were laid, and their walls rose and their balconies were bolted on and the promise of a multitude of customers grew more solid.

The till was dirty brass, scrolled with an intricate floral design, the drawer yawned on its hinge. The front door, hung with magazines, comics and knitting patterns had been locked from the inside, but the rear entrance, where the wholesalers' vans unloaded stock from time to time, stood wide to the night. Whoever killed them locked the front door, rushed it shut and shot the bolt. The Fairbairn sisters were still doing business when he came: still open because they had a customer: a child called Susan, aged four. Susan McLelland, fair-haired, who may have talked of going to school next year, or of the paints she expected in her sock, while her hand opened and dropped the wooden thrupenny bit on the counter and her eyes picked out the largest toffee-apple on the tray. Then what? She kept it, I expect, as children will to comfort her on the cold walk down the long street back to her house where her Mammy waited for her with pyjamas toasting on the fire-guard and the big baking bowl and the sponge out ready and the towel. Perhaps one lick. She could hardly have seen him as he slid in through the back door, or identified him against the beady arc of coloured lights over the coal bin. But the sudden stillness of the old ladies arrested her, scratched her curiosity and by then it was too late. There were no words, no demands, just the three sounds of the gun, then a moment's silence before the crash of the till and the brisk metallic noise of hands scooping change out of the drawer. A good day it had been with forty pounds there, a little more maybe, counting all that he took, every sixpence, every penny, every halfpenny. He went away again and no one saw him. He might have been invisible, passing like a bitter wind, and no one might have known except for what he left behind: the gaping till, a shattered jar embedded in a heap of lentils, and the stone-dead bodies of two meek old ladies and a four-year-old child, who in the end had dropped her toffee-apple into the blood-puddle which covered the floor.

I put on my wet gloves and moved away from him. "Bob," I said. His eyes were quite alive, suddenly, and he showed his teeth. He turned full towards me. "I'm going to bring him in," he said. "And I'm bloody-well going to hold him here all night, and all tomorrow and all the next night, until I get what I'm looking for—and his old man and his mother and his friggin' sweet sister."

"Suit yourself," I said. "I'll draw the warrant and try the house again while he's clear."

"Do that," Booth said, and went down and out of the swing doors into the rain.

3

Joseph

SO, I NEVER even got to see Arnold. A hell of a time at
night this to start dragging folks away from their ain fire-
sides. Sitting holding your peace while they sweat somebody
else before you. Just like the American pictures, except they
keep the big light on. I can smell the smoke of all the cigarettes
they've burned in the last three years. I wonder what they
did with Arnold. Booth, the bloody whore, he pushes out the
chair for me to sit on, and kicks the electric fire round to face
me. I know them, keeping the waiting-room freezing then
bringing you in here where it's warm, so's you'll ease up and
get sleepy and let the buggers put words in your mouth. Not
my mouth. I know what happened that night, and I know
they've got it in for Arno, and that's good enough for me. I'll
keep my eyes open all week, if that's what they want: my
eyes open and my wits about me, and neither Booth nor old
Muirhead's going to make me run off.

"Sorry we had to keep you waiting, Joe," Booth says. "Been
a bit of a rush on our services lately."

"Get on with it," I says.

"You know what it's about?" Booth says.

"I'd be daft if I didn't."

"Fine," Booth says. He walks round back of me where I
can't watch him without screwing round, and there's nothing
tires a man out faster than wheeching round and round in

138

his seat, so I'll sit tight and listen and that's all. He's saying, "Now, we know each other pretty well, Joe, and I know just what you think of the law, but that's beside the point at the moment. I want you to look at it from our point of view."

I'm bloody well not replying to that: soft-soap shit.

"All right," he says. "We've got a problem on our hands. This time it's a stick-up man who does in a couple of old hags and a kid. I mean, is that right? Does it strike you as right, that anybody would do that for forty quid? That was all he got away with, Joe. Just forty lousy quid."

"I've known worse done for less," I says.

"No doubt," Booth says. "But we want to get who did it. Not, mind you, just because that's our job, but for this person's own good too. It's not natural to go around shooting harmless people in cold blood, just for a few quid. And then again, you remember poor Harriet Calder?"

"I should. You rubbed it in enough at the time," I says.

"Did it never strike you that it might be the same person?"

He stops. He comes around the front of me again, so close that he hits my shoulder with the flap of his jacket. He stands in front of me and says, "Somebody broke into a house in Abbotshead Road, early last Friday night: do you know anything about it?"

"Not me," I says. "I was in Kerrigan's pub."

"That's not the point. I said, did you hear anything about it?"

"Nope."

"All right then," Booth says. "We'll just assume that it was the same man as done the break-in there, who shot the Fairbairns and the kid."

"Assume what y'like," I tell him. "You know a friggin' sight more about it than me."

"I just hope so, that's all," Booth says.

Muirhead says to me, "Then there was the break-in at Newtonard eight or nine weeks ago."

"I read about it in the papers," I says.

"You wouldn't be mixed up in that either, I suppose?" Muirhead says.

"You'll be asking me next if I'm the one that poisoned that horse at Ayr last year?" I says.

"Did you?" Muirhead says, lifting his brows up.

"Get on with it," I says. "I've a home to go to, and work in the morning."

"You'd call yourself a conscientious citizen, I suppose," Booth says.

"I would."

"Well, it's your duty to assist the police in any way you can. You know that."

"Get on with it then!" I tell him.

"These . . . goings-on," Muirhead says. "I wonder if Arnold would be able to help us?"

"You've already asked him."

"Arnold's not . . . well, not like you. I think he's a bit recalcitrant," Muirhead says.

Before I could ask the old bugger what he meant, Booth says, "He doesn't like busies."

"Who does then?" I says.

"Elderly ladies in lonely shops," Booth says. "We give them a sense of security."

"What: after they're dead?" I says.

"By nailing whoever did it, so that he can't do it again," Booth says.

"You want t'know where I was that night, is that it? I've told you bloody once, but I suppose bloody once isn't enough for you. Okay, I was in the public house, Samuel Kerrigan's. I stayed there in the saloon bar from the hours of seven o'clock to near on ten, then I went down the road with a man called Sanny M'Meichan and went into his house and his wife made pie an' chips and tea and I stayed there until midnight, then I went home. Arnold was with me, all the time too, if you're interested. Ask anyone in the pub, or M'Meichan or his wife. They'll tell you."

"Arnold was with you all night?" Muirhead says.

"Except for a couple of times he went to the piss-house."

"You didn't go with him then?"

"He can wipe his own arse now," I tell them. "Can't you?" They're quiet for a minute, looking at each other.

"How long was he gone?" Booth says quiet-like.

"Ten minutes."

"And the second time?"

"A couple of minutes the second time: ten minutes the first time."

"You seem hellish sure of that, Joe," Booth says.

"I noticed," I tells him, "because he was away for a long time."

"You thought he was away for a long time then," Booth says, "but it turned out to be only ten minutes. Ten minutes isn't a long time."

"It is when you go for a slash," I says.

"But it might not have been . . . he may have been in the closet," Muirhead chips in.

"Ay, he was," I says.

"How do you know that? Did you see him?" Booth says.

"He told me himself."

"You asked?" Booth says.

"I asked him if he'd been sick, or anything, an' he told me he'd been for a crap."

"All right, all right," Booth says. "We won't go into the subject of Arnold's bowels. Tell me, who else was there?"

"Where?" I asks.

"In the bar," Muirhead says.

"Me and Arno, and M'Meichan and Alex Brown and Wee Robertson and M'Meichan's boy, Larry, and some others—all at different times, y'understand."

"When Arnold went out, who was there?" Booth says.

"Me and the two M'Meichans, and Alex Brown."

"Right," Booth says. "And they don't know how long Arnold was out of the bar. They can't remember."

"I'm not surprised," I tell Booth. "Sanny was bleary by that time, and Brown wasn't much better."

"So, we just have your word for it that he was in the lavatory for ten minutes, and not half an hour, or an hour," Booth says.

"I reckon you could see if anybody else missed him," I say. "Or saw him in the piss-house."

"I reckon we could," Booth says.

He goes in behind his desk and opens a drawer and takes out a box of fancy cigarettes and hands it over to me, open. I take one from it, and Booth hands the box over to Muirhead who shakes his head. Then me and Booth light up and Booth sits down in the tilted chair and puts his feet up to rest on the open drawer. His voice is soft as a chamois leather. He's going to try and con me again. I wonder what Arno told him.

"Joe," Booth says. "Joe: your boy's in bad trouble."

"First I heard of it," I says.

"Take my word for it, Joe. I've seen them come and I've seen them go, but I've never seen anyone running so fast into a condemned cell as that boy of yours."

"He's old enough and ugly enough to take care of himself."

"I don't think you really mean that, Joe," Booth says. He does a wee thing with his fingers that flicks ash on to the carpet. "Now, if you're screening him. I mean if you know he went out and shot those two old dears. . . ."

"Christ, what d'you take him for," I says. "I mean t'say, going out and doing a daft thing like that, then coming back in and joining his father and his mates in another pint. I mean, what sort of lunatic d'you take him for, that could do a thing as cool as that."

"Either cool, or crazy," Booth says. "That's what I want you to think about, Joe. Because I know you know whether it really was him or not. And the same with the Calder girl. You're the one that knows whether he really did it or not."

"You've got your big bloody knife in him," I tells Booth.

"Not without reason," Muirhead says. I'd forgot about him, sitting in his chair like a kangaroo in its pouch.

"Forty quid," I says. "He doesn't need the money that bad, what with him holding down a good job an' all."

"Money's always useful," Booth says. "But I don't think he did it for money."

"Naw, well, what then: because he wanted to?" I says.

"That's right," Booth says. "Because he wanted to."

"Well, if you think that why don't you haul him in and charge him?"

Booth smiles. "You know we can't."

"Bloody true, you can't," I say.

"Get him to come in now and give himself up and I swear to God I'll get him off with his neck. He's as crazy as a coot, and well you know it, Joe."

"Well I don't know it," I say. "Frig off a mile, and do your own dirty work. If you're so bloody sure you're persecuting the right bloke, why bother with all this palaver: why not just find out and go and bring him in. There's nothing I can do to stop you. Go on, bring him in then. Hit him with anything you fancy hitting him with. Try him for his neck, and see how far you'll get. But you won't do that, will you, because you want to make sure you get him for good, and right now you can't even find out if he was within a mile of that shop. Well, I know better than you. I know he was in Sammy Kerrigan's pub all night, so you can stuff that information up your backside."

"He's insane, Joe," Booth says. "It's been coming for years, why blink the fact."

"He's no more insane nor you and me," I tell him. I had the feeling he'd try that one, to get me to rat on my own son because I'm afraid of him swinging. Arno knows everything he's doing, and even if I wouldn't do them things myself, what right have I got to turn him over. Get him put away for treatment: the only place Booth would get him put away to would be the sinner's unhallowed grave, with his neck broke and burned.

"You know he'll do it again, don't you," Booth says. "Think about that when you're lying in bed at night. Who it's going to be next. You'll be as much to blame for the next one as he will. Maybe a bit more so."

"Balls," I says. "Arno's been a terror in his time, just wildness like all boys have. He hasn't killed nobody, and he isn't going to kill nobody. You just want a' easy scapegoat, that's what you want."

Booth sits up straight in his chair and grinds out his fag in the tin ashtray. "I just want whoever killed the Calder girl, and the two Fairbairns and Susan: and until something happens to make me think differently, I'll continue to consider Arnold as the right man to fill the bill. In other words, Skinner, I want your son for four killings, and I'm bloody-well going to get him."

"Right," I say. "Okay, Mister Booth. You get him. That's all I say to you. Just you get him, but I'll tell you this for no extra charge, you'll not get him through me. That you will not."

"We thought you might be interested in saving yourself a great deal of grief," Muirhead says. "You and your wife."

"Keep her out of this," I says. It might just be a threat. I don't think they can do nothing to her, or to Rosemary.

"It's a shade late in the day for that," Booth says. "I'm afraid she's already in it."

I could tell him what I think of him. Right this minute I could even go so far as to lay hands on him, but that's what Arnold can't do that I can. I can stop myself coming up to his bait.

"Get on with it," I says. "And let me get home."

"You can go now," Booth says.

Muirhead slouches out of the settee and opens the door for me. Booth's busy lighting another cigarette.

"How about Arnold," I say. "Where's he?"

"He's safe enough," Booth says. "But I wouldn't wait, if I were you."

Muirhead starts to close the door on me, putting me out into the waiting-room again where the constable is. "No," Muirhead says too. "We might be some time with him yet."

4

Booth

"RIGHT, SKINNER," I said, after Muirhead had brought him in and left again. "I think it's about time we got down to brass tacks, you and I."

"Again," he said.

"You know what I'm talking about," I said.

Skinner said, "I've a vague idea, yeah, but I'm not the man y'want, y'know."

"On the contrary," I said. "You're just the man we want. I've not only got the shop killings lined up against you, but I've still got the file on the Calder girl laying open, and, what's more, I think I'm going to stick you with them both."

"That's nice," Skinner said. "But I wouldn't want t'bet on it, Mister Booth."

I said, "First things first; we'll have you out of a job for a kick off."

"An' that won't worry me at all."

I began to edge round the radiator under the window, to see if he'd follow me with his eyes, a gimmick to let me know if I'd said anything to perturb him as yet, but like old Joe he simply sat there waiting for me to come round into the direct line of his vision, sitting quite loosely, his arms folded and his legs crossed.

"I wouldn't be surprised if I managed to hang a couple of break-ins on you first," I said.

"N'doubt, y'could," he said. "If you pulled strings."

"I'm sure I could," I said.

Skinner said, "But y'wouldn't want t'do that."

"Why not?" I said. "It'd put you well out of harm's way."

"But not for keeps," he said. "An' I don't think you really want t'settle for anything that's not by way of bein' kind of permanent, eh?"

"Small beginnings," I said.

"Come on now, Mister Booth," he said, with a note of sarcastic impatience in his voice. "You an' me both know that the pokey doesn't scare me none. Beside which you'd be pervertin' the cause of justice."

"Leave the big words to me, please, Skinner," I said.

Grinning at me, he said, "And with me inside forbye, you'll have no chance'f settlin' all them other nasty crimes."

I sat down, not behind the desk but on the kitchen chair a little to the left of him, so that there was nothing between us. I lit my cigarette rather slowly to give him time to wonder from which direction I would come in at him, for he must have known that I wasn't going to waste half the night making him reiterate what we already knew.

"You've got a younger sister, haven't you, Skinner?" I said.

"I have that," he said. "A teacher she is, more's the pity."

"So I heard," I said. "It wouldn't look too good on her record card, if you got sent away. I don't suppose all the activity round your humble home of late has exactly filled her with delight."

Without anxiety he said, "That's a matter private between her an' me, Inspector."

"Not unless she happened, just by chance, to be nabbed for distributing the stuff," I said.

With not a trace of bitterness or anger showing yet, he said, "What stuff are y'talkin' about?"

"Property stolen from one or two houses round here in the

last couple of months, or money taken from the till in the
Fairbairns' shop."

"How can she be nabbed for distributing stuff she's never
even heard of, never mind seen," Skinner said.

"You know well enough how accidents can happen," I said.
"With the best will in the world."

"Sure, y'could make it work," Skinner said. "Nobody's
denyin' you're one'f the best fiddlers in the business, Booth,
but I'm still thinkin' you'd need t'find this stuff before y'could
plant it on me, or on her for that matter."

"We've recovered some of it already or will shortly," I said.

"Think so," he said. "I know you won't."

"Because you've hidden it yourself?"

"Naw," he said. "Because I know who did the jobs an' where
the stuff is, and that's that."

"But you won't tell me, I suppose?" I said.

He waved his hand in the air, as if swatting at a persistent
wasp. "Christ, I thought y'knew me better'n to mark me
down as a toady."

"Not even to save your own neck?"

"That'd be a different story," he admitted. "But as m'neck's
not in any danger, I'm sayin' nothin'."

"But you do know who did it?" I said.

"Did what?" he said.

"The Fairbairn killings and the kid."

He said, "Sure. I know. Same bloke as did the robbery at
Newtonard, for which I've got a lotta witnesses t'say I wasn't
even in the County that night."

"The same gun," I said. "But not necessarily the same hand
on the butt."

He uncrossed his legs and bent forward towards me,
stabbing his finger for emphasis, as he said, "D'you want information or not? I'm tellin' y'for a fact, it was the same
bloke."

"Supposing," I said, "I intend to charge you with the shop

killings, right here and now," I said. "What could you do, Arnold?"

He really smiled this time, broad as a gollywog. "I'd be on that phone t'Rumsey an' he'd have me walkin' out'f here free as a bird before mornin'."

"Yes," I admitted, "I think you're probably right."

He pressed his advantage, forcing me to listen to him toting up familiar points of law, wagging his finger at me dictatorially, as if he was conducting a lesson for my special benefit. It was not, even at that moment, the slur on my professional abilities which I resented, nor was it, as he—and Muirhead too—believed, any twisted animosity towards Skinner himself. I hated him because he was not human enough to be afraid of us, or the law, or of himself. He drew us together, him and I, into the same foul-smelling web. True, we were bound by mutual interest, bound one to the other by the law which says one man shall steal to live and another shall prevent stealing for exactly the same end. But with Skinner, I resented his implication that we even breathed the same air. He was not a desperate man, not even a man who loved money enough to fight society to get it. He killed because he wanted to kill, for self-glorification, and for the love of blood, and that exempted him from any sympathy I might have had left to give. To stop him I felt I had only to hate him enough not to undervalue my hand. But, because I am what I am and he was what he was, I had at least to search for the weakness upon which I could work. To stamp him out, kill him as one would an infected rat, or any other piece of vermin.

"I know a thing or two, Inspe'tor," he was saying. "I know as much about the law's you do yourself, an' I'm tellin' you, if you go an' bring me up without a case I'll make you the laughin'-stock of the whole'f Scotland."

"By pleading insanity," I said.

"You've never known me hit the ceiling yet," he said, in a muted voice now. "Nobody has. That'll never wash. By Christ,

I've met m'share of head-shrinkers an' it'd take better'n them t'put me away in the padded cell. I'm as right as you are up here." He tapped the side of his head briefly.

I nodded.

"Well, remember that," he said, and left it. I watched him struggling to curb his tongue, but before I could encourage him to keep talking, he got himself under control, and sat back with enough rigid defiance, and triumph, in his posture to tell me I'd missed my chance. I didn't really create another that night, though I kept him with me for an hour, going over again and again his alibis, falling back in the well-tried technique of switching rapidly from one to the other. It was all just a formality, an excuse to keep him out of the way, while Muirhead ransacked his house. It was a conviction rather than a premonition that nothing would come to light to assist our case against him. Just before I called the duty sergeant to get rid of him, I bore back upon the threat of persecution. Even there he bested me, at least to his satisfaction.

"And remember you've got a sister, Skinner," I said abruptly out of the shadow of a pause in the staccato of question and answer. "Think of her."

He was on his feet by this time, and his parting shot was much better and, because he was Arnold and not Joe, held an undeniably sinister threat.

"An' so've you, Inspector," he said.

For an instant I didn't quite make the connection, and asked, rather stupidly, "What?"

"A sister," he said. "Remember, you've got a sister too."

I let it go at that, for the time being.

5

Howie

W H A T   W I T H Christmas looming near, I was working like the hammers for the overtime bonus. The yards being busy there was much extra money floating around. Six to six I was on that week, and not a whole day at home for nearly a month. A good thing in a way; it kept my mind off McNally. Somehow once I'd got the two hundred quid salted away, I seemed to have no urge to rush out and do another job. Besides, like I say, I was working too hard, and making good enough money without raising any ulcers trying for more outside the law. The next stunt would have to be the Railway yard itself and I wasn't mad on that idea. I mean, if anyone was going to get hooked, I knew who it would be. I'm not daft altogether. What was it all for anyhow? I stopped sometimes to ask myself, what was it all for. Still, it kept my mind off Skinner too, and I just didn't want to think about him then.

Seven in the morning I got home. I was done in; proper bashed. Another week and it'd be Christmas and I was damned if I was going to chalk myself up to work on Christmas Day. Not with the kids in the house. I had two hundred quid put away safe in the bag inside the cistern, and sooner or later, when the fire went out around the Carsehorn district I'd be able to take it and put it in the bank.

It was bloody cold that morning, somewhere between raining and snowing, the frost falling just as thick as snow against

151

your face like it had been for full three days. I was thinking
that after I'd got Jean and the kids out of the house on Christmas Day, and away over to their Granny's, I would build up
the fire, take one of the Ne'erday bottles and all the comics
and Westerns I could find and go back to bed for the rest of
the afternoon. That's what I was thinking when she opened
the door to me, and I went in.

Right off I knew something was the matter. She didn't look
angry, but she had that whiteness around her mouth. I
thought it was one of the kids had been up all night, ill, or
something: I thought that first, then I thought next, and
with a bit of jitteryness that she'd found out about me and
the two jobs. Then I thought the cops had been. I went right
into the kitchen still with my coat on.

"What's wrong?" I asked her.

She stood beside the grate, picking lumps of coal out of the
bag and putting them on the fire. When I saw that she was
dressed already, I started to jitter again about the police.

"For Heaven sake what is it, Jean?" I said, touching her.

"A man came to see you last night," she said, in a hurry.

I sat down in the armchair, fighting it hard. I knew my voice
was high when I asked her who.

She seemed better now, as if in having told me she'd got a
whole load off her chest.

"He said he was a friend of yours. Said his name was
Skinner."

I sat back, then I got up and started to take off my coat, talking to her while I did it, as if Skinner was all right.

"What did he want then?" I said.

"He wanted to see you," she said.

"What about?" I said, then said, "Maybe you could get the
breakfast up while you tell me, dear. I'm knackered."

She went over to the cooker and lit the gas and took
down the frying-pan. Then she put it down again and turned
round.

"I didn't like him the least little bit, Brian," she said. "I didn't know you had friends like that."

I said, "I don't know him all that well. What was he after?"

She stood still with the frying-pan in her hand as if she was getting ready to pitch it at me.

"He wanted to see you."

"What about?" I said.

"He didn't tell me."

"Then what are you getting yourself all worked up for?" I said.

"I'm not all worked up."

"All right," I said. "But I'm not blind, Jean. I can see he annoyed you."

"I told him you wouldn't be home until the morning, but he asked if he could come in for a while and wait. I mean, I told him you were on the twelve-hour shift but he insisted on coming in."

I stood beside her and soaped my hands and started to wash them. She poured me some hot water from the kettle.

"You should've shut the door on him, if you didn't like the look of him. Skinner's all right, though. He's all right."

"I didn't like him," she said.

"Did he. I mean . . ." I was watching her, to see if she'd give anything away. Skinner was the last person in the world, next to the cops, that I wanted to come in my house and bother my wife. He's not the sort you pick to come into your house at night when the wife's alone. Meeting him in the pub's fine. He's a hard man and he's all right, but I didn't know what to think of the way Jean was acting.

"No," she said. "It wasn't anything like that really."

"What was it then?" I said, washing again.

She put the pan on the stove and switched on the current.

"Och, it's nothing, nothing really," she said. "But I mean he just came in and sat down. I didn't offer him tea or anything—and he talked and played with Fiona then he went away again."

"What did he say?" I asked.

"Just blethers really," Jean said.

I said, "What sort of blethers?"

In a sort of burst, she said, "He said I was to tell you you weren't to worry about anything because he wasn't going to ... shoot his mouth off. I asked him what he meant, but he just said you'd know. Brian, what did he mean?"

"Search me," I said. I wondered vaguely if he was going to put the screw on me to keep his trap shut about my being involved in the last two jobs.

"He must have meant something," Jean said, planking the rashers into the pan.

"Honestly, I just don't know. He's a bit on the queer side actually."

"He looks it," Jean said to herself, more or less.

"He's all right though," I said. "He wouldn't do you any harm."

"You should have seen the way he looked at me," she said in her busy voice.

"How d'you mean?" I was beginning to get angry. I was tired I suppose. That would have something to do with it, but the thought of him made me begin to get angry.

Jean shrugged her shoulders. "I don't really know," she said. "Just peculiar. It made me feel uncomfortable."

"He's a bit shifty right enough," I said. "But I wouldn't worry about him. If he comes again, just don't let him in."

"I won't," she said. "Don't worry."

The bacon was smoking nicely. I dried myself and sat down at the table. My back was sore and my neck felt strained. I'd been working too hard. Jean broke eggs among the bacon and plugged in the kettle. The fire was roaring up the lum and I could feel the heat on my back, relaxing me, like taking a bath, seeping through my sweater and trousers.

"Have you known him very long then?" Jean asked.

"No," I said. "I hardly know him at all."

"He must have had some reason for coming up here."

"Well, I'll find out next time I see him, though the Lord knows when that'll be," I said. "How're the kids? Sleep all night?"

"Yes," she said. "You know what he did before he went away?"

"What?" I said.

"He gave me this to buy the kids a present." She put the two pound notes down on the table in front of me. I looked at them.

"That was nice of him," I said. "You can put it to good use, no doubt."

"I didn't want to take it, but I mean, what could I do?"

"Stop worrying about it. He does things like that. Perhaps he likes kiddies."

Jean said, "He seemed quite taken with Fiona."

"Did she behave herself?" I asked.

"She was just on her way to bed."

"I see. When did he come then?"

"Half-past eight," Jean said. "He stayed for an hour."

"Hurry up with that fodder, dear," I said. "I want to get to my pit before the girl wakes up."

She served my food and sat down opposite me to have her cornflakes. I decided, while I was eating, that I wasn't going to let Skinner worry me, and that there hadn't been anything important behind his visit. Then she said, "He's funny right enough. He said we had a nice bathroom."

I put my knife and fork down.

"How did he know?"

"He used it," she said. "He asked me if he could."

I didn't start eating again, until she said, "Why? Shouldn't I have?"

"No, no," I said.

I bolted through my food then while she was clearing away the dishes, I went out and into the bathroom and locked the door. Behind me in the bedroom I heard my daughter starting to bawl, then the younger joining in, bawling. I was shaking when I got up on to the pan and lifted down the big metal shroud from the cistern. The package was still there all right, but just to make sure I drained the water away and held the ball up to keep the tank dry, tore the plaster away and lifted the plastic bag up from the bottom of the tank. I could see that it hadn't been opened. I hadn't time to check it all anyhow, so I put it back, taped it on again and let the cistern refill itself. I don't know why but I looked in the cupboard under the bath, but it was just the usual rubber ducks and packets of Vim. I wouldn't have bothered with the big cupboard under the stairs at all, if I just hadn't happened to notice that the latch had been put round the wrong way and the door not shut properly. I opened it and struck a match and went in on my hands and knees. I moved a lot of the stuff around, the old bar-bells and the shoe-last and other junk. My two bottles of whisky were okay, still where I put them on top of the dross behind the wooden partition against which we stored spare coal in paper bags. I didn't notice anything odd about it at the time, I just had that funny feeling.

I flushed the toilet again and came out. I went into our bathroom and got out my Christmas money from the tin in the stud drawer and took a couple of notes from it, then I went back into the kitchen. Jean was through getting the kids up, I could hear them making a fuss. I don't know why I did it, but I put my two quid on the table and lifted the notes Skinner had left and threw them in the fire. I even stabbed them down with a poker, so they would burn away faster. Then I went away through to my bed in a hurry, before Fiona got a chance to see me. I lay and thought about it all for a long time before I got to sleep. I didn't like it very much really, but I thought at the time I was just being daft again.

6

Ruby

THE TELLY said it was snowing all over the country, and showed pictures to prove it. It was going to be a white Christmas after all and the bairns would be pleased. I reached out of the bed and pulled the curtain back a bit, so that I could see over to the houses opposite. True enough, the roof was white, the ledges hung with thick snow. The trees in the room windows were lit already, although it was still only mid-morning. I heard Mike cursing the fire in the kitchen and I shouted through to him to put the kettle on. He swore at me half-heartedly, but lit the stove. Ten minutes later he brought me in tea and a slice of toast. I told him to leave the door open so I could watch what came on the telly next. The house was dismal at that time in the morning. We didn't have any sort of excuse for a tree in the window. Mike had put some glass things and holly round the mirror and I'd slung paperchains from the light shade to the corners of the room. But even that didn't help to make the house cheerful at that time in the morning. When the fire got going and breakfast down it would be better. I never did like the Christmastime much, because it put me in mind of Sally. One thing George was good for and that was organising a fine old time at Christmas: fussing with all the trimmings. We had a tree, a real live one, in a tub, with fairy-lamps on it. It meant a lot of extra work, but it was nice in the long run. Mike didn't believe in

157

Christmas though. Like all his mates he fancied saving up his money and his energies for Ne'erday.

I lay in bed for an hour, waiting for the fire to burn up bright and warm the living-room, and thinking as how I'd like to do something special that night, just to chase away the blues. I shouted through and asked him what we were planning, and he shouted back and told me nothing. We could go out to Sammy's if I wanted later on. I didn't want to really, but it was better than staying at home.

I got up about half-eleven and cooked breakfast. Mike'd got the papers and we sat round the fire reading them for a while. The sky was dark outside the window as if it was gathering itself ready to snow again. If I listened hard I could hear the bairns shouting in and out the closes and up and down the street outside, playing in the dirty patches of snow in the backcourts, and on the wash-house roofs. I was beginning to think I'd go out and walk round the park or maybe take the bus into Argyle Street just to see the fun, when the door bell went. I looked at Mike and he looked at me.

"It's maybe the postman," I said.

He nodded, and got up to answer the door. I heard him say, "Well, my God, you're an early bird," then he put his head round the edge of the living-room door and told me, "It's Arnold, get some clothes on."

I went into the bedroom and shut the door. I could hear them talking in the living-room. Arnold's voice was high and chirpy, talking nineteen to the dozen. I put on my woollen dress and stockings and slippers and did my hair a bit, then I went into the living-room again. The first thing I saw was a big paper bag sitting on the draining board at the sink. I could see the parcels in it wrapped up in fancy paper, the shape of the bottles and gold-foil tops sticking out.

"Santa Claus," Arno said, getting up and coming over to buss me on the cheek. I glanced over his shoulder at Mike, but Mike just raised his eyebrows and smiled at the performance. Arno went past me rubbing his hands together and singing under his breath.

"What brings you out at this unholy hour?" I asked him.

He peered into the parcel and without turning round held up his hand, the palm flat and fingers spread open to shush me up. He poked in the bag and came out with a fat bottle of Cherry Heering, and a holly paper packet. He gave a long bow that made his hair spray down over his face, then snapped up again jerking his head to shoot his hair back into position in its thin shed.

"Ruby," he said, "Merry Christmas and many of them." He gave me the packet and handed the bottle to Mike.

"Well, thanks right enough, Arnold," Mike said, holding the bottle and looking at it. "Y'shouldn't've bothered."

I did as Arno told me and opened the parcel. Four pairs of black nylons.

"Right size, I hope, Ruby?" he said anxiously, watching me.

I gave him a pleased smile, and told him it was. I don't know how he knew.

"D'I not get another cheeper for that?" Arno said.

I bent forward and brushed his cheek with my mouth.

"Lovely," he said. "Lovely. You're a lucky man, McNally." Mike waved the bottle up triumphantly, and said, "I am that."

I put the nylons in the drawer, and asked Arno if he'd like some breakfast.

"Nah, nah," he said. "No time for that."

"Something on then?" Mike said. "Is that why you're not working?"

"Work," Arno said. He plumped himself down in the arm-chair. "Only mugs work at this time of the year."

"Y'seem t'have struck it rich," Mike said.

"Well," Arno said, and spread his hands like a fat Jew pawn-broker. He hadn't taken his coat off and he plunged his hand into the pocket and took out a fifty box of Capstan. "Have a fag," he said. We all took one and lit up. Arno was sitting forward in his chair.

"Right," he said. "I hope you've nothin' special on t'day."

Mike and I looked at each other again. There was something in the wind.

"Not that we couldn't put off," Mike said warily. "How?"

" 'Cause I've a car outside," Arno said. "An' I thought we could all go for a run in the country, maybe have a snack and a tipple in some of them plush hotels out by Aberfoyle or Drymen or Ardingarth. Eh?"

"A car, have you?" Mike said.

Arno leapt to his feet, like a cat with its paws on a griddle. He was grinning all over his dial. "Hired it," he said. "Don't worry your head about it bein' knocked. It's mine all right, all legal and signed for, more or less. I've got it on trial for a week from a fellah I know, and I'm thinkin' of buying it, if I like it."

"Cars now," I said. "Going up in the world, Arno?"

"Y'never said a truer word," he said, serious for a second. "Sky's the limit."

"I see," Mike said, stirring himself. He put the brandy down on the mantel, and said, "Well, I don't see why not. Good'f y't'invite us, Arno." He looked at me. "Feel like a ride in the country, Ruby?" he said.

"Sure," I said.

Arno leaned on the table like a minister. "Right," he said. "Get dolled up an' let's go."

Mike stood up and stretched himself, then told Arno, "There's just one condition, mate. The grub'll be my treat. Okay?"

After a bit of hesitation, Arno said, "Okay then, Mike."

"Right," Mike said. "Let's get drawn t'gether and get the show on the road."

We hustled round and got ourselves ready. Before we

went we had a glass for the road from Mike's bottle.

The car, when I could see it properly after the bloody kids
had scattered from round it, was a nice second-hand Hillman,
in good nick too by the look of it. Mike was all for having a
shuftie under the bonnet but Arno talked him out of it and
we climbed in. Mike and Arno were in the front and I had the
back seat to myself. We drove up the street and stopped at the
traffic lights long enough to let Arno turn round from steering and say, "Y'look like Lady Muck sitting there in your
furs, Ruby. How's it feel?"

"Drive on, James," I said, waving my glove at him.

We drove into Glasgow and across the river and out the
Dumbarton Road to Balloch. Outside the city there was a blink
of sun now and then and the fields and the hills all blue and
white with thick soft snow. The inside of the car was warm,
and the snow made it exciting. I felt like a girl again, sitting
in the Hillman, looking out at the scenery.

At Balloch we stopped and went into a hotel and had our
dinner, then we went and sat in the lounge looking out over
the Loch and the bonnie banks. The place was full of stuffed
shirts and young couples, but Arno knew how to handle himself all right and we got service when we wanted it. Arno
and me had a drink or two, then stopped because he was driving, but Mike must have tucked away a good few. Big meal
or not he was beginning to look just a bit glazed when we came
out and got in the car again. Him and me sat in the car, while
Arno went back into the hotel again. Mike put his arm round
me, "Are y'havin' a ball, honey?" he said. I told him I was.
"A great kid's Arno, isn't he not now?" Mike said. I agreed
with him. The water of the Loch was like pink velvet but not
soft, and the light had started to fade away from behind the
big high mountains, so that the shadows fell long and pigeon-
coloured on the soft banks of snow. All the trees were stripped
bare and fine, except for the thick patches of firs black and
shaggy like expensive rugs on the hillsides. The house-boats

that we could see were mostly shut up for the winter, but away out on the Loch, near the far shore, a speedboat was cutting a pure white furrow and making a noise like a lazy bumble bee. What with the food and the liquors I'd drank, I was so relaxed and peaceful I could've curled up and gone to sleep with my head on my old man's knees. Maybe I would have too, if Arno hadn't come back and handed us a full bottle of gin.

"T'keep the cold out," he said, and started the engine. "Get wired in."

Mike let me go and began to open the bottle.

"By Christ, Arno, you're a white man indeed," he said. "How d'you manage that?"

"Ways'n means," Arno said, staring over his shoulder while he edged the car out of the parking lot and took it down gently on to the main road. Mike loosened his tie and undid the top button of his shirt, then with his hand against the back of the seat tipped the bottle to his mouth and drank about an inch of neat gin. Gasping he put the bottle down again.

"Ruby," he offered, but I said I didn't want any.

"Arnold, then?" Mike said, pushing the bottle over Arno's shoulder.

"Not just now," Arno said. "I'm not wantin' t'run this buggy int' the bloody water."

"Ach well," Mike said and knocked off another mouthful.

I was glad to see him cork the bottle and put it on the ledge under the rear-view window. I can't stand him when he's filthy drunk and I'm sober.

Where exactly we went I don't know. Arno was enjoying himself driving and I suppose he was driving fast enough to have frightened us if I hadn't been so sleepy. We ran close beside the Loch for a long time, with the water sometimes almost right below and the banks of snow and the trees right over us, the road twisty as a snake beside the Loch between the big mountains with the sun shining bleak and sad-like only

on the high parts of the hills opposite. I felt my head nodding
and went right off to sleep.

When I wakened we were still driving, and it was full dark.
Arno's face was lit from the dash-light and in the half second
it took me to realise where I was, it gave me a bad fright. He
was driving hard, his mouth open and his cheeks drawn tight
back to show his teeth, his head held forward and cocked. I
put my hand out and touched Mike's knees. He was splayed
back against the seat, dead to the world. I felt stifled inside the
car and my head was throbbing. My mouth was dirty and I
wanted nothing so much as a big cup of tea.

"Where are we now?" I asked Arno.

"Ah, you're back t'life then, Ruby," he said. "Did y'have
a nice forty winks? By God, y'don't half snore."

"Where are we then?" I said.

"We'll be in Ardingarth in about five minutes," he said.
"How?"

"I could do with a cup of tea," I said.

"There's that gin there," Arno said.

"Tea," I said.

"You're a great one for your cuppa," he said. "Okay, we'll
stop off an' have some."

When the car stopped outside a place called "The High-
lander", Mike woke up. He came round with a start and as
soon as I'd told him we were going into this hotel, he started
feeling like a glass of lager. That's always been his sure cure for
feeling low, a glass of ice-cold lager. Arno got out of the car
and opened the door for us. We bundled out and stood in the
cold, breathing in the air. It went right down to my stomach
and filled my head with blood, but after a minute or two I
began to liven up again. Mike was in fine fettle, for he still had
enough of the booze in him to make him rare for action. We
walked over to the long front door of the place and went into
the hall. This wasn't like the other hotel, but modern and
slick; trees of nylon with electric candles on them all down

the hall to the door of the dining-room, and women in long gowns and men, one or two of them in monkey-suits, flitting back and forth between the bar and the lounge. I could hear the mutter of voices and the music from the telly in the lounge. A gentleman came forward and asked us if we wished to register, or to have dinner. I could see him eyeing us up and down and though there was nothing said or even in his face, I could tell right off he disapproved of the likes of us. Maybe it was Mike stinking of spilt gin. Arno put him in his place though and the gent showed us into the lounge, as if I'd been the Queen of Siam, or Arno the Rajah of Bengal. We settled down at a wickerwork table and a youngster in a white bumfreezer came over and took our order. Mike had decided that he'd better have a whisky along with the lager, just to clean out his stomach. Arno settled for a Carlsberg and I got my pot of tea. The clock said it was half-past six, and I was surprised for I thought it would have been much later.

"Well, Arno," McNally said. "It's been a grand day right enough."

"Sure," Arno said. "This is the life. You should get out more often, you two. Now I'm gettin' a car we can buzz off for the weekend whenever y'fancy it."

"Ay," Mike said. "There's nothing like it."

The waiter came back and put the tray down and poured my tea for me and the drinks for the men.

"Here's to you then," Mike said.

Arno lifted his glass, "T'Ruby," he said.

"I'll drink t'that," Mike said: big-man voice. "Ruby."

The tea was just what I needed. I took a squint round me at all the people enjoying themselves. Arno and Mike were talking.

"I hear Howie's wee bit play was worth while," Arno said.

"It was that," Mike said. "That's another thing we've t'thank you for."

"Well," Arno said. "It's no loss what a frien' gets, is it?"

"If there's anythin' can do for you, any time," Mike said. "Say the word."

"Y'did enough gettin' Howie off my back."

"Is it soon then?" Mike said.

"As soon as Booth gets out'f m'hair," Arno said.

Mike was getting confidential, his elbows on the table. "Ay, they've really got it in for you, Arnold," he said. "Right enough though, it's been a hell of a time in the district. D'you know, I mean without givin' away any secrets, d'you know who did for the old women and the wean?"

"I've an idea," Arno said.

"Y'have," Mike said. "Who?"

"Don't ask me," Arno said. "I'm on my oath t'keep tight about it."

"Go on," Mike said. "I'll not breathe a word."

"Sorry," Arno said. "It's more'n m'life's worth."

Mike nodded, his eyes full of sympathy. "Like that, is it?"

"Yep," Arno said.

Mike ordered another whisky to chase his lager, and after that another. His voice was loud all of a sudden, and his arm shook when he took it off the table.

"Heh," he said. "But y'd have had a goodly giggle at young Howie up at the Kissock place."

"Hold your tongue, Mike," I told him.

"Ach, away, nobody's bothering with me," he said.

"Tell us about it," Arno said.

"Don't encourage him, Arno," I said.

"Let him alone, Ruby," Arno said, though smiling with his mouth while he said it. "I'm interested."

Then it struck me that he was a damn sight too interested, and I began to think that maybe the whole day had been nothing but a cover-up for this sort of question. Getting my old man half-cut, or well oiled, is one sure way of getting him to blab. Now Arno had him just where he wanted him, and if I was right, and Skinner did want to find out about the two last jobs we'd pulled then he had the best chance he was ever likely to get.

"I think it's time we were going, Mike," I said.

"Another half, Ruby," Mike said. "Have one t'keep's company."

"No thanks," I said. "Come on let's get out of here."

"Are y'hungry, Ruby?" Arno said. "We can have a feed here, if y'feel like it."

"I think we'd better get home before he conks out on us," I said.

Mike said, "For Jesus sake leave me alone, woman."

Arno nodded a little bit as if to say he agreed, or to tell me that he knew what he was doing. I'll bet he did.

When Mike had been furnished with another half and a lager, Arno asked him outright, "Did y'make much off the Matheson place? I mean, in terms of hard cash?"

"D'you know," Mike said, his nose almost touching Arno's, "D'you know, there was six hundred odd quid sittin' in a bag on the table as if the silly bastard had done it up special for us to come in an' lift."

Arno whistled through his teeth. "Six hundred, eh?" he said. "That's a good night's screw."

"Bloody good," Mike agreed. "Half it down the middle and there y'are; only . . ."

"Only what?" Arno said.

"Only I took a picking or two before we did the split," Mike said. "Don't tell your frien' Howie, though."

Arno laughed heartily and patted Mike's arm. I wanted to get them out of there and to get shot of Arno now as soon as I could. I thought that maybe I was being silly in suspecting him, but he kept on and on asking questions until I was sure I was right. I didn't know why he wanted information, because it could do him no damn good now, unless he had plans for Howie, but for some reason of his own he was very anxious to know our business. I wondered if Howie had told him anything at all. I had the suspicion that the boy wasn't so keen on sharing secrets with Skinner as he had been a couple of months ago, that the gilt was off the gingerbread quite a bit since Arno had palmed him off on Mike and me. Still, I wasn't in a fit state to do wee sums in my head then, all I wanted was to take Mike by the scruff of the neck and haul him out of there.

"You're a right twister," Arno said. "I like that though. Makin' the bugger pay for his learnin'. I'd've done the same m'self."

"Well," Mike said, smiling and pleased. Just like all the rest of them he was falling for Arnold's line of patter. No matter how much he talked about not wanting to mix with Skinner, down there at the bottom he looked on Arno as someone to be envied and respected and someone whose good opinion was worth having. And as I looked at the pair of them sitting there I started to think of George and Sally again and wonder where they were and what they were doing. She'd be a big girl now, with no stockings to hang up in the fond belief she'd get them filled by Santa on the night of Christmas Eve, but she would still be young enough to go out and enjoy herself without looking for anything other than the lights and the presents and the snow and all that stuff. She wouldn't be sitting with two men, afraid of one because he was shallow and weak and afraid of the other because he was the very opposite. She wouldn't have anything yet to fear, unless it was that someone else dear to her would go away and leave her as I done all them years back. Left her at school and kissed her and gave her a half crown and walked away knowing that unless George was more of a man than I thought he was, I'd never see her again. Hating her then because of what she done to me, and hating her and loving her without even knowing what she had grown up to look and behave like, in a swank hotel with two men I was afraid of. But it's too long a way to try going back.

"I want to go home now, Arno," I said. "I don't want him flaking out on me here."

"Ay, okay," Arno said, still with his hand on Mike's arm. "In a minute."

"One more," Mike said. "While I tell you about what he did. Y'heard about the dog."

"A bit," Arno said.

I got up and said, "I'm going now anyway. I'll wait for you in the car."

"Ach, Ruby, sit down," Mike said. "We'll go in a minute."

I went out through the room with people staring at me, and through the hall and out into the courtyard. There was a sort of light off the hills as if some of the sunshine'd been held by the snow; a snippet of moon away over the trees behind the hotel. I stood beside the Hillman and looked at it. I don't remember what I was thinking: just thinking. I waited five minutes, then I got into the car, which he hadn't locked, and waited another five minutes until they came.

"What happened t'you," Mike said. "I thought y'wanted fun."

"I'm tired, that's all," I said.

He pushed in beside me in the back seat and got the bottle of gin out, then humphed himself over the back of the seat into the place beside Arnold. Arnold was laughing to himself.

Mike turned to him and put his face up into Arnold's. "Funny i'n't it?" he said.

"A bloody riot. If it'd been me with him I'd've kicked his arse from hell t'breakfast," Arno said.

There was some ice on the road now and perhaps for that reason Arno drove slowly out of the village away from the hotel. Mike was scoffing gin again straight from the bottle. I knew it would hit him hard in five or ten minutes and that when it did he'd go out like a candle. The side of the road was dark and not much passed us in the way of traffic. I didn't know where the hell we were. The road wasn't clear of snow here and I could hear it whooshing under the car, and on the corners see the gold colour of the banking as the headlights glossed over it. We hadn't gone more than five miles before McNally was away with it. I heard the bottle hit the floor, saw Arno stooping down quickly to pick it up and cork it. without taking his eyes from the road. Mike's head rocked back and slid all the way down the door until it hung, like a sheepshead on a butcher's hook, with his nose against the window handle and his temple jammed against the glove compartment.

"He'll suffer when he wakes up all right," Arnold said. "D'you want t'take him in the back and spread him out?"

"Leave him," I said. "He'll not come round now for a while."

"Suit yourself," Arnold said.

We drove for another fifteen minutes, or maybe more, without saying anything. Then I began to suffer for all the tea I'd drunk. I thought we might be near home, but there was still precious few houses on the roadside and when we came out from between the trees at a stretch I saw nothing all round but snow and the hills drifting back into the sky. I couldn't wait any longer and asked Arnold to stop for a minute.

"Are y'sick?" he said.

"No," I told him. "I want to pay a call."

"At least you'll not need a penny," he said.

He slowed the car to a crawl and cut the engine and let the thing trundle down a slope in the road and round a corner, then cut off the road a couple of yards and put on the brake. The wing was touching the snow and I had just enough room to push the door open and get out. It wasn't as dark as I thought it would be, and the blobs of snow on the fir-tree branches helped me to see where I was going. I went back about ten yards and crossed the verge and climbed a low dry-stone dyke into a field. There were trees about ten yards away, a black mass of them, thick, growing up. Everything was quiet. Absolutely quiet. I crouched behind the wall and did what I had to. I stood up again to adjust my dress when I heard the noise: just a scuffle like an animal might make as it darted between the trees. I half turned round, frightened of what I'd heard about rats and weasels and stoats in the winter country, but I didn't turn round far enough. The first thing I knew the hands were round my throat and I was falling backward into the black snow.

The pressure was instant. Though I tried to cry out the sound was bottled before it reached my mouth. The impression of strength was instantaneous too and even though I writhed, flailing with my arms against his legs I could find no purchase which would help me to break the grip. The snow was cold and wet, like thrashing about in shallow water, my hands beating at it and my legs, beating against suffocation. Thumbs squeezed into my neck like two rivets, and my lungs swelled to bursting point: everything whirled and danced and then crushed itself into a ball. That was the sensation, as I remember it, the whole of life balling up and shrinking as if someone had taken me and crumpled me down and down like a fine silk handkerchief into a tight hard lump the size of a walnut. I blacked out. I thought I was dead.

When I came round again, and it couldn't have been more than a couple of minutes really, all my attributes were inflamed, not stilted as you'd think they would have been. And I just lay there, knowing where I was and what had happened, lay still as a corpse with the ice-cold snow packed against my feet and calves and thighs, touching my frozen hands and my neck and cheek, drawing the long deep breaths down into me with a desperate sort of violence, swallowing the burning glot at my throat over and over. A bitterly chill breeze stirred along the surface of the snow and I heard the black trees moving in response to it. Funny but when he spoke, hunkered in the snow beside me he must have been, leaning against the wall out of the wind like a hunter inspecting some

poor creature dying in a trap, when he spoke, saying, "Ruby,
Ruby?" twice like that in the rhythm of a question, I wasn't
afraid of him. I didn't have the guts left to even be full of
fear or enough of the stuff of life to want to crawl away.

I said, muttering through my raw throat, "What, Arnold?"

"Get back t'the car," he said.

"What for?"

"Unless y'want t'catch pneumonia," he said.

"Help me," I said. "For Christ sake, help me to get up."

I must have gone under again there, for the next thing I
remember is him pushing me over the wall like a sack of potatoes. I could see the ground sloping away, then felt him catch
me round the breasts and bring me down. My feet had no feeling in them. I was all head, floating. He carried me back to
the car, and that must've been a comic sight, I suppose. Him,
squat, carrying me, long, down the deserted road through the
snow, staggering, my head and my legs drooping over the
ends of his arms like a giant bairn, or the bride of a dwarf.

He propped me against the car while he got the back door
open, then he pushed me inside. I could hear him breathing
short and fierce, the blow of breath from his nostrils against
my face while he stretched over the back of me and fished out
the bottle from the front seat. He took a shot himself first, I
think, then the rim of the bottle was clinking against my
teeth and the gin was carving down into me in a long flood.
Mike lay like a slaughtered pig in the front seat, only his rasping and farting to tell me Arnold hadn't done him to death
before he started on me. We didn't speak at all, not a single
word. He fitted the shape of the bottle into my hand and
clenched it for me. The door slammed like an explosion and
the engine started up again. The Hillman rolled a little way
then got up enough power to take off and we were moving.
I seemed to be moving at a different speed from the car altogether, floating along inside it, two different kinds of move-
ment and two speeds taking me home. I suppose I blacked out

again after a while, for the next thing I remember is seeing
the streets with the strings and strings of bright metal lights
shivering in the wind out of the window of the car, the straining jerk and start repeating itself as we drove down through
the crowded basin of Glasgow. I shut my eyes, counting the
turns and the twists and the duration of the stops until I
knew where we were exactly. He halted the car finally.

He turned right round in the seat.

"Key," he said.

"Mike's coat," I said.

He fumbled through Mike's pockets and came out with the
key.

"Can y'stand up?" he said.

"I'll manage," I said. "Get him first."

Skinner's movements were brisk now, smooth, like the way
a doctor moves in a hospital ward, hurrying without hurrying. He latched open the offside door and grabbed at Mike's
arms as Mike fell out head and shoulders first. I saw them
going across the pavement and into the close. The woman
Mulholland coming out with a shopping bag stopped and
stared as Skinner dragged Mike across the pavement and I
heard Skinner say to her, "Been celebratin'."

I sat back against the seat, as the Mulholland woman tried
to see who else was in the car. After a bit Arnold came back.
He stooped down and peered in the door, his shoulders closing off the harsh light from the street.

"D'you want a hand?" he said.

I shook my head, and shifted my legs over and dropped them
to the kerbstone, bent double and, with my head swimming,
got out of the seat into the air. His fingers closed on my elbow.
"Lean on me then," he said. I told him to go to hell, and managed to walk across the yard of pavement and down the close
to the foot of the stairs. I knew he was standing in the arch
of the close watching me, maybe waiting for me to fall down
again, so I kept going upstairs, holding the banister with one

hand, pumping up all them steps to the first landing. The gas-lamp purred and made fluttering shadows yellow and brown across the whitewashed steps. Our door was open. I went inside and closed it behind me by pressing against it until it sagged back with me and the lock clicked. The living-room was crossed by squares of light from the street outside and the fire was out, so that the whole place was as cold as the grave. Mike was full length on the hearth rug, his feet splayed out like a cod's tail towards me, his hands folded under his face, sleeping sound through the thick phlemy breathing. The paper chain bell against the alcove, the colour of a ripe lemon, snatched a band of the street-light to itself and seemed to hang there in dark space like the face of a ghostie, bodiless and vacant. I thought I was going to take my coat off and start lighting the fire again and make a cup of tea and put McNally to his bed with a hot-water bottle, but I didn't. I buckled down on my knees beside him and put my face against the roughness of his coat and cried. I can't remember very well now but I think I cried for him to wake up and help me: and I think I cried for my wee girl Sally. I think I did, but I was so done-in I can't remember now. All I know is that I must have wept myself to sleep, dressed as I was and laying across the old man's back, for when I wakened it was midnight and I was bitter cold.

7

Joseph

I W A S just hitting my stride when he came in. Not that I
wasn't glad to see him, for his friends is my friends and my
friends is his and always has been, but it was an older crowd
that night and some of them was not exactly well-disposed
to him just at that especial time, with the busies hanging
round his neck. He came right over to me without crossing
to the counter first. It was about half-eight.

I said hullo son to him and asked him if he was drinking,
but he came right out and said, "Mam asks y't'come home,
because Uncle Frank and Aunt Mattie've arrived with the
boys."

"You should've brung them up here," I says.

"Aunt Mattie'd've none of that," he says.

"Christ!" I says.

"Will y'come. I've got the car."

I said, "What car?"

"I've got a car on trial," he says.

Archie asked him, "Thinkin' of buying it then,
Arnold?"

"That's right," he said. "Hillman. It's a bargain."

Archie pursed his mouth and looked at Bertie in that way,
as if to say where the hell did Joe Skinner's boy get the brass
for a car.

"Have y'got it here?" I said.

"Outside," he said. "If you're comin', you'd better come now. I mean it's your bloody brother."

"I suppose it is," I said.

I wasn't much in favour of spending a night at home with Frank. Nothing against Frank, he's my own flesh and blood after all, but his bloody wife rankles me, with her bloody pious don't-do-this and why-did-y'do-that. It was aye the same at the Xmas time, folk we never saw from one year's end to the next, and half of them we never wanted to see at all, banging on your door and expecting you to entertain them. So Arno's got a car now, I thought to myself. That was a right one in the eye for the half of them.

As if it was the most natural thing in the world, I finish my half and said to the lads, "Well, I'll need to away. If I can talk m'brother into it, we'll maybe drive back for a small refreshment later on."

"Ay, right," Archie said, and the others went on drinking and looking green at me and Arno as we went out.

We got into the car and he started it up and we talked about it on the way down the road. The inside fair stunk of booze and I gave him a word of advice about that sort of caper, but he told me it hadn't been him that'd been sousing. I didn't like to ask him who it was, for if he'd wanted me to know, he'd have told me himself.

When we got into the house, there was Frank and Mattie and my nephews Tom and Alex and a couple of their girl-friends. One of the dames had a sort of blonde haircut with it piled up on her napper like a busby, and her face was that small and pale under it that when I first got into the room I could've swored her whole head was transparent. Tom and Alex are a couple of fine big lads though. I didn't mind shaking hands with them, or the two dames, but Mattie's hand gave me the shivers. It was like taking a fistful of old haddy. Nora was fluttering about setting the table, harassed-looking and done up in her new frock.

"Didn't take you long," she said. "I thought Arnold'd've needed to prise you away from that place with a crowbar."

I let them laugh for a minute, and then I said, "Well, we came down the road in a couple of minutes."

I let that sink in.

"Get a lift then?" Frank said, and I knew Arno had kept it under his hat even from Mam.

"Och no," I said. "Arno's car."

Arno was sitting on one of the hard chairs over against the curtains at the window, watching me with his eyes lowered and trying not to smile. He was giving me the carpet to leak it out as I liked.

"Oh," Mattie said, "We didn't know Arnold had a car."

"Ay," I said. "A Hillman."

"You must've had a whack of overtime, Arno," Tom said.

"Enough," Arno said.

"We thought of it, y'know," Mattie said. "But what with our Alex getting married . . ."

"Yes," Nora said, while she put out the cups. "It's a right expensive ploy getting married these days."

Then we got safe split up, me and Arno and Frank talking about cars and things and the women about getting married and the two Dunsmuir lads playing with their lasses.

It was the dark-headed one that took Arno's fancy. All the time we were talking and having supper he was looking at her. It wasn't open sort of, not as would give offence to any of the company, but I noticed it. He'd no time at all for the blondie, but she was a skelf anyhow compared with the other. Joan was the handsome one's name. I don't know really why he bothered for she'd no time for anyone else but her fiancé, making cow-eyes at him, putting her hand through his arm as if to trumpet to the world that she'd got him good and hooked, sugaring his bloody tea for him. There was none of that sort of public carry-on when I was their age. It was sit tight in the parlour and keep yourself to yourself until the mother-in-law went to bed or you went to walk the lassie home. It gave it an edge too, the holding yourself in all night: and there were none of them advice columns in papers to tell you that a wee bit off the corner of the candle'll cause you to turn frigid at the end of the honeymoon, or churchmen dressing up the plain fact that we all just want a wedge as fast as possible ring or no ring, sacred rite or no sacred rite. If I'd been ten years younger I'd've been keeking at the Joan creature myself and maybe wishing I was Alex Dunsmuir. Still, it was a passing fancy with Arno. I reckoned if he'd wanted a girl like that, he could've got one any time, a well set-up young chap like himself. But he knew what the cost was. Ay, that was it, and always had been. He knew fine well what it would have cost a man of his calibre to take a wife for ever and ever, and he'd started paying up his instalments, in a manner of speaking, on another thing. It was easy to forget it on nights like that, to think of him like Alex or Tom, but then when I looked at Frank and saw him chalk and me cheese and both of us spawned out of the same womb, then I knew it wasn't possible by then, not with thirty years under the bridge and his life set to a strange mark. But there was no harm in looking at her, the firm tight bum under the skirt, or the diddlies poking the cardigan, or the red mouth and the dark eyes. Another one placed there to remind you of all that went missing all that time ago, and that'll never be now. Just the same as looking at the old football photos and wishing you had taken it up and trained and practised serious. Ach well, I said to myself, there's ways and ways, and if one isn't as good as the other, there's nothing an old buzzard like me can do to change the way of the wide world.

When it came ten o'clock and they'd eaten all that was on the table and drunk all the tea going, Mattie said it was time to get away home. I said Arno'd run them down to the bus-stop, and he said he would. Then Alex spoke up and said he and the girl Joan really wanted to go on to another party over in Holmhill direction. I don't know why now but I just knew Arnold would offer to run them there. I thought that perhaps he was hoping they'd ask him in to the party, and that he might find another wench like Alex's Joan only not affiliated to a man already. It just crossed my mind that it might be something of that nature. He offered right away.

First he took my brother and his wife to the bus-stop, then ran the blondie and Tom round to the station, then he came back and picked up Alex and the girl. Nora and me went out on to the step and waved to them, giving Nora a chance to get a look at the car. I knew she was pleased too, underneath being worried where he got the money to pay for it. We stood and waved and I was dead positive we'd see no more of Arno that night. I was wrong though, cause he was back in an hour, as large as life, coming in and sitting down at the table and wolfing into the last of the cakes on all the plates. We talked for a while and about midnight we went up to bed. Arno was sitting in the living-room reading a book when I came in to put up the fireguard. I remember what he asked me. He says, "Where's Rosemary?" as if he'd just missed her. I told him she'd gone up to Glasgow to stay with a girl-friend for a couple of days. Nobody had told him yet that she was moving out, but his Mam wanted me to wait 'til it was all fixed and settled. He looked at me for a minute, blinking, then he says, "Is she coming back?" and I says, "I bloody-well hope so," and he nodded.

There was only Nora and me in the house with him, and I know she was asleep. Nobody else could have heard him then, when he opened the back door. I don't know what came over me, for as I always say, he's big enough and ugly enough to gang his ain gait, but I slunk out of my bed and looked out the window through a scrape in the frost-skin. It was Arno right enough and in the wee glimpse I got of him as the light from the street outlined him when he was leaping the fence, I knew he was using the gardens to get on to the fields. What the hell he was playing at I hadn't a bloody clue. Since he'd been riding around in a car all day long I thought maybe he just felt like a walk.

Part Four

DECEMBER

1

Booth

I ENTERED the building shortly after eight-thirty. Walter was hanging about the doorway, a clip-board in his hand.

"Yes," I said.

"Chief wants you," he said.

"In his office?"

"Ops. Room," he said.

To give him the benefit of the doubt, I imagine that if I had delayed a moment he would have warned me what to expect, but I walked on past him and left down the corridor out into the new wing. The corridor, though concrete, was liberally lined with heaters which had been blazing solidly for the last five weeks. The effect was of walking through scalding fog. The Operations Room was no better.

The first thing I saw as I slid back the door, was Paige. He was facing me against the map-screen. He had on his horse-blanket coat, his hat was thrust far back on his head. Sitting on a high stool, like a disciple, was Strachan.

I strolled into the room as if nothing unusual was taking place, and threw my hat on to the vacant desk in front of them. Out of the corner of my eye I saw McAlister straightening himself from the screened line of phones. The metallic humming of mechanical detectives was at its normal pitch.

"Good morning, gentlemen," I said. "And what can I do for you?"

I stood between them and offered each a cigarette from my case. Paige accepted and lit both cigarettes from his lighter. I heard McAlister speaking quite sharply to one of the operators. A group of uniforms was assembled in the far corner, drinking tea. The map behind Paige showed the Northern sector of the County, but it bore no markings or push-pins as yet. It was just there, like Everest, silent and secret.

"Not what you can do for us, Bob," Paige said. "It's what we can do for you."

Lingering in his accent still the faintest irritating touch of West Highland origins. I had known him as a bobby when the accent was as thick as porridge.

"I gather you've been summoned," I said.

"Now, now, Bob," Strachan said, "there's really no need to take that attitude."

"What attitude?" I said.

"We know you've been having a lot of bother with Skinner," Paige said. "We've done business with him ourselves. Besides, there's been another development," Strachan said.

"In your province?" I asked.

"Holmhill," Paige told me.

"What?"

"It looks as if it may be another killing," Strachan said.

"Looks like?" I said.

"A Missing Persons thing," Paige said. "The old story, No Body: No Crime."

"A girl?" I said.

"A girl," Paige said.

"Last seen?"

"Ten-thirty or thereabouts last night," Paige said.

"And it's now . . ." I glanced at my wrist-watch, "now eight fifteen."

They understood immediately. Strachan shifted himself off the stool. His shoes were very light brown and highly polished. They made his small feet look even smaller. He held his hat in his hand, like a bowl, a pair of knit and leather driving gloves in it.

"There's some rather special circumstances, Bob," he explained.

They were both on their best behaviour. In another couple of years when the process of retiral opened posts for them, they would be at each other's throats, but, for the moment, they presented a solid front of patient, slightly disparaging, efficiency. It was one of the few things I admired in the lump sum of their attributes.

"What special circumstances?" I said.

Paige nodded. "We're pretty much in the dark."

"Parents?" I said. "Have they been . . . ?"

"Muirhead's out there now," Strachan said. "We thought we'd better go easy just for the minute. You know, not throw the whole county into general panic. There may be nothing in it anyhow."

Paige disagreed. "I have the feeling it'll be one for us, all right."

"We'll just have to wait and see if it ties in with the other killings," I said. "Presumably you're bang up to date on the reports?"

"Unless you've anything you'd like to add to what went down officially," Paige said.

"All right," I said. I looked round to see how long McAlister was going to be. He saw me and held up his hand with five fingers open. I sat on the desk top and debated the advisability of confiding in them. If the wolves had been brought in, I decided, I would have to play wolf myself. The days of the fox were over.

"Sure," Paige said.

I smiled at them. I could feel their inward keening after information. I was being frank with them because I wanted them to co-operate with me and help me to force McAlister into a decision which would not meet with his approval. They didn't know that at the time. They thought I was being gracious and properly spirited.

"Skinner's as good as admitted he did it," I said. "It doesn't go down on paper very convincingly."

"Reading between the lines, I'd say you're right," Strachan said. "Did you get anything from the nether regions?"

"Information received," I said. "No. Not a cheep."

"Nothing with us either," Paige said.

"Skinner says we daren't bring him to court."

"He does, does he," Paige said. "By the sound of it Skinner hasn't changed much in the last seven years."

"Ay, he has," I said. "He's gone over the top. That's the point. He's clever enough to get away with it."

"Bluff," Strachan said.

"Not bluff," I said. "It cuts deeper than that. It's rigged somehow. If it weren't rigged he'd be making a lot more song and dance about persecution and defamation. No, Skinner is sitting quite happily on the top of this shit-heap laughing up his blasted sleeve because he knows he can afford to take us all the way and still come out on top: not just vindicated but as pure as a new-born lamb."

"How in God's name do you make that out?" Paige said.

"It's simple," I said. "It's just the old business about a second line of defence. I mean you know the type as well as I do. They commit a felony and do everything in their power beforehand to make sure nobody catches them at it."

"There's a rudimentary statement, if you like," Strachan said.

I went on, "But Skinner kills on impulse."

"And depends on his luck, which might run as good for him as it seems to do for most kinks," Paige said.

"Then the fun begins," I said. "He creates a plausible doubt. Admittedly, I don't know how, but he's backing two horses, not one. He's bargaining that we won't be able to fix

up a decent enough case to arrest him, but he's feeling quite
secure behind this second fence, an intricate and probably
thoroughly plausible alibi which won't fool either you or me
or a judge and jury but which will under the magnanimity
of the law get him off Scot-free."

"Interesting," Strachan said. "A bit up in the air though."

"That's as may be," I said.

"Maybe you should change direction," Paige said.

"Exactly," I said. And left it at that.

After a moment or two of silence McAlister came up behind me, and put his hand on my shoulder.

I said, "I've just heard."

He nodded his head briskly two or three times and said,
"Come into the office."

We walked back along the corridor. McAlister opened the
door and ushered us in. There was a thin layer of grime over
everything, as the cleaners hadn't been in over Christmas.
We took chairs and sat in a ring facing him. He looked up
from his desk and said, "Give me a cigarette, will you, Bob?"

I did as he asked, but before I could feel for my lighter,
Paige had his held out. McAlister lit the cigarette and looked
at us searchingly, as if he was trying to find out how things
stood between us. I said, "It's all right"

He nodded once more, again curtly.

"Damn the bastard," he said. "Damn the bastard to hell."

We waited. He got up and went and sat on the broad ledge
under the window.

"The girl's name is Irene Pettigrew. She left her home, in
Lauderton Road, Holmhill, at eight. She walked to the Church
Hall at the corner of Lambert Drive and Holmhill Road. She
joined a group of young people there—Youth Fellowship, or
something—and they went out Carol singing round the district. They got back to the hall about a quarter to ten, had a
cup of tea and a chat, then went home. She walked down
Lambert Drive in the company of a young man, a boy, called

Rankine and another two girls. The girls turned off to catch a bus at the end of the Drive, and Rankine walked Irene on down the Parkway. He didn't go home with her, but they stood talking at the corner of the Parkway and Launderton Road until half-past ten, perhaps a bit after, then the boy friend cut back the way he had come to his house in Holmhill Road."

He blinked at us through the cigarette smoke and took a long drag on the filter tip. "Can you visualise this area, or would you rather I ran down a map?"

"It's okay," Paige said.

"The girl didn't arrive home. About half-past twelve her old man finally got panicky enough to start calling round her friends. He took out his car and toured the district, finally winding up at Rankine's. After he heard what Rankine had to say, he went back to Launderton Road and called in at every house down the line. None of the neighbours had seen her. At two-fifteen he arrived at the station. We sent a constable with him and told him to phone up anyone he could think of that might know where the girl was. He was particularly emphatic that his daughter wouldn't stay out for the night without telling him. The constable did the usual things and we checked out the hospitals and the accident cases throughout the County. No trace."

"When did Muirhead get in?" I said.

"We called him at six," McAlister said.

"You'll have set a net?" I said. "Or have you another reason for holding on?"

"No," McAlister said. "I believe the father. He's a banker by the way. He seems convinced that his daughter wouldn't do anything daft."

"You know fathers," Paige said. "And daughters."

"Anyhow," McAlister said. "I'm not prepared to chuck this one in as Missing Persons: not with things being as they are around here. The Pettigrew man hadn't forgotten about the

Calder case either. He reminded me of it, rather pointedly. I think he was embarrassed at making a fuss, but his attitude just convinces me all the more that, as far as he and his wife are concerned the girl has definitely run into some sort of trouble not of her own making."

"It might be a snatch? No?" Strachan said.

"Not likely, I should say," McAlister said. "He's only a branch manager. The whole thing's too coincidental anyhow."

"She may have met up with some friend, of course," Paige said. "Young girls are witless."

"Two minutes walk from her home," I said. "She'd hardly just breeze off for the night without calling in first."

"Well, anyhow," McAlister said hastily. "We'll have more details when Muirhead gets back. I don't imagine we'd be jumping the gun to go ahead and set up a search. Do you?"

"No, sir," Strachan said. "It's this malarky about not knowing who to begin with. Rankine, then the neighbours. How about Rankine?"

McAlister humped his back grotesquely. "Let's be honest, gentlemen." he said. "We're not really looking for a missing girl, we're looking for a body. I know, I know, that's committing the deadly sin of assuming we not only know of a crime but that we've a fair idea of the type of man likely to be involved."

"You mean Arnold Skinner?" Paige said.

"Yes."

"Arab slave-traders again," Paige said. "History repeats itself."

"No it doesn't," I said. "Not this time."

"How?" Strachan said.

"Leave Skinner out of it," I said. "Discount him. Concentrate on finding . . . her, and then watch what happens."

"He may kill again," Paige said.

"He may. That's the risk."

McAlister, in a low voice, remarked, "I think we've already allowed him more opportunities than we should have. Our job . . ."

"I know," I told him. "Is to prevent crime."

"If you want him," Paige said, "we can get him."

"What on?" I said. "A capital charge?"

"It's got to be that, hasn't it?" McAlister said. "Why must it?"

"Because he's guilty."

"Prove it then," McAlister snapped at me.

"I'll get him for you," I said. "He'll shoot his bolt."

"You just can't ignore him," Strachan said. "I mean to say."

It was Paige, surprisingly enough, who saw what I was driving at, and who came out on my side. He sighed deeply, and said, directly to McAlister, "Maybe we should after all. It might tempt him to show his hand."

McAlister thought for several minutes, facing the window in traditional style, scratching the frost with his pinky. "Well, if you like to try it," he said. "All right."

I got up. "In the meantime . . ." I said.

"We'll move heaven and bloody earth to find the Pettigrew girl," the Chief said.

2

Muirhead

IF SHE would cry it would make things simpler. I think it would ease him too. If she would just stop being brave. Come to think of it perhaps this is her nature. And Pettigrew too. He sits back in the chair, with his hands in his lap, giving me his full attention. It's probably the same sort of pose he'd adopt if I was sitting in his office at the bank asking him for a loan on unsatisfactory colateral. A small man, breaking his heart behind that façade, I expect. Breaking his heart at the thought of what might be happening to his girl. The morning has hardly begun, and yet I feel as if I'd been here in this room with them for an eternity. She is bigger than he is, but they have similar features, sharp and angular, as if they were in fact brother and sister, rather than husband and wife. I continue noting down his answers in my book. The frame from which they have taken the photograph sits horribly vacant and empty on the table to my left. The milk wagon purrs up the drive and stops at the house and a whistling milk-boy clinks up the path, plays his tune with the milk bottles and goes off again. The woman listens to it too, quite intently, with her shoulder lifted and a wary expression on her face. There is an unnatural tidiness about them and about the house itself as if they had spent some time grooming it, and changing their clothes, in expectation of my visit, just as if I was the parish priest, or minister, on a social call. Pettigrew unfolds

191

his hands and touches the side of his nose lightly with his forefinger. He wears a Sheaffer pen and pencil in the breast-pocket of his suit in front of the rigid white linen triangle. Singleton shuffles his feet and stares at his shoes. We have nothing else to ask or say. The girl is missing. The girl is dead. Such an equation is more obvious to them than to me, because they knew her. Certainly they can tell me, vehemently impressing it on me, that she is not the sort who would go off without telling them, but I can't accept it. Morally I'm obliged to disbelieve them and in doing so to make light not only of their faith in her character but also of her fate. A very pretty girl. Irene Pettigrew.

"I'm sorry to have to put this so bluntly, Mister Pettigrew,' I say, addressing myself pointedly to the father, "but has she ... your daughter ever been in any kind of trouble? I mean anything, no matter how trivial."

"None at all."

"That you know of."

"There is no reason on earth for me to suppose she was leading a double life, if that's what you mean," he says.

I say, "I wouldn't have put it as strongly as that."

"Perhaps not," he says. "But I think it best, under the circumstances, if we don't waste time with the niceties."

"Right you are," I say.

"We're not holding anything back," the woman says. "I mean it."

"Did you encourage her to bring her friends to the house?"

"We do," Pettigrew says, leaning heavily on the tense.

"So you're pretty well acquainted with her friends?"

"Almost them all, I would say," Pettigrew replies.

His wife is hardly conscious of my questions. She has gone drifting off again into a blank world. I wonder if I penetrated that world if it would give me something I could use to make them hope she's still all right.

"And how many of them have you contacted?" I ask.

"Every one—at least excluding a few whose addresses we don't know."

He puts his hand in his jacket pocket and produces a small leather diary, blue morocco, gilt-edged, fastened with an elastic band.

"I went through this—systematically," he says.

I take the book from him, and open it.

It contains a multitude of names and addresses, telephone numbers, kept with meticulous care in small neat open handwriting. The girl had been unusually full in her details. It wasn't a question of a nickname and a phone number. She had provided, in alphabetical order, a comprehensive directory of her acquaintances, and, almost more than we could have hoped for, her relations.

"It's all in there," Pettigrew says.

"And you've contacted every one of these people?"

"Four of them were out. Probably out of town," he says. "The others have no information."

"Did your daughter go dancing much?"

"Only to Church socials and the like. A school dance at the end of term," the woman replies.

"Dance halls—the Plaza, that kind of thing?" I ask.

"Never," the woman replies.

"Did she drink?"

"No."

"Not at all?"

"Not at all," her mother says.

"Or smoke?"

"No. She hated the very smell of smoke in a room."

"Now, Mrs. Pettigrew," I say. "I don't want to sound like a policeman, but you seem to me to be very didactic about your daughter's habits. I'm wondering if she kept something back from you. I mean she seems just a little bit too much like a ..." I was about to say paragon, when the woman strains forward. Her mouth is momentarily vicious as if I'd just challenged her honesty, or, worse, the daughter's chastity. Pettigrew lifts his hand, palm out, to silence her, and he replies, "I'll admit she isn't one of your usual girls, and that I may sound just like any other foolish father, but we're merely giving you the facts as we know them. And furthermore we know them to be true. I'll admit it is just possible that Irene had some sort of . . . liaison going on behind our backs, but it's most improbable. Don't think me foolish when I say this, but Irene is far too honest, and far too fond of us to do anything wrong which might bring us unhappiness. All my life I've tried to give her a sense of security without . . . well, without playing the heavy father, and she is as she has made herself, not as we've made her. Do you understand me?"

"I think so," I say. "Is that the reason you called us so quickly?"

"Yes," he says. "And because of the . . . things which have been happening in the County lately."

"Of course," I say. "But I don't think you need worry about that."

I close my book. Singleton gets to his feet, takes my hat and gloves from the table and hands them to me. Pettigrew gets up as I do. The woman sits still, looking up at me. She says, "What do we do now, Inspector?"

"Wait here," I say. "In case we come across anything."

"Goodbye. Thank you for coming so promptly," she says.

I say, "I wouldn't worry unduly about it, Ma'am. It's quite a common occurrence. I'm sure she'll turn up safe and sound in an hour or two."

Singleton goes out of the room before me. Pettigrew opens the front door for us. Outside in the cold street the car waits. Singleton goes on down the path. I turn to Pettigrew.

"I promise I'll let you know the moment we have any news." Cliches come easiest in a situation like this. No one is keen to force it out in words not worn by use, to be brutal.

He puts his hand on my arm.

"Tell me truthfully," he says in a soft voice, "Are you going out of here to look for Irene, or to search for a . . . for something else?"

"I don't think your daughter's dead, if that's what you mean," I say quite harshly.

"I don't believe you," he says.

"That's up to you," I say. "What you or I believe, or hope, or think, won't alter the situation one little bit."

"I'm sorry," he says.

I shake his hand, then, just as I begin to turn away, I glance at him again and ask him, "The name's not in the book, I know, but did you or Irene know anyone by the name of Skinner. Rosemary Skinner, or Arnold Skinner, perhaps?"

He thought hard for a moment, but without the false contortions of concentration. I believed him when he told me, "We know no one of that name. I don't believe Irene did either. If she did it was never mentioned. Shall I ask my wife?"

"No," I say. "That won't be necessary. It was just a thought."

"Who is Skinner?" he asks with almost fiery interest.

"No one in particular," I say, rather lamely. It's early, and I'm only half-slept, and I've had to ask too many questions and tell too many lies already this morning to rattle another one off the tip of my tongue.

I follow Singleton down to the car and get in. The interior, smelling of leather, is pleasantly warm. Singleton has already lit a cigarette for me and passes it to me as soon as I close the door. As we take off from the kerb I can see Mrs. Pettigrew standing at the window, one hand holding the curtain down, watching us drive away. Even before we change gear, I can see her attention leave us, as her eyes wander towards the naked frost-pricked fields at the end of the avenue, the deep grass dead and white and brittle, and below them in the hollow of the low hills the silent quarry pools stoppered with night ice, old railway sidings, ash-pits and a thousand other holes large, deep and secretive. And as we pull up to the top of the hill, I can see as far as the river, the stone-coloured water flowing through the screened fields all the way down to the pastureland of Pickering where Harriet Calder died, not even half a year ago.

3

Pettigrew

I AM alone with her, the house quiet as a church. Irene is not coming or going. We have stopped waiting for her and there is a vacuum in the house now. She's no longer part of my future, only of my past. Unless somewhere she's being forced to stay alive. I shouldn't wish for that, out of my own selfishness, hungering for something to come back to me no matter how horribly she must suffer, to live through for her to return to our world of honour and chastity. The whole point is honour, chastity, charity, love, truth, hers without stigma no matter how she has preserved in terror all her innocence. I know of such things.

To Agnes I say, "She'll be all right."

Agnes stares back at me out of some fund of determination which I could not have foreseen.

She replies, "Yes, Walter."

Her obedience is automatic.

The telephone squats between us on the glass surface of the coffee table by the minister's cup.

"What more do you wish me to do?" I ask of her.

"Nothing," she replies.

"You're content to sit here and wait. A whole day gone."

"Don't," she tells me.

"I can't help it."

197

She moves the cup precisely one inch towards the cake-tray.

"I know you can't," she says.

I wish to Heaven she would permit herself to cry like any normal woman. It's not knowing which cuts so deeply. She would have married and left us, but she would still have been ours to pretend for. She may not be . . .

Lord God, I can't but admit she's dead. Killed.

The police know it too. The detective this morning was as good as telling me, and was only being mistakenly kind to deny it when I quizzed him. She hasn't run off: there's nothing for her to run from, or to. She was a happy girl here, with us.

To conceive a child, to work out one's days in the rut to feed and clothe and comfort her, only to have her snatched away.

"Shall we pray now, Walter and Agnes," Lamb said, kneeling on the hearthrug and clasping his hands. We knelt with him to pray. I was with him in his mumblings and his mutterings, when I should have refused. This is no time to come and offer promises to God. God the Father can do nothing for my girl now.

"We must never give up hope, you know," Lamb said. "Never, never give up our faith in her safe return."

As if his damned incantations could conjure her up out of the scratched ground, draw her feet back along the avenue to the main road again, make her choose to walk by the way in which the man wasn't lurking.

And what of us now, Agnes and I: of the bank now, of the church now. How is it going to be possible to stroll into the clubhouse and drink a glass with my friends, or step out to the first tee with my bag on my shoulder. Pretending. Is that what going on living means, learning to do such things. Now, it's too late to unlearn all the habits that I put in there to substitute for living.

It cheats us all horribly. Did he feel cheated too, cheated

in cheating me out of all I had in this life worth the pretence?

Where is she at: spilled somewhere, lonely in her death. No God would put that loneliness on to her, the loneliness of this day passing for her. Not even us: each to the other driven. I can't do it for Agnes alone. It's too much to ask of me. Perhaps in time, when we have her back, and she is our own child to bury as we will.

God, if they don't ever find her. Never knowing, living with the hope, no matter how hard I strive to convince myself that she is: not. Not ever knowing if she still walks on the face of this earth, if round the next corner she's standing, waiting. Not knowing if you look at a strange face in a holiday town if it's going to alter the change and melt to show you hers, there, blinking out of the back of the grave. God, I hope she is:

I can't sit here thinking about it. They won't let me go to the bank tomorrow. I couldn't be at peace there either, anywhere within a mile of a telephone.

"I'm sorry," I tell Agnes.

"It's all right," she tells me.

My only vulnerable spot in all these years: Irene. Every other thing was safe enough, and doubly insured, insured because to lose it meant nothing, just as having it meant nothing, except for what it gave to her.

Agnes yawns, straining against it, as a normal woman has to strain to hold back tears.

"Is the stuff he gave you taking effect?" I ask of her.

"I can't help it," she replies.

"I think you should lie down for an hour," I tell her.

"No."

"If anything happens . . ." I tell her. "Go on. You can't do anything just sitting there."

She rises, very old in her movements, like an old, old woman all of a sudden, all her erectness and poise sloughing off. I place my arm around her shoulders and draw her body to mine. The drug the doctor pricked into her arm is taking effect. I kiss her forehead.

"If anything does happen . . ." I tell her.

She leaves the lounge and goes into the bathroom. The toilet flushes, clicks, then hisses in the silence of the other rooms.

From the window I look at the gardens, at the gate, at the path.

The sound, a low thin wailing, comes from the bathroom, rises and falls at once. And then begins again, thinner, higher, rising.

The path, the gate. She doesn't come back to me.

Lying lonely, after pain.

The first day has gone by of its own accord. The first day only.

Irene, my beautiful girl.

4
McNally

ENOUGH, AS I always say, is enough. A knock on the door. I open the door and there he is, as large as life, cocky, grinning like he'd just been voted Mister Universe.

"How's my friend McNally?" he says.

"What the hell do you want?" I asks.

"Nothin'," he says, leaning a bit with one hand on the wall, "Just nipped up for a bit of a chat."

"Well, you can just nip off again smartish, Arno," I tell him.

His brow wrinkles. He puts his hands in his pockets. I still haven't opened the door wide enough to let him in. Ruby's come quietly through from the kitchen and stands out of the way by the lobby door.

"Now, now," Skinner says, "that's no way t'treat an old comrade in arms."

"Comrade in arms nothing," I says. "I'd be obliged if you'd get t'hell out of here."

"How?"

"You know how," I says.

He says, "Because you got plastered, is that it?"

I say, "It's nothing to do with that."

This piece of information gives him some sort of relief, as if he'd been worried by the thought of me lying blotto on the kitchen floor for a night. Surely it's entered his head that he's taboo at the moment, bad company for any self-respecting anti-

201

law man. The busies do, and the busies are running through clients like a dose of salts.

"Aren't y'goin' t'invite me in then?" he says. "I'm half frozen t'death."

I look out into the close to make sure there's not half a dozen burly cops leaned up against the wall taking down our every words, then I say, "You'd better come in for a minute, I suppose, just 'til we get a few things straight."

He comes into the hall. Ruby fades through the kitchen and goes into the bedroom, closing the door. She thinks he killed that kid in the shop, and she's bloody positive he killed the girl that's missing too, but I'm not going to let that affect me or swing my judgment. A man's entitled to the benefit of the doubt. It wouldn't be the first time the busies've bayed at the wrong bloke and hounded him into an early grave. But if Arno is drawing busies to my door, then I can fairly do without his company; for a while at any rate, until he cools off again.

I decide not to take him into the kitchen, because it'll be easier to get rid of him if I let it be known he's not welcome and keep him sitting in the lobby.

I deliberately close the door to the kitchen.

"Ruby havin' a bath, or somethin'?" Arno says.

"What I have to say," I tells him, "I'll say quick, then I'd be indebted if you'd take yourself off."

"What's eatin' you then, McNally?" he says.

I say, "I'll tell you what's eating me, Arno. You're a very unpopular laddie at the moment. . . ."

He interrupts, "Why? What the friggin' hell've I ever done t'you or yours?"

"Listen," I tells him. "You're not stupid, Arno. Whatever else you are—and that's not for me to express an opinion— but whatever else you are, you're not stupid. You've got a noddle on you, I'm the first to admit, so how about using it for once, and making a few guesses, about why the hell I want you out of here, eh?"

"Has Ruby been puttin' ideas into your head?" he says.

"I'm not influenced by woman's blethers," I tells him. "Sure, I know what the word is about you."

He throws back his head, standing just inside the door, half-leaning against it, his hands in his coat pocket. He wears a brand new silk shirt and a dark silk tie, which together must have set him back about a tenner. "What's the word then, McNally?" he asks.

"The word is you're not clean. That shop killing."

In a voice as thin and edgy as a Gillette blade, he says, "I see. What else?"

"This muff that's missing: they're after you for that and all."

"Are they?" he says. "First I heard about it."

"Well, I've had two special visits from the high-ups, putting the screws on me about you."

His chin tilts sharply, but his voice is calm. It never struck me until this minute that maybe he didn't know they were spreading a wide net to pin him down.

"Who? Booth?" he says.

"Glasgow Branch men," I tell him. "Two of them. Paige and Strachan."

"Paige an' Strachan, is it," he says.

"I didn't tell them anything," I says. "You don't have to worry on that score, but I'm getting sick to death of living here like a monk in a tower. I'm telling you, Skinner, just because we've done a bit of business together and had a few drinks, I'm scared to go out to the piss-house in case they nab me as an accessory, or something."

"Your nose is clean enough," he says, sort of vaguely, as if he's not listening to me just for the minute. "Paige and Strachan, is it now?"

"A couple of hard nuts," I tell him.

"They've got nothing on you, McNally," he says. "Yet."

"What d'you mean by that?"

He says, "By what?"

"By saying 'yet', as if you thought they might be able to dig up dirt on me."

"Well, they might, I reckon, if they work hard enough at it. There's plenty of dirt on you kickin' around, Mike, if they look in the right places."

I crowded him into the door a bit, not too obviously, but just enough for him to get the message.

"Are you makin' threats, Skinner," I says. "I hope not for your sake."

He grins again, coming up in spirits like a rubbery ball bouncing off the pavement. "Threats? I never threaten people. What did they want t'know?"

"Things," I says. "The usual."

"Was Ruby here?" he asks.

"No."

"Just as well. T'be frank, Mac," he says, "I don't trust your old woman. I've the feelin' she'd stab me in the back as quick as look at me."

"She'll do what I tell her to," I says. "But anyhow, the less I've to do with you the better, so how about taking off, eh?"

"In a minute," he says. "I'll go in a minute. I want t'ask you something first."

"What?" I says.

He says, staring at me full in the face, he says, "D'you think I'm a killer then?"

I'm standing very close to him, for the lobby is narrow and I haven't shifted back from the time before when I was inclined to defend myself. I fold my arms carefully, and let my shoulders drop back against the press door. "That's none of my business," I say, after a wary minute. "What I think's got nothing to do with it."

"Do you?" he says. "Do you think I stuffed that bint at

Pickering, or blasted the old dears and the kid in Lauderton?
D'you really imagine I've done away with this Pettigrew dame
that the papers are screamin' about?"

"You're crafty enough for it, Arno," I says.

"That's not what I asked you," he says. "I asked you if
you thought any of them crimes was done by me?"

"The busies seem to, that's what I'm bitching about,"
I says.

He stoves out his hands, they appear from his pockets as
if by magic, hardly visible at all to the eyesight, and presses
them against my shoulders, hard. I swing up my fingers and
snatch his wrists and we stand there like that: him, sly and
small and mad angry and me big, holding each other like two
judo-mongers posing for a photograph.

"Frig you, McNally," he says. "D'you think I done it?"

"What if I do," I says. "What difference does it make?"

He sighs, a long explosive sigh, as if I'd hit him in the guts,
and folds back from me. I let his hands go and he puts them
back in his pockets.

"Open the door, you slimy bastard," he says, grinning
again now, "Come on, open it up and I'll clear your pitch."

I open the door and he takes the handle from me and pulls
it wide and steps out on to the mat on the landing. It's freezing cold out there, and me in my shirt-sleeves, shivering. Even
in the close, his breath clouds on the air. He stands half in
and half out, one finger jiggling the hanging chain of the
safety latch.

"I did do them," he says in the same voice he might tell
me he liked draught better'n bottle, quiet and casual like. "I
did them all. I did this Pettigrew dame too. But they'll never
take me for it. Not till I'm ready to go."

He stops playing with the chain and jerks his head round
until he's staring at me again, his eyes round and hot. "But
by Christ, when they do, I'll create such a Godawful stink in
this town that even the Woolworth's tanner-knockers'll shake

in their shoes. They'll never hang me, y'know, Mike," he says, stepping out of the way at last. "Never hang me."

I close the door on him fast. I stand in the half-dark lobby, trying to light the cigarette, though my hand's shaking. I have to straighten myself and throw my chest out like a guardsman, for my breath can't seem to come fast enough: panting I am, as if I'd just completed the mile in four minutes, or climbed the highest mountain in the world. I push into the kitchen, just as Ruby comes out of the bedroom.

"Mike," she says, "what's ailing you?"

"Nothing," I say. "I'll be okay in a minute. I think the cold out there. . . ."

She takes my hand and presses it to her cheek.

"You're chittering right enough," she says.

I sit down in the armchair and manage to light the fag.

"Has he gone?" she says. "Skinner?"

I nod.

"What did he say? Come on, tell me what he said that set you in a state?"

"He didn't say anything," I tells her. "Nothing much."

"He won't be back, will he?" she says.

I take the glass she gives me, and tell her, "No: he won't be back here again: never."

5

Muirhead

THE LIGHT has almost gone now. I can hardly see the Land-rover twenty yards away let alone the cars by the roadside. The neon lamps over at the boulevard have just come alive and glow dull red as they warm up. Vince is bringing up the last of the netting now, more by touch than sight. The rowing boat spins slowly round as the two constables haul on the ropes. Their hands must be raw with cold, and with the touch of the sodden rope. The hook metal will burn too. I can hear them grunting and cursing, heedless now of Booth and McAlister. The hooks splash loudly and Vince moves back, his body hunched against the faint light of the frosty banking on the other side of the water. A new thin scum of ice is forming already over the broken fragments. Up on the hill, like a small army, the others are drying off and cleaning up before Yum-Yum marshalls them over to the vans.

McAlister and Booth have stopped talking, and are standing still, like two large chunks of coal, while behind them the little man waits, as he's waited every day, for us to finish so's he can go home to his wife again and tell her that there's still some hope. Some hope. Not a hope in hell for the poor fellow.

Vince shouts across the water, telling us that there's nothing showing but muck. He has a bass voice and it carries in the cold air.

"All right, Sergeant," McAlister calls back, "Bring in the

tackle and I'll send down a squad to lug it up to the lorry. You four can call it a day at that. You've had your share."

"Andy," Booth says.

"Yes."

"Nip up and tell McCorquodale to let's have a half dozen large constables to cart the stuff. Shan't keep them more than a minute or two."

"Right," I say.

I skirt the pond. The mud has frozen hard, cakes of ice like cobbles, treacherously scattered in the ruts. My Wellingtons skate in it and I hold my arms out to keep balance. Once I get on to the side of the quarry it's easier and I force myself up it at a run in the vain hope of restoring some heat to my limbs. Yum-Yum has them about ready to move off, but he stops when I appear and shouts to the men to hold it. He comes over to me.

"What now?" he says. "What fiendish ploy has Big Chief dreamed up?"

"Wants six of the big fellows to lug the boat," I tell him.

I can see the vans already lighted and the bus, warm-looking, pulled back off the highway. Behind them the three detached cottages show their windows through the trees.

"Frig the man," Yum-Yum says pleasantly.

"You can take the rest over to the transport," I tell him. "And hold them there for a while. It won't take long."

"I suppose Vincent drew a blank?"

"He did."

Yum-Yum nods flatly.

"I suppose you know my opinion?" he says.

"I should by this time."

"She ain't here at all," he says.

"You'd better get that squad down," I tell him. "Let's get out of this place."

"Bloody cold, i'n't it?" he says, then turning roars out

vigorously, "Right then, my lucky ones, I'll have six of you
rugger types. Come on then, I know there's six of you in
there some place. Rugby," he says, "that bloody mad game
with the oval ball. Six of you huskies, out here."

Six of the men detach themselves from the serge mass and
come, not enthusiastically, forward and make a ring round
Yum-Yum.

"Down to the pit again, lads," he tells them. "Carry the
ship up to the lorry, then come back to the bus. Right."

The men start off down the slope. I can barely see the group
on the quarry floor now, only a flicker of reflection of a torch
on the water of the pond. The boat appears to be drawn up
on the banking. Another torch lights. The whole scene is
desolate, a miserable and pointless charade.

"Okay," I say. "See you in the morning."

He says quietly, "Is the lass's dad still there?"

"Yes," I say.

"Ay," Yum-Yum says. "It's a grim business."

I tap him on the coat-sleeve and start back down the hill,
his voice bellowing at the men loud above me.

The huskies have the boat already up on their shoulders
and are treading daintily across the ice with it in the direction of the west gate where the lorry is parked. Booth and
McAlister have walked on a little way towards the cars, but
Pettigrew remains behind, watching the final dark mass of
the searchers disappearing from the horizon, as if he really
thought they were giving up for good.

Booth turns and says, "Are you coming, Mister Pettigrew?"

Without turning, Pettigrew tells him, "Yes."

As I come over, I can't help stopping by him and saying,
"We'll be shifting to another area tomorrow. There's nothing
here."

He sniffs in a breath, coughs, holding his gloved hand up
politely to his mouth. He moves with me, walking step in
step back up towards where he's left his car.

"You go to a lot of trouble for one girl, don't you?" he says.

I don't quite know how to reply. He appears to be in complete control of himself. I let him continue, for I can feel he wants to talk. Booth and the others have got around to ignoring him rather of late: not intentionally but simply because he seems to prefer to be alone, to watch, to wait, but not to be in the way. Strictly speaking we could clear him off the area if we wanted to, but even McAlister wouldn't do that, and with such evident self-effacement there's no need. I can understand it, I suppose. He wants to be where the action is, to feel he's doing something, even if it is just hanging around watching the police get on with the job. It must be sheer hell for him and her.

"How long do you keep this up?" he asks.

"As long as is necessary, Mister Pettigrew," I tell him.

"Until you find her?"

"Yes."

"Supposing . . . let us assume you don't . . . find her?"

"At least we'll do everything we can to . ."

"Do you think my daughter's dead? You've got children of your own, haven't you? I'm sure you'll tell me the truth Do you think Irene's dead?"

I don't hesitate. "Yes. I'm afraid I do."

He is silent. "Thank you," he says.

We walk on silently up the slope to the fence and I hold the wire strands wide for him to slip through. Booth and McAlister are seated in the car, waiting for me to join them.

"My car's over here," he said. "Can I offer you a lift?"

"Thanks all the same. I'll have to go back to the station now."

"Have you no idea at all who could have . . . ?" He hasn't come through the wire yet. I let the strand fall, for even through my glove I can feel it like a hot steel rod pressing the flesh of my fingers.

"None at all, I'm afraid. That's the truth," I tell him.

"You mentioned a man called Skinner," he says. "How about him?"

"He'll be questioned in time. Don't you worry. If he knows anything about it, you can depend on it we'll ferret it out."

"Of course," Pettigrew says. "I just wondered. Is it likely?"

I opened the wire again.

"You'd better get through now. I'll have to be on my way."

"Certainly," he says, and obligingly comes through the gap. "Is it likely?"

"Likely?"

He has positioned himself between me and the Jag, and without being positively rude I can't very well get past him.

"Is this Skinner likely to be of use?"

"Arnold Skinner's always ..." I began, then I stopped myself. "He's quite a local character," I say with a half-hearted laugh. "He often helps us out."

"I see," Pettigrew says. "Well, I won't detain you any longer."

"Goodnight, sir," I say.

He walks away. I hurry over to the car and let myself into the front seat beside Caldwell.

"What did he want?" McAlister asks.

"He wanted to know how long we kept it up," I say.

Booth says, "I suppose you told him for ever, if necessary?"

"More or less."

"Quite right," McAlister says. "No sense in depressing him more than's needful. Bad enough for him as it is."

The thought struck me rather suddenly just now, and I turn round in the seat.

"Bob," I say, "did you mention Skinner to him?"

"Who? Pettigrew? Of course not," Booth replies.

"I ... he seems to have picked up the name from somewhere," I tell him.

"I'm not surprised," Booth says to McAlister. "It was bound

to happen sooner or later. I'd rather he hadn't of course, just for his own peace of mind."

McAlister leans forward and taps me on the shoulder. "You didn't tell him anything about Skinner, did you?"

"No, no," I say. He grunts. I take it approves of my reticence. God, it seems a small point in the middle of this mess.

6

Booth

I SHOULD have known really, but then again, it was without precedent in my experience, and I had put the conversation behind me, buried it but not forgotten it. I was thinking of something else, lying there in my armchair listening to my sister making the evening cup of coffee. The book was on my lap, open, but the people in the story were stupid and I couldn't concentrate so I just lay there, dog-tired, letting the ache seep out of my bones into the leather. I heard the telephone ringing but I didn't move. Anne answered it, but I had the shutters up, hoping that it wasn't what I knew it would be, a call from the station. Anne came to the lounge door, the pan of coffee in her hand and the ever-fresh crinkle of sympathy in her face.

"It's for you, Bob." she said.

I buttoned my braces and went through to the hall. It was cold there. I lifted the receiver from the desk and drew the pad over and fiddled out the pencil from its pocket.

"Booth," I said.

"Mister Booth?" a man's voice said. He was very close to the mouthpiece. It sounded as if he actually had the instrument halfway down the back of his throat. I did not completely place the voice.

"Yes," I said.

"This is Watson. Y'know Willie Watson, from the *Arms*."

"What do you want, Willie?"

Apologetically he said, "Look, Mister Booth, I know this's none o'my business like, but there's somethin' goin' on up here I think y'd be better takin' care of."

"What?" I said.

"Well, there's a man here goin' round askin' people if they know . . . well, if they know Skinner."

"What does he look like, this man?" I said.

"I know who he is," the barman said. "It's that girl's father."

"Pettigrew?"

"Uh-huh," Willie said. "I wish you'd come over, Mister Booth. I mean it looks bad, y'know what I mean." He was talking nineteen to the dozen in the muffled voice. "I mean, he's puttin' people off. Jack wanted me t'get a constable but I didn't like. Besides he's not makin' a riot or anythin'."

"Is he drunk?" I said.

Willie replied, "No, no, he's just goin' about quietly and askin' people if they know a man called Skinner."

"He asked you, Willie, didn't he? What did you tell him?"

"Well . . ." the barman said, "I didn't tell'm anythin'. He's not drunk, y'know."

"I'll be right over," I said. "I'll come to the brewer's entrance and you can let me in through the restaurant."

"When?"

"Ten minutes," I said.

I pulled on my jacket and coat and Anne brought out my shoes. She didn't ask and I said nothing because I wasn't thinking about her. I took my car from the garage and managed to start it without too much trouble in spite of the cold. I drove very quickly indeed, slowing only when I came into the last hundred yards before the pub. I stopped back at the turn-in to the bowling green and walked down and through the car park round to the back of the building. Willie, a very

young man who had once been to Art School for a couple of
years, was waiting outside the door, hugging himself into the
soiled white jacket and smoking a cigarette. I could hear the
hub-bub from inside the Public, and the strident intermittent
notes of the Lounge piano as if someone was walking up and
down the keyboard. Willie threw away his cigarette. For a
young man he had sad eyes, wise but not cynical.

"I'm sorry I got y'out," he said.

"I'm glad you did. Who gave you my number?"

"Jack had it. He wants rid of the man."

We stopped in the intersection of the corridor. Another
barman came out of the side room with a bottle of *Vat. 69*
in his hand. He glanced at Willie and moved on. The corridor
was packed with noise and through the tangerine-coloured
frosting of the Lounge-Bar door I could see the blurred and
bloated faces of the press at the bar, the steely slivers of the
pumps and the white sails of the jackets rippling back and
forth.

"Listen," I said, touching his arm to stop him going on into
the Public, "Who's been in tonight that might know
Skinner?"

Willie pursed his lips. "A few."

"Arnold or the old man haven't been in?"

"Christ no," Willie said. "They don't come here. Jack
doesn't encourage their kind."

I grinned at him. "I know. Don't worry."

Willie went quite hostile on me suddenly. "He's in there,"
he said curtly, pointing at the door of the Public. "Get him
out of here. Too many folk know who he is. It's like havin'
a . . . like havin' a . . . I don't know—a ghost in there. Get the
bastard out."

I touched Willie's shoulder. "Okay," I said, "I'll get him
out. Thanks."

Willie brushed past me and went into the Public. As the
door flapped open I caught a brief glimpse of the room, but

I did not see Pettigrew. I found the way into the small restaurant, closed on week-nights, and went through it and opened the door a little bit. I looked at the faces in the long room. The men at the bar itself were not looking round. On the chairs round the wooden tables down the long wall towards the fireplace, the men sat crooked, angled round away from the fireplace corner. Now and then one would turn and glance furtively over his shoulder. I went into the room. Several heads turned, turned away, then back, then bobbed down to the beer glasses. I went over to the bar and without crowding lifted my finger. Jack impassively drew a Guinness and I reached over and grasped it. I gave him the florin. The shoulders at the counter dipped down away from my arm, but no one looked at me fully. I turned and glanced around the place, sipping the Guinness slowly. I began to edge up towards the fireplace. The silence was not complete, but the lessening of noise was apparent. I came up to the edge of the tables and saw him. He had not noticed me yet, but stood, almost rigidly with one foot on the brick kerb holding the short drink in two hands. Even as I watched him, he stepped over the kerb and across the fire. Two old farmers were supporting the far end of the bar and he stood by them, his chest almost touching the right elbow of one, until they stopped talking and both turned to stare at him. Their faces, all three, were impassive: the farmers' planed and fine-skinned and uniformly russet—they may even have been brothers—and Pettigrew's quite different, drawn and sallow, his eyebrows already raised in involuntary politeness and apology. I watched him ask them and the stony uncomprehending stare, and the two heads shaking. Pettigrew leaned a little towards them and tried to smile. He really fought for that smile but without any success. One of the men spoke, monosyllabically and Pettigrew scooped up his own whisky glass and drank some, searching the two old faces over the rim of his cupped hands. He said, "No one of that name?" The farmers turned and put four elbows flat on the counter and gazed at the bottles three yards away as if each was alone at the gate of a great field of black and beaten wheat. Pettigrew paused then stepped back over the hearthstone and took up his place against the wall. As his eyes flickered up and down the men at the bar, he finally saw me.

I didn't know how I was going to play it. I smiled and went over. "Bit out of your neighbourhood, this, Mister Pettigrew," I said. He turned the little glass round and round in his fingers.

"I'm waiting for a friend," he said. His eyes had sunk back into the dark circles and all the blood seemed to have drained away from his face so that it was the colour of tree-fungus.

"Are you?" I said, and drank more Guinness. I still didn't know how to play it. The bar was almost dead still now, except for the shuttering of the door as men left.

"I'm waiting for a friend," Pettigrew repeated. He opened his mouth with great effort as if his lips were lined with lead, but his voice was light, and his diction perfect. Then I felt angry. I said, "Come on, I'll take you home."

"No thank you," he said. "I'm waiting for a friend."

He glanced at his watch, spilling whisky over his sleeve.

"I can't make you," I said. "But I think you should."

"No," he said. "You can't make me. I've done nothing. I'm doing nothing wrong. You've no right."

The two farmers edged out of their corner and left. Pettigrew and I were almost alone now in the region of the hearth.

"I'm telling you to get out," I said.

"No. Not until I'm ready."

"You're making a bloody fool of yourself," I told him.

"That's my own business. Please," he said. He hadn't moved from the wall yet. He now shifted the glass into his left hand and spread his right down behind him, opening his fingers to the fire.

"Have you a car?"

"I don't drive when I'm drinking," he said.

"Then I'll take you home."

"I've a perfect right to be here." He hesitated, then blurted out, "Unless you want to arrest me. Would that do? Arrest me."

I put my arm out and clenched my fist over the edge of the mantel-shelf so that I could say what I had to say without anyone hearing.

"You've asked enough questions for tonight. I *can* stop you. I can do what you're trying to do, if you want me to, but I'm telling you, Pettigrew, this'll get you nowhere."

"I'm waiting for a friend."

"Christ, stop saying that," I said. "Now, come on."

He finished his whisky, looking past me, down the length of the bar.

"You're not doing any good," I told him, murmuring. "In case you don't know it, all you're doing is giving this man one hell of a laugh at you."

Then his face was bright, oily bright. "Which man?"

"You know who I mean."

"I know his name."

"No, you don't," I said.

"Yes, I do."

"No one knows his name. No one knows who killed your daughter."

"Ah," he said, then cramped forward a little. "Yes."

"Look," I said. "If you let me take you home I'll give you some information."

His chest heaved and he ran his tongue back and forth across his lips. "All right," he said.

They watched us now, quite openly, the few who were left. I took the glass from him and put it in mine and pushed them over the bar to Jack, who nodded once as we went on past and out through the door into the car park at the front. He walked ahead of me, small though he was.

"My car's down the road a bit," I told him.

"Tell me here," he said.

"What for: so you can try a few more places. How many pubs have you been in tonight?"

"Three," he said.

I pushed him lightly on the chest and he stepped back. We were at the entrance to the car park now, on the road almost, and I pushed him again so that he stepped back on to the verge and we both were off the tarmac standing under a big faded evergreen which screened us from the pub door and held the neon lamp's glare in shiny layers all down it, now silvering with frost.

"I can do as I like," he said.

"Can you?" I said. "Listen, you're searching for Arnold Skinner. What do you do if you find him? Say, *Please, Sir, where's my daughter*? Is that what you say? Do you know what this Skinner's like? Have you any idea at all? He's not a man . . ."

"Yes," Pettigrew said sharply.

" . . . he's not a man like the men you know, like the men you deal with in your bloody bank, or the men you have lunch with, or go to Church with. He's not like these at all. He's not even like the men in there," I swept my hand at the pub. "He's not like that at all. You would get nothing from him." I stopped. He was listening to me. His face bunched about the eyes which were round and almost girlish in the yellow glow: or not girlish, more like the eyes of a small marsupial transfixed by the beam of a powerful torch. "He would love you," I said. "Yes. He would love you. He would welcome you, because . . ." I couldn't tell him the reason. Only I knew the reason, the real reason, and I couldn't find the words to tell this stupid, hurt little man. He thought it was all about his daughter. He was all bound up with his own intensely selfish sense of loss. I didn't blame him for that, but it made my pity less: nil.

"I'll find him," he said. "I'll know then."

"All right," I said. "Supposing she isn't dead. Supposing he —this man, whoever it is, has her somewhere, what do you think. . . . ?"

His head began to jerk back and forth, hideously. For a moment I thought he was going into some kind of fit.

"Your girl is dead," I said. "She's dead. You can do nothing."

"Jesus. Jesus. Jesus," he said.

I gripped his arm at the elbow. "If you try to find this man again, yourself," I said, "know what I'll do? I'll watch him stamping on you. I'll watch you asking him, begging with him, and I'll watch him laughing at you and seeing the joke in you that he saw in her. Now, do you understand me? I *will do that.*" I released his arm. He lurched to the low wall that held the car park sign and went down on his knees in the grass before it, folding his arms over it and tucking his head away, so that I couldn't see his agony. I stood behind him, not touching him, waiting, while the cars coming and going on the highway lit us up in passing and the drivers chuckled or perhaps snorted, thinking that he was nothing other than sick drunk. I waited until the sounds stopped coming. Then I said, "You think I wouldn't do that. I'm capable of it, Pettigrew. I will do it too, if you push me to it. It doesn't matter to me what he does to you."

He drew himself up against the little wall, the roughcast tearing against the material of his overcoat, then he sat on it, hunched forward, the cloud of his breath hanging in front of him and his mouth open, panting. His cheeks were streaked with tears, but he had stopped weeping.

"I'll drive you home now," I said.

He pushed his shoulders back and stared at me out of the face like a crushed sponge. "No," he said, "I'll walk."

"You're in no fit state . . ." I began.

He got to his feet. "I'll walk," he said. "I won't ride with you. I'll walk. I know the way."

"All right," I said, and turned about and went back to the car, leaving him there against the upright of the sign. When I passed a couple of minutes later, he had already gone.

7

Pettigrew

I N A way I had been expecting it, and consequently it was no great shock to me when it did come: I might almost go so far as to say I welcomed it, as one would welcome a thunderstorm after a period of intense heat. I had had my time of grieving; hers was still to come. It occurred inevitably late at night, in that hour or two of almost agonising retrospection which we had to suffer alone together and which now, in all decency, we could no longer pass in close silence. The silence had no power to unite us, for we were not one in suffering. She blamed me for this, and I can't truthfully claim that she was wrong to do so. If any man deserved the punishment, I did then. I had played the fool. She had no call however to accuse me of more, even by her total reticence. I had done everything that was possible at that time: and deluded her, as well as myself, into thinking that my daily occupation with the police served another purpose less cruel and much less subtle than merely keeping us apart. Or that the ministrations of neighbours and friends in the fore part of the evening was actually and of itself comforting to either of us. Grief and anguish do not work in that way. There was nothing we could properly bury, save hope and neither of us would admit to the other that we had reached the lowest depth by discussing a life without her. I did it for her. Not to save myself her reproaches, and certainly not spurred by her outburst, but because it was the only thing, the only form of foolishness, which was concrete enough to substitute for the tenderness I could not simulate.

She emerged from the kitchen carrying the tray with the two beakers of hot milk upon it and the neat white pillbox beside them. Neither she nor I would resort to sedatives in spite of the doctor. Perhaps, she, like me, felt that to deaden ourselves to the gnawing pain of fear and sorrow would entail some sort of betrayal. Perhaps it was just another kind of penance as meaninglessly brave as her ability to go on with cooking and cleaning and laundering in the face of it all. I was in the hall, at the telephone table, rummaging in the drawer there in search of the writing pad, when I heard her calling my name.

I did not reply immediately and she came out of the lounge, having rid herself of the tray, and stood in the lounge doorway and asked me if I had switched on the television set. I replied that I had.

"Why?" she asked.

I told her that I wanted to watch it for a little while. The set had been unused for almost a week.

"What is it that's on?" she asked.

"I've no idea," I told her.

"Must we have it on, at a time like this?"

"I want to do something for a change," I said.

"Do . . ." she said. "Something."

"I don't know what's on, and I'm not much interested either, but I'd like to watch."

"I see," she said. "Are you trying to tell me you think it's all over."

I seated myself in the armchair directly in front of the set. The volume of sound was very low, but the image was clear enough. I sat still, looking at it but not seeing it. I had hoped that in time I would find myself focusing on it. The probability is that I would have given up after a little and turned it off,

but when she objected I became determined to have my own
way. I left the writing pad and the stub of the pencil on the
arm of the chair beside me. I knew she was still standing close
to the door. I reached out to the tray and took up the beaker
and drank a mouthful or two of the insipid milk. I did not
touch the pillbox.

"You want to do something!" she said quietly. I held my
tongue, and she continued, "Are you going to sit there and
watch it?"

"I don't know," I said. "Come and sit down."

"I don't want to sit here as if . . ."

"What?" I asked her.

"As if it was all right."

"No," I said. "I know, but come and sit down."

She took her seat, kicking the pouffe away almost viciously.
She lighted a cigarette and smoked it rapidly, while I lay in
the chair waiting for her to speak again.

"What are you going to do?" she said abruptly.

"I'm sorry," I said. "I can't think of anything else."

"I mean . . . if Irene doesn't . . ."

"Nothing," I said.

"Will you leave me?"

"Of course not, Agnes," I said. "Don't be idiotic."

"You've given up, Walter, haven't you?" she said. "You've
given it all up."

"No, I haven't," I replied.

"You don't believe they're going to find her at all."

"I don't know that any more than anyone else." I said.

"If we never see her again," she said, "never at all, what
will we do?"

"I think Irene is dead," I said. I turned to face my wife.

"How do you know that?"

"She's dead, Agnes," I said. "You've got to reconcile yourself to that fact."

Then she was standing in front of me, one hand resting in

the crook of her other elbow, the cigarette still jutting from her fingers across the wedding ring.

"But I don't know that," she said. "And what's more, I don't want to know. I can read your mind, Walter, don't think I'm so stupid. I know what's going on. You don't want her to come back now. You just don't want her to come back to me."

I said nothing. I watched her. She went on, "Tell the truth for once in your life, Walter Pettigrew. You're not deceiving me with your . . . lies. It's just a game you're playing, out there with the police all day . . . and last night. You left me *alone* last night, while you went off . . . drinking. I could smell it off you. Is it? Am I right, Walter? Is it some kind of horrible game?"

"Sit down, Agnes," I said. "Please."

"You hated her," Agnes shouted.

"Sit down, for Heaven's sake."

I had no feeling of anger, bore no malice towards her, just a numbness of spirit, a kind of deadness which gripped the fibres of my reasoning and wouldn't let go. I was fully aware of what I was doing, but I couldn't explain the reason. "Sit down, Agnes," I said quietly.

She slumped on to the sofa. I understood her well. I finished writing the names of the bars on the notepad, tore off the leaf, folded it and laid it neatly on the table. Then I gave her my attention: not, however, stretching the fallacy too far by taking her hand. I leaned close enough to speak softly to her.

"Now, listen to me, Agnes," I told her. "I've made a damn' fool of myself already. I may not be much in your eyes—in fact, I know I'm not—but I've done what I can. Only I can't help *you*. That's the one thing I cannot do. You've got to think of yourself now. I'm sorry, but that's the way it is. You must look out for yourself. And I must. . . ."

"You're my husband," she said "You're her father."

"Yes," I said.

I lifted the pillbox and took out three of the pellets and swallowed them down with the milk. Then I got up and, leaving her there, I went into the bedroom and began to undress.

I was lying in the darkness, smoking a cigarette when she came into the room. I could see her clearly against the escaped light from the lounge. She held the square of paper in her hand.

"What is this?" she said.

"Nothing," I said. "But keep it."

"They're *public houses*?"

"Yes," I said.

"Walter?" she said.

"Just keep it," I said.

"It's . . . to do with . . . Irene, hasn't it?"

I did not tell her. She said, "If it's to do with Irene, why haven't you told them about it?"

I closed my eyes. "Booth knows," I said.

"Walter?" she said, her voice a blur across the darkness in front of my closed eyes. "Walter?"

"Just keep the note," I said.

She went away then, and after a little while I fell into the first real sleep I'd had for five nights. I would have slept on until daylight too, if the telephone hadn't disturbed me. I wakened on the first ring, coming straight out of sleep into wakefulness. I felt Agnes stirring beside me, mumbling, and looked at the pillbox on the bedside table standing open beside the water glass. I counted the tablets quickly. She had taken four, and she was fortunately in the fore-part of her sleep, still, I suppose, under the influence of the drug. The telephone rang again. I slid rapidly out of bed and opened the bedroom door. The hallway was cold and my bare feet hissed on the cold linoleum until I stepped on to the rug at the phone. I was trembling, I remember, as I lifted the receiver.

"Yes," I said. I thought I knew what to expect, but I was

quite wrong. The relief perverted my judgment, made me calm, almost ebullient. I heard the voice, full of a purring tranquility, say, "Mister Pettigrew?"

"It is." The voice broke slightly, into a lazy chuckle. "Who's calling?" I said.

"Me?" the voice said. "You don't know me really. I mean we've never met . . . formal like."

"What is it?"

"Ach, no, that's my question, Mister Pettigrew. What d'you want?"

"I don't understand," I said.

"Did y'just want t'stand me a pint then: a gesture of hospitality, is that all it was? I wish I'd known sooner. Still, I'm sure a generous man like yourself'll not mind me callin'— just t'say how sorry I am I wasn't around t'give y'my company in your time of need."

"How did you know?" I said.

"People talk," he said.

"I'm sorry," I said. "I don't think this is the time."

Then his tone changed, becoming for a single moment as rasping as a whetstone on blunt iron. "Ay," he said. "It's the time. The right time." Going back to what it was before, silky and bland, saying, "Unless you've given up, right enough. Know what I mean?"

"Can you help me?"

"Help you?"

"I don't have to explain."

"Yes, y'do have t'explain. Y'have t'explain what you were up to even breathin' my name out of your mouth," Skinner said.

"I only wanted . . ."

"Wanted what then?"

"Do you know where she is?"

"Who's that?" he said.

I said, "My daughter?"

"Oh, is that what it's all about: her. What was her name —Irene, was it? A nice name that."

I pulled the phone round on its cord and sat on the hall chest. I had stopped trembling.

"Are you still there?" he said.

"Yes," I said.

He said, "It's a nice name. Y'gave her a good name. Is that her Mam's name too?"

"Can you help me?" I said. "I have money."

"Money."

"I can pay for information."

"Oh, I get the picture. You thought I could give you information?" he said.

"Sell," I said.

"So you've got money. Well, that gives y'a head start on some of us. A bank manager. Good job that. A bank manager." He paused and I heard him striking a match. I held my tongue between my teeth, and listened for Agnes, but she was still asleep. I could feel the cold draught seeping in under the front door, almost visible, like vapour thick in the dark hallway. The house was strange, alien then, as if I had never been there before. I peered at the vague outline of the calendar on the opposite wall wondering what the picture was. On the other end of the line, I listened to him drawing on the cigarette.

"You've a nice voice," he said with shocking abruptness. "Did y'take lessons in talking? I bet y'do a lot of talking in your job."

"Listen," I said. "I want information."

"Try Inspector Booth," Skinner said.

"This has nothing to do with him."

"I thought you an' him were very pally."

"I met him by accident, if that's what you mean."

He laughed. "Some accident!"

"I see," I said.

"What d'you see?" he said.

"Nothing."

"Ach, you're just bein' coy. Did she take after you?" He paused. "She did, I think. I think she took after you."

"I'm going to hang up now," I said.

"No, wait," he said urgently. "Maybe we should ... co-operate, in a manner of speaking."

"If you have any definite information," I said.

"It's definite," he said. "I'll tell you that for nothing."

"Very well," I said.

Again he was quiet, waiting, listening to me. I put my hand over the mouthpiece.

"You're goin' t'phone Booth and tell him I called, aren't y'now?" he said.

"I might."

"That wouldn't be very friendly."

"I'm not friendly," I said.

"All right then," he went on. "I think you an' me might be able t'do a bit of business. But I wouldn't want them t'know about it."

"What sort of business?"

"I might even know who ..."

"What?" I said. I felt desperately ill now, almost to the point of collapse.

"I think I can help, we'll put it that way."

"Why should you do this—for money?"

He laughed once more, heartily. "Ay, why not."

"How much?"

"We can discuss all that later on. Tell y'what I'll do. You hang around t'morrow, and I'll give y'a wee buzz on the phone—make sure you answer it—an' we'll come t'some arrangement. Eh, no busies, of course. I mean, I'm stickin' m'neck out t'help you here, so you gotta play fair too. Okay?"

"Very well," I said.

"Very well," he said. "Very well. That's fine then."

He gave a low half-suppressed, whimpering giggle. "Y'know somethin'," he said. "You really have got a nice voice. A lovely proper voice." Outside the first hint of dawn had outlined the fan-light over the door, ash-grey, faint. I watched it, waiting. He said, "Just like hers," and hung up.

I put the receiver down and got stiffly to my feet. I went into the kitchen and put on the kettle and lit the plates on the stove. I stood over the stove and warmed my arms and chest until the kettle clicked, then I made a beaker of coffee and smoked a cigarette. It was quite light by that time: quite light for winter. I went into the bedroom and looked at Agnes. She was still asleep, but shallowly, restlessly. Her mouth was open and she snored a little. I went quietly out into the hall again and to the telephone which was where I had left it on the chest. I sat down and began to dial the exchange. I stopped. I wasn't afraid. I wanted perhaps to make a fool of myself, as some sort of penance for all the things I hadn't said or done, or all the tiny trivial incidents that I could never forget, or begin to make amends for. Agnes called from the bedroom. She called awkwardly at first, as out of delirium, as if my name was the only concrete recollection of reality she had to hold on to for a second. Then she called again, querulously, then sharply. "Walter, Walter." I stood up and replaced the phone on its proper place on the table, and went down to the bedroom to reassure her that nothing had happened while she'd been asleep.

8

Howie

H E W A S in the bath howling blue murder. I was holding
the towel, warm from being across the fireguard, while my
wife soaped him down. The other one, so I thought, would be
hiding out as usual to avoid going into the tub. I was worn
out and tired and beginning to turn crabby. Jean had had a
wearing day with the pair of them too, and she wasn't making
matters any better by smacking the wee chap's bott every
couple of minutes to make him shut up. I'd thought of going
out to Kerrigan's pub in the hope of seeing McNally, but I
didn't much fancy it really. What I honestly wanted was a
couple of cups of tea and away to bed. Jean looked up sharply
over the wee chap's head.

"What's she up to now," Jean said. "She's too quiet to be
up to good."

"She'll be all right," I said.

"Will she?" Jean said. "You go and see what she's up to."

I draped the towel over the front of my chair and went
through to the kids' room. I couldn't make her out in among
the jumble of stuff that we keep stored in their room, but after
a bit I saw the shape of her head moving over behind her
rocking horse. She was always sitting in the dark. It didn't
seem to worry her, the dark didn't.

"I see you," I said. I went over. "And what are you doing
hiding there?"

231

"Funny lemonade," she said.

I switched on the lamp.

She had the cork off the bottle and about half a pint of the whisky puddled on the floor. She was dipping her fingers in it and sucking them. She hadn't decided whether she liked the taste enough to have a go at the rest of it or not. I snatched the bottle off her. I was tempted to belt the daylights out of her but I knew it was my own fault for leaving the stuff where she could get her hands on it.

"Did you drink any, Fiona?" I asked her.

She stared at me, not sure if I was going to larrup her or not, and shook her head.

"You're sure."

"Yes, daddy," she told me solemnly.

"Just off your fingers?"

She nodded her head bigly to tell me it was the truth.

"Right," I said. "Go on to your mummy and don't tell her what you were up to. I'll be through in a minute."

I watched her going into the kitchen, then I went into the bathroom and got out a cloth and went back into the bedroom and mopped up the spirits. I carried the bottle and the cloth back into the bathroom. I syned out the cloth in the sink and put it away, then I wiped the whisky bottle and opened the cupboard under the stairs.

I got down on my hunkers, put my head and shoulders into the cupboard and reached over the back of the boards to hide the liquor in among the coal dross. I worked the bottle down into the dross until it stuck. I hoisted it up again and tried once more, and this time I heard it clink on metal. I'd never been right sure about that cupboard since Skinner's visit, and that was why I went inside it and started burrowing in the coal. It was hid deep, but a few big handfuls uncovered it. I brought it out and looked at the paper. The barrel was sticking out. I didn't have to bother unwrapping it to know what it was. I went in again to the cupboard and felt around in the dark pile until I got the other parcel, and brought it out into the light. I placed them on the altar seat and snibbed the door, then I unwrapped them. The gun all right, and the bullets. I counted them. There were four missing. I wrapped them up again as they'd been and put them on the floor. I sat on the seat and thought about it. I got the polythene-wrapped parcel down from the cistern and took out the money and counted it, then I wrapped it up again too with the trinkets and put the lot down with the gun. A long time I spent looking at them, then I unlocked the door and went out into the hall. I laid the stuff on the umbrella-rest at the foot of the hallstand, and went back into the kitchen.

Jean had the wee chap on her knee, in his pyjamas now and happy that the bathing was over. His bottle was already teated and stood waiting on the mantel. Fiona was standing in the bath, ready for Jean to wash, as soon as I came to take Iain. I took him from Jean. He was starting to get his strength now, and he leaned back from me and took my nose in his hand.

"What's going on?" Jean asked, laying about Fiona with the sponge.

"It's all right," I told her. "She'd got my New Year bottle and spilled some, but she didn't lip any."

"Did you?" Jean said, to Fiona, shaking her slightly to wheedle the right answer out of her.

"I didn't," Fiona said, appealing to me. Her skin was all fine gold in the light from the fire, and she was pretty and funny all at the one time, the way kids are.

"It's all right," I said. "I wiped it up and got rid of the bottle."

"She might have drunk it and killed herself," Jean said.

"She might have, but she didn't," I said.

"Give him his feed," Jean said.

I cuddled Iain into me, and wrapped the pram quilt round him and gave him the teat. He sucked with his eyes closed and even after he'd gone to sleep, he continued to suck. I could feel the tugging quite hard against my grip. He was warm against me. All the time Jean was getting Fiona ready. Both of them co-operated with each other through the drying and the ear-cleaning, the pyjama bit and the hair combing, then Fiona was sitting on Jean's knee, leaning back against her, drinking her milk from the Mickey Mouse cup and watching me with heavy sleepy eyes, watching me and her brother through the Willie Winkies.

I carried Iain through to his cot and put him down and tucked him in. I carried Fiona through to her bed too. She was all weighty with sleepiness. Then they were both down, asleep, and I went through to the kitchen again. Jean was tipping out the bath-water, and she'd already put on the kettle for my cup of tea. I sat down in my chair. I didn't know how I was going to tell her, so I just started and hoped it would go on. I was sure enough of her to know she wouldn't try to stop me.

"You remember the man that came here that night before Christmas?" I said.

"What about him?"

"He left a gun and bullets in the bathroom press," I said. "I've just this minute found them."

She came away from the stove and stood behind the table, drying her hands on the dish-towel. I didn't wait for her to have time to ask anything.

"I think he maybe killed with that gun."

"The Sweetshop Murder," Jean said.

"Yes," I said. "I think so. Now I'm going to take the gun to the police. Right away. Right now."

"You'll have to, Brian," she said.

"Ay, I know," I said. "But it's not that easy. You see, I'm mixed up in it too. Not the murders, but I . . . well, I helped another man burgle a house and a dog got shot with that gun."

Jean came slowly round the table and stood in front of me, watching me. I was unsure just for a couple of seconds what she was going to do or say. I just lost the feeling that I could trust her for those couple of seconds, then I was all right again.

"And if I take the gun to the police, there'll be no chance of my getting off, I mean, they'll have me for housebreaking. D'you understand that?"

"Yes," she said. "Couldn't you leave the gun somewhere else, where they'll find it?"

"He's killed with this gun," I explained to her—for I'd got it all clear in my own head in the bathroom. "But they can't prove it. This gun isn't going to be any use to them unless they get some method of tying it in with Skinner. I mean, that gun being here, him hiding it here, means that he did it. He did shoot those folks in the shop."

"What did you do?" Jean asked. "Why didn't you tell me about it, Brian?"

"I broke into a couple of houses, along with another man and his wife."

"Who were they?"

"McNally his name was. Her name was Ruby."

"Did you do it for her then?" Jean asked.

"I did it to get money," I said.

"And did you?"

"About three hundred quid," I said.

"And who did you spend it on?"

"I didn't spend it on anyone. It's out in the hall."

"All of it?"

"Every bloody penny."

"And you want me to tell you what to do?"

"No," I said. "I'm telling you what I'm going to do. I'm taking the whole lot to the police."

"They'll put you in prison."

"Yes," I said.

She waited. She wasn't depending on herself being able to
look at me for a while, so she got up and went to the stove
and turned off the gas, and stood in the alcove with her face
to the wall. Then she whipped round.

"Go then, you silly man," she said. "Go on."

"What'll you do?"

She was crying, not in her voice like, but with the tears
rolling down her cheeks. I kissed her and held her, while she
told me what she thought of me, and kept on crying, until
she wasn't talking any more just crying.

"I'll be all right, darling," she said. "I will. Don't worry."

"You can go to your mother's."

"I'll be all right," she said.

I didn't wait long with her, because it would get harder
and harder all the time. I put on my coat, picked up the stuff
and crammed it into my pockets and went out in a hurry. I
didn't go into see the kids. If I had, I'd never have brought
myself to do it, killer or no killer, Skinner or no bastard
Skinner.

9

Pettigrew

H E C A L L E D again late in the afternoon. Agnes's sister and her husband were with us. We stopped talking when the phone rang and looked at one another in mute and mutual fear. Keith, my brother-in-law, said cheerfully, "It'll be the damned newspapers again. They never give you a minute's peace. You'd think..."

I went out to answer the phone, Agnes following me with her eyes. It was, as I'd anticipated, Skinner. I asked him to hold the line and returned to the lounge. I smiled saying Benson from the bank had called. I closed the lounge door firmly.

"What is it?" I said.

He was brisk this time, perfunctory. "Do you know Redburn at all?"

"A little," I said.

"Right. You'll know the Bakehouse Square. Meet me there at ten tonight."

"Why should I?"

"You want her back?" he said. "Well, I don't know, mind you, but I can take y'to a bloke that can *maybe* help. I'm makin' no promises. And no busies. If the busies come, then it's all off. I'll just say I never phoned y' nor nothin'. Got that."

"I understand," I told him.

"The Bakehouse Square in Redburgh, at ten o'clock. Bring

237

money too, just in case this joker's interested in sellin'. Not everyone's as big-hearted as I am myself."

I said, "How much money?"

"As much as y'can raise."

"How do I know I can trust you?"

"Christ," he said. "Y'd think y' didn't want this girl of yours, t'hear y'goin' on. Listen, Mister, I've gone t'a lot of trouble over this. You be there."

I let him wait. "I'll be there," I said at last.

"An' bring the cash."

"Of course," I said.

He hung up then. I couldn't overlook the fact that he might be telling the truth. I tried, but I couldn't rid myself of the last shred of hope that Irene was not dead at all. I had little or no money to take with me. He should have considered the bank hours when he was making his arrangements. I went into the lounge again and told them lies as to what Benson had supposedly said to me. I sat down and waited half an hour. My sister-in-law had an uncontrollable bout of tears and Agnes went out to make tea.

The evening, after the in-laws left, went by very quickly. On the pretext of hearing the sound of running water and suspecting a burst pipe, I drew down the Slingsby ladder and climbed into the loft. This would be about eight. While I was up there, the minister called once more and Agnes took him into the lounge. I found the ancient toy box that my mother had insisted I bring here after my marriage. In the bottom, in a metal box, I found my father's old revolver. It was clumsy and heavy, the mechanism red-rusted in spots. I brought it down with me and, in the bathroom, cleaned and polished it as best I could. I had no ammunition for it. It would be impossible now to find ammunition for it, I suppose, even if I had so wished.

I put it safely in the pocket of my coat, which hung in the hall cupboard, together with ten pound notes. In the kitchen,

I wrote out a careful memo simply reporting the gist of Skinner's instructions, and sealed it into an envelope. I addressed the envelope to my wife, stamped it and put it too in my coat pocket. Then I returned to the lounge and allowed Lamb to guide us in prayer. Inside me, as the pastor's voice droned on and on, I experienced only anger, the only emotion which I dared allow myself to feel. But my anger was not self-directed, nor did it involve Skinner. It cofused on her, on Agnes and on Lamb; on Booth too, and on Muirhead. I hated them for pretending to understand, for even having the temerity to attempt understanding. I didn't want it put safe into compartments in that way: to have Booth's cryptic grasp of the mechanics of crime thrust on me, or Muirhead's spaniel-eyed oozing of pity, or the man of God spewing out his platitudes and useless panaceas as if we had a lesson to learn from our suffering—the neighbours, friends, relations, the newspaper reporters each seeing our grief as something different, divorced from that blunt, hellish source. When Lamb had finished praying and sat back on the sofa, his hand across his face still, I asked him if he would do me the favour of sitting with Agnes for a while. I told him that I wanted to call on Booth at the Station, and that I might be gone for some time. He smiled his patient smile and patted my arm replying that he would be only too pleased to do this. Agnes accompanied me to the door.

Whispering she said, "Where *are* you going?"

I said, "I've told you. I'm going to see Booth."

"No, you're not. Why?"

"Don't you want to know," I said. "Don't you want to know what's happening?"

Her face was pinched, her lips wet and I thought she was about to speak again, but she did not. Instead—the action was provoked by pure habit—she kissed my cheek curtly, then closed the door on me.

I fetched the car from the garage and drove slowly and

carefully over the slippery roads to Redburn. The Bakehouse
Square lies at the heart of the old town, round the squat clock-
tower; above it the high banking and the shrub-shrouded
path to the Chapel. The roof of the Chapel and the curvature
of the railings round it stood out against the dull suffusion of
the lamps on the other side of the knoll. The bakehouse, an
old building, stretches down one whole side of the square.
Under the clock-tower are public lavatories, and on a small
muddy obling of grass in front of them, a bench where old
men spend their mornings in fair weather. I had visualised
him waiting on that bench, but saw no sign of him in its
vicinity. I did not stop the car, or even slow down. Children
were playing on the broad pavement, their cries shrill as they
clustered and broke in tag, like avifauna down to scratch the
earth, around the warm yeasty region of the bakehouse door.
The pub on the East side of the square, closing, released its
clients two by two. I braked rapidly as a couple staggered off
the pavement. I went round the square once, but I could not
spot him anywhere. I felt I would recognise him: that there
would be some sort of attraction between us, that, at least, his
very immobility would point him out for me. But he was not
there. I forked away out of the square then, turning back to
the main thoroughfare by another way, but drove back in a
half circle to tour round the area again, more slowly this time,
peering into dark shop doorways, and intently at the group
of young people who dallied outside the café door. I could
find no trace of Skinner at all. It had been merely part of the
fun then—as Booth had tried to explain—bound up with the
man's black humour. Guiltless or not, this was his show to
run as he pleased. He was there, hiding, watching me, not
out of caution or fear, but for the simple pleasure of imagin-
ing my anguish as another avenue of hope closed. I could
hear the laugh again in my mind's ear. Once more I steered
the car around the square. Above me the small windows of
tenements looked down, alight, and I could envisage him in

a room there, his arms on the sill, his face against the parted curtains revelling in my desperation, perhaps already designing his next phone call, framing the time and the place of the appointment he woud drag me to next. I stopped the car in front of the lavatory and got out and went inside. I used the urinal and came out again. Deliberately I hesitated at the kerb, then crossed to the café. The coffee bar was closed and the short counter had before it only some children buying sweets. I purchased a packet of cigarettes and came out to stand on the pavement at that corner and studied the streets to right and left. I could see no one who might conceivably be Skinner.

Of the five streets which feed into the square I had already explored four. Now I drove down the West side and turned right. As I made the turn I glanced behind me to watch for traffic coming directly through from the road by the Chapel. And then I saw him. He emerged from the black canopy of a drinking fountain set in the tower wall behind the toilets, and, with a single swift angling of the head at the back of my car, walked smartly across the cobbles by the café and into the narrowest side street of all. I could not turn just there, so I accelerated, pushing the car on round the long uphill curve of the old road past the Chapel Knoll. I knew it was him, not so much by the slyness of his movements, but by their very briskness. He walked off, like a man with an urgent and fixed destination, in a district where, at ten at night, no one goes anywhere but home. It was a deserted street this, running between small factories and houses vacant and awaiting demolition. I spun the wheel at the first right turn and dipped the car down into a lane, in spite of the large notice prohibiting vehicles. The roar of the engine shuttled back at me from the high walls. I cut and drifted down the gradient to the bottom. The exit on to the next street was barred by three ancient horse posts. For an instant I was possessed with enough blind frustration to drive the car at them point blank, then I regained control of myself and backed the car up into the deep part of the lane and set the brakes. I put off the lights and climbed out, walked down the lane and stood in the shadow of the wall, pressing myself in against it. It was then that I began to wonder at his motive, and to concern myself with the question of his sanity. He had taken the risk of phoning me, to taunt me, to reimburse himself perhaps for having received short measure from his killing. I clung to the projecting stones behind me, pulling on them with my fingertips as if I wanted to bring the whole wall down upon me, to bury me from all of this.

A minute later he came by, walking fast, swinging his short arms in a manner almost military. I listened to the light click of his heels on the pavement as he strode past the lane on the opposite side. He glanced up into it only briefly then turned his face to the front so that I had no more than an instant to take in his features. I let him go on until I was sure he was well past me before I put my head out and saw, as I had hoped, that the street he was on ran under the railway bridge, without a turn-off, on to the main road once more. I hurried back to the car, started it and reversed up hill again and drove, more leisurely now, the full length of the Chapel road on to the main Redburn Road. The buses and the motorcars comforted me. I drove across and turned into the traffic stream and cruised with it, until I passed the long street in which I knew Skinner to be. I drove fifty yards beyond it and parked the car, watching in my mirror all the while to make sure he didn't emerge before I could be ready. I strolled back along the pavement towards the street, stopped at the glass and marble front of the post office building and put my letter in the box. When I turned again he was coming out of the street, diagonally across the thoroughfare from me, no more than thirty yards away. He turned left on the same side and slowed his pace. I followed him on the opposite pavement, keeping myself well behind him. Almost at the Cross he used a Zebra and came on over the road. I hesitated, thinking that somehow he must have become aware of my presence and that he was coming to. . . . But he went on down into a wide side street, flanked high by tenements and well enough lit. I stopped on the corner at the big supermarket window there, watching him out of the corner of my eye and making ready to go after him again once he was far enough away. I had no need to do this, for, quite suddenly, he swerved into a close-mouth and was gone. His disappearance shocked me. I filled with dread at the thought that he might be running among the back courts, traversing the maze of closes and wash-houses through which I could never hope to follow him. I counted the lamp-posts to the close into which he had vanished, then I ran back to the car and brought it up into the street. I drove down the full length of the street and back again and parked fifteen yards or so behind the close, facing the car towards the main highway. I sat quite still then watching, neither afraid, nor angry now. Quite still, the dud revolver in my lap and my hands on the steering wheel, waiting for him to come out again, whenever that time might be.

10

Muirhead

YUM-YUM PUT his head round the canteen door and jerked it at me, unceremoniously indicating that he wanted to speak with me in private. "Come in, man," I said.

"You come out," Yum-Yum said. "I'll guarantee you won't mind missing the rest of that scrambled egg when you see what I've got for you."

"All right," I said.

I put down the knife and fork and stood up. As a last minute afterthought I lifted my teacup and drank off the tea hurriedly. I was still hungry, but I knew Yum-Yum well enough to realise the last thing he would do would be to summon me from the haven of the canteen unless he had good cause. I went out and joined him in the corridor.

"Well?" I said.

Yum-Yum jerked his thumb back down the corridor in the direction of the waiting-room.

"Guess what just turned up?" he said.

"Never mind the game," I snapped at him. "Tell me."

"A gun," he said.

"Where?"

"In someone's coal-hole."

"Whose?"

"He's down there now with the blessed thing wrapped up

in a parcel. He says he's damn' well not parting with it to anyone but you."

"Who is he?" I asked, already starting down the corridor.

"Name of Howie. Brian Howie. He lives in Abbotshead: Valentine Road."

"What do you know about him?"

"Nowt," Yum-Yum said. "When he said he'd found a gun, I came and got you."

"I suppose you didn't think to ask him if he was still under the impression that an amnesty existed."

Yum-Yum grinned at me, with a disagreeably savage lip. "Now you should know better than that, Andy."

"What makes you . . .?"

"He's a friend of Arnold Skinner's," Yum-Yum declared.

I left him in the corridor and opened the waiting-room door.

He was a young fellow, pale, tired-looking. He sat with his knees together, a parcel, wrapped in holly-paper, lying in his lap. He had one hand on it as if he was holding it there by force as one would restrain a small wild animal. His eyes were turned towards the door even before I entered. In his left hand he had a cigarette, holding it almost beneath the seat as if he was committing a breach of the rules by smoking on police property.

"You're the lad with the gun, are you?" I said.

"Yes, sir," he said.

"Come into the office."

I led him into my office. The wall clock told me it was half-past nine. Booth had gone home and Paige and Strachan had been missing for some time, presumably snuffling after trails too involved to be trusted to mere provincial coppers like myself. I pulled out the straight chair for the young man and went round behind the desk.

"Sit down," I said.

"Thank you," he said.

He was well enough spoken, and there was no air of applied innocence about him. He was genuinely scared, and unsure of himself.

"Go on," I said. "Sit down, we won't eat you."

He sat down cautiously on the edge of the seat, putting the parcel in his lap as before, and holding it there.

I withdrew a notepad from the drawer, and switched on the desk-lamp.

"Name," I said.

"Brian Howie."

"Age?"

"Twenty-four."

"Occupation?"

"I'm in the Railways: Goods Yard at Milligan Street Depot."

"What do you do there?"

"I'm a clerk in the Parcels Office."

"How long have you been with the Railway?"

"Eight years, nearly."

"Married or single?"

"Married."

"Family?"

"Two," he said.

I held out my hand to ask him for the gun, then I changed my mind and lifted my pen again.

"You'd better give me your address," I said.

"Seven, Valentine Road, Abbotshead, Carsehorn," he replied, closing his eyes briefly as if striving to remember a rehearsed role.

"You've never done a bit, have you?"

"No. Never."

"Now," I said, sitting back with rather the same air of serene power as Booth would have used. "Let's have the weapon."

He lifted the parcel and held it in front of him for a second as if to make sure he had the right one, then he leaned forward and laid it on the desk.

With an effort I restrained myself from grabbing at it. We sat looking at each other blankly for almost a minute, then I reached for the parcel and ran open the sellotape binding with my thumbs. The gun fell out on to the desk in a little shower of coal-dust.

"Did it come in the bag?" I said. "Is that your story?"

"What?" he said, with an expression of horror. "What?"

I pushed a pencil into the barrel and lifted the weapon from the desk and examined it. Obviously it hadn't been in the coal-pile very long, but the oiled parts had attracted a fine even coating of the dust. I squinted at it, and saw that it wasn't loaded. I carefully replaced it on the paper.

"No name with it?" I asked.

"Yes," he said.

He delved into his coat pocket and produced a manila envelope with a British Railways stamping across it. He hesitated again for a moment then opened the envelope and removed from it a flat packet done up in newspaper but unsealed. The packet sagged limply and almost split open as he offered it to me. I accepted it in both hands and flipped it open to admire the cartridges.

"Very nice," I said. "Were they wrapped like this when you found them?"

Howie nodded.

"And just where exactly did you find them?"

"In the dross under our stairs."

"Give me a bit more information please," I said.

He said, "We got a cupboard in the bathroom that takes up the space under the stairs. We got a sort of—partition—thing of wood there and we store coal behind it, you know, bags and dross an' that stuff, in case we can't get delivery some week. You know?"

"All right," I said. "Where was the gun?"

"Stuck in the dross. Buried in it, but not very deep."

"Bullets too?"

"They were under the gun, deeper, if you see what I mean, and wrapped up in the bit of paper there."

"Very well," I said. "Who found them?"

"I did," he said.

"When?"

"About . . ." he glanced at the clock to make sure he wasn't to be trapped into the smallest lie, "about a half-hour ago: no, maybe nearer an hour."

"You came straight here?"

"Yes," he said.

"Why didn't you wait until morning?"

"I wanted to get rid of it as soon as I could. I thought . . ."

"Go on, son," I said. "You don't have to worry about me."

"I thought it might have something to do with . . . the murders."

"You did," I said. "Well, you were perfectly correct in bringing the gun to us right away."

He sighed, quite audibly, his shoulders relaxing. I offered him a cigarette from my case and lit one for myself too and waited until we had both settled to the tobacco, then I asked him, "What were you doing digging in the coal?"

"Actually I was hiding a bottle of whisky," he said. "I had it out on Christmas Day for a dram or two and I forgot to put it back. My wife doesn't like me to leave liquor lying round the house, in case the kids . . ."

"That's reasonable," I said. "And when you put the bottle back you discovered the gun. It was quite a shock then?"

"It was that," he said.

I was coming very close to it now, and I could feel the nerves in my stomach growing taut. I placed my hands flat on my knees under the desk to stop them trembling, and fired the questions at him with great rapidity.

"So you've no idea how long it's been there?"

"Yes," he said.

I let it pass unnoticed, as if he had replied in the negative. "Or how it got there?"

"I said yes, I think so," he replied with a note of desperation. "Or who put it there?"

"Hell yes," he said. "I think it was Arnold Skinner. D'you know who I mean?"

I stopped. Carefully took one hand from my knee and reached very quickly for the cigarette in the ash-tray. I allowed myself to go back in the chair slowly.

We had him now. I said respectfully, "Tell me."

And he did. Everything.

11

Ruby

HALF-PAST EIGHT at night, the door-bell rings. Arnold Skinner's standing on the doorstep.

"What do you want then?" I ask him, not even bothering to take off the safety chain.

"Thought I'd come up for a blether. Mike in?"

"No, Mike is not in," I inform him.

"I see," he says. "I don't suppose you're goin' t'ask me to wait for him."

"That's right," I say.

I looks back down the stairs, and I make to shut the door again. He puts his hand up round the jamb.

"Come on, Ruby," he says. "Open up."

"Look you," I tell him in no uncertain manner of speaking. "What gives you the idea that either me or Mike ever wants to clap eyes on your ugly mug again."

"Because of what happened?" he says, hurt.

"That and a few other things."

"Like what?" he says.

"Like things I've had on my mind for a while now."

"Like what?" he says again harder.

"You should know," I say.

He leans his shoulder against the door. Not pushing on it, but getting himself into the position to apply his weight.

"I'm just not letting you in, Skinner," I tell him. "So you

250

can buzz off. In fact if you take my advice, son, you'll steer
well clear of Mike for a long while to come."

"Did y'tell him then . . . about what happened?"

"That's between Mike and me."

Skinner smiles. "I thought y'wouldn't."

"What did you want t'kill me for?" I ask him outright.

"Kill you," he says, in an amazed voice, as if nothing like
that had ever entered his innocent head. "I was just havin' a
bit of a go at you. Never knew you yet t'pass up a good offer."

"Well, I'm getting fussy in my old age, put it down to that.
Now clear off. Go on."

I can feel him leaning against the frame now, testing the
strength of the chain-holding as best he can without making
it too obvious. His face is pressed up against the opening, and
he still has his hand in there so that I can't close the door.

"Ruby," he says, whispering. "Let me in for an hour or so,
for ol' time's sake."

"Why should I?" I says.

In a quick rushed angry whisper he tells me, "Because the
friggin' busies are all over the place."

"Well, I hope they find you."

"Come on, Ruby. Give's a break," he says, pressing hard.

"Not in your bloody life," I tell him.

He relaxes suddenly. "I want a place to wait," he says. "A
safe place. An' d'you know what I'm waitin' for? I'll tell you.
I'm waitin' for them."

"Who?" I say.

"Them. Christ. Them. All of them. I'm ready for them,
near enough. Ready t'take them on."

"You're nuts, Skinner," I say. "What do you mean?"

"They think they done it themselves That's what they'll
shout when the time comes. But you'n me'll know different,
dear. We'll know that I just . . . I just decided it was time."

"Oh God, Arno," I say.

"But not just yet. I'm, not just ready yet, y'see. It's not quite time yet. I can still pick an' choose just when; see. Nobody calls the tune for Arnold Skinner. No bloody busie. No bloody prissy-arsed dame makes me look stupid."

He put his hand across his breast as if he was swearing a Bible oath. "Only Arno does for Arno. It's my choice. Y'see that, Ruby."

"Ay, Arno," I say. "I see that."

"An' I'll even tell y'why." He stopped, and his face was soft just then, like a boy's face, unmarred by trouble at all, and the mouth quiet, full. "Because I'm fed-up. I'm just plain fed-up. I'm bored, Ruby. I'm bored t'bloody death."

"You did all these things, didn't you. Arno?" I say.

He stares at me, hard now, all the sadness gone, just furious mad. "An' who else did y'think?" he says. His forearm thuds against the wood. "So let me in t'wait a while. I'm not just ready for them yet."

"Go to hell, Skinner," I tell him.

He hits the door full with his shoulder, resting in behind the blow to speak again. "You stinkin' old whore," he says. "You'd bloody shop me."

"Try Brian Howie," I say. "Maybe he's still soft enough to put you up."

"Stinkin' old bag. Bitch," he says.

I slammed the door hard on his hand. Hearing him yelp like a stuck pig did me the world of good.

Then I pushed the big linen chest up against the door and couped it on its end. I went through into the bedroom and squinted out of the window, to make sure he'd gone. There was a car there, drawn up beside the lamp-post about twenty yards from the close. Arnold came rocketing out of the close, hesitated a minute, looking up and down the street just exactly like a man waiting for the pounce, then he turned off towards the town and walked fast. The car ground along behind him and just before it passed out of my range of view slowed to a stop. I couldn't see how many were in it, but one

of them got out and after words Arnold went round and slipped
in. The car drives off. Seeing him actually lifted right there in
front of my house doesn't make me feel bad either, though,
by God, if they charge him there'll be trouble enough for the
rest of us. Knowing Skinner, he'll run off at the mouth like
an iron lion on a fountain. That's what he meant, I'm sure.
That's what the bugger meant about being just plain bored.
I start jumping into my coat and boots to go off to find Mike.
The longer we have to cover the better for all of us.

12

Booth

I CAME into the station in the car, at seventy all the way. Muirhead was already waiting for me on the pavement, with Paige and Strachan. They got in fast and, leading the whole fleet, we headed for Skinner's.

"Tell me," I said. "Did you find the girl?"

"Not so far," Muirhead replied.

"It was a character called Howie," Paige intervenes from the back. "Ever heard of him?"

"Never," I said.

"Nor me," Paige said.

"Not surprising, really," Muirhead said. "He's never been netted before. I gather his association with Skinner was more or less social, until a couple of months ago."

"Go on, get to the meat," I said.

"Howie discovered a gun hidden in his coal-closet. The gun and the bullets. He knows almost for sure that Skinner planted them there. It's fairly typical of Skinner. Howie used the gun, which he got from Arnold in the first place, to give him Dutch courage at a housebreaking. . . ."

"Kissocks?" I asked. I was already a jump ahead of Muirhead, but I allowed him to continue. I was already searching my mind to discover if Skinner could have been tipped off. Singleton was relief man on the tailing job we'd set up at the beginning of the week. He had instructions to let us know

254

where he was and what Skinner was up to, just as often as
seemed feasible.

"Yes, the Kissock place," Muirhead said. "It was Howie who
shot the dog. He panicked somewhat then and returned the
gun to Skinner. It happens to be the same weapon as was used
on the two Fairbairn women and the child."

"Then Skinner calls at Howie's and plants the thing well
out of the way. The lavatory being the logical place?" I
said.

"That's it," Muirhead said.

"Quite enough to hook him on," Paige said. "Don't you
think, Bob?"

"Definitely," I said. "How far will Howie go?"

"All the way, I should think," Muirhead said. "He feels
he owes a debt."

"Why, what did Skinner ever do to him?" I asked.

"Nothing. I suspect that Howie's just discovered the truth
of the old adage that crime doesn't pay—at least not when
you still retain a few shreds of conscience, in the dour old
Scottish Presbyterian sense," Muirhead said.

"He must be a youngster," I said.

"He is," Muirhead said.

"All right. Where's Singleton?" I asked.

Paige answered that one: "Unfortunately he lost Skinner."

"How?"

"The usual caper," Paige replied. "Skinner led him a dance
in that car of his. Parked the car at the dockside at the foot of
Hope Street in the city, and went for a stroll. Your sergeant
played by the book. Left his mate to check on the car and took
after Skinner on foot."

"Which store did he lose him in?" I asked.

"Lewis's," Muirhead said. "You can't blame Singleton."

"Where is he now then?" I asked.

"Who? The sergeant?" Strachan said. "He stationed one

of our lads at the parked car, then dived back to Skinner's house. He sent his mate up to Kerrigan's public bar, just in case. I suppose it was all he could do under the circumstances really."

"I suppose so," I said. I had the feeling that Skinner wasn't going to be sitting waiting for us.

"I've covered the exits," Muirhead said.

"So if he isn't at home," I said, "we've got to hang on until he shows."

"Or go out and find him," Paige said.

"His places of retreat are covered," Muirhead said. "That character McNally is being brought in, by the way. He's apparently been the source of some of the house-jobs—according to Howie."

"Everyone's going to just love this Howie," I said.

We broke the fleet just outside Carsehorn and converged again at the street. Singleton was waiting for us. He had no idea, of course, that anything urgent had occurred, and I could see him mentally kicking himself for having let Skinner slide away.

"Is he in there?" I asked.

"I very much doubt it," Singleton told me remorsefully. "It's as quiet as the grave. I think the family's in bed. Bedroom lights went off about three-quarters of an hour ago."

"You look frozen," I said.

"I am," he said. "Twelve hours wasted."

"Come back to the car now," I told him. "We'll take the lot in at once. If he's here it won't do him any harm to let him see we mean business, and if he's not, it might serve to panic the women-folk into telling us his whereabouts."

"Okay," Singleton said.

We walked quickly back to the lead vehicle stationed at the blank end of the street under the railway embankment.

As Singleton crushed himself into the front seat with me,

Paige said, "What's t'do, Bob? Are you going to the house?"

"That's it," I said. "Are you ready?"

13

Pettigrew

THE REVOLVER, large and formidable-looking but completely useless was perfectly steady in my hand. I recall quite vividly being startled at my own composure. I remember thinking, for instance, that my emotional numbness had certainly picked a fine time to begin wearing off. Under different circumstances I might even have been thrilled by what we are led to believe is an exhibition of cool nerve, but my pride was not that rampant or inviolate. Inwardly I was sick with desperation and fear.

I managed to climb out of the car and came round the bonnet with the pistol at my side, hidden in the folds of my coat. He had emerged from the close very rapidly indeed and if I had not been so keyed up I doubt if I could have brought the car to life and negotiated it alongside him with such precision. He appeared to know it was for him and stopped, standing stock-still in the middle of the empty pavement facing me. As I got out and moved round towards him he never ceased watching me, the inch of cigarette in his lips working up and down slightly as he pursed his mouth. An old science-master of mine had the same habit of smoking, constantly and with forgetful enjoyment.

"What the hell d'you want?" he said to me.

"I want you to get into my car, into the driver's seat," I said.

"What for then?" he said to me. "What the hell do you think I am, a bastard free chauffeur?"

"Please, get in," I said to him.

He spat out the cigarette end and peered at me closely, his head held on one side.

"You're not the busies," he said. "Don't throw me none of that official shit. If y'think I'm gettin' into a buggy that. . . ."

Very deliberately I raised the hand with the pistol clenched in it and pointed it approximately at his heart. I held my elbow bent to prevent a tremble developing and to maintain a safe distance between the nose of the weapon and his hands.

His mouth sprang open suddenly into a delighted leer.

"You're her old man," he cried.

"Yes," I said.

"Pettigrew," he said.

"I do know how to fire a gun," I told him. "And I won't hesitate, if you don't go quietly into the driving seat of my car."

"You've saw too many duff movies, mister," he said. "That's your trouble."

But all the same he started to move in the correct direction. I stepped away from the bonnet and glanced briefly up the street to make sure no one had remarked our exchange. Some children were playing round a filthy close-mouth and, of course, a steady stream of pedestrian and vehicular traffic passed along the main transpontine thoroughfare at the street's end. He passed between the pistol point and the front fender. I studied him closely as he reached the open door of the car, then I inched close enough to shoot him dead through the head without the bodywork protecting him. He stared at me flatly and I motioned to him to enter the car. He crouched and slid into the seat passively, nodding his head repeatedly and smiling slightly as if I amused him intensely. I darted round the front of the car and let myself cautiously into the rear seat. I trained the pistol over the back of the cushion of the front passenger seat.

"Close your door and start the engine," I told him.

He did this.

"Where to, Sahib?" he asked.

"I think you know that better than I do perhaps," I said.

"Where to, Sahib?" he repeated.

"Take me to my daughter."

"Ay," he said. "Take me to your leader."

"Come on," I said. "I know you're aware of her whereabouts. You told me so."

"Me!" he said. "I never spoke t'you in my life."

His hands rested lightly on the wheel, but he showed no sign of starting to drive. I knew he was watching me in the driving mirror.

"Because you know where she is," I informed him.

"Who says?"

"You did. On the telephone this morning. Come on."

"Supposin' I say I think you're a bloody nut, an' tell you t'go an' work your pop-gun, then what?"

"Then I'll shoot you through the back of the head."

"You haven't got the bloody guts."

"If you don't drive this car directly to my daughter, I will, I promise you."

"Supposin' I told you I do know where she is, an' that I know who put'r there, you'll go right to the busies, won't you?"

He swivelled round suddenly. Frantically I snatched the pistol back and got myself into the corner of the seat so that he couldn't reach for me.

"Hey," he said. "Did that bitch Booth set you up t'this?"

"No," I said. "He knows nothing about it. I told you I wouldn't contact the police, and I didn't."

"Sure," he said. "An' m'granny's an orangeman."

"We're going to fetch Irene now," I told him.

"Frig off," he said, swinging towards the door and feeling for the lock handle.

I said, "Skinner," and as he brought his face round towards me again I drew the barrel of the pistol twice, forehanded and backhanded, across his cheek. As his arm came up, on reflex, to protect himself, I withdrew the pistol and sat stiffly back. The gun-sight had cut him and the blood flowed freely. I didn't feel sorrow at having hit him, only trepidation in case I had gone too far: but I had completely lost perspective. Only the fact that this man knew where my daughter was existed for me. There was no horizon beyond; no niggling guilt or quibbling thought of recompense, only Skinner and myself and my daughter in a straightforward geometry of need and fulfilment. Though my last wraithlike hope of finding my girl alive had deserted me the instant I clapped eyes on him, I wanted her then more desperately than ever before. It was, I suppose, the need to make the want tangible, comprehensible to this man, that caused me to strike out at him, and not hatred or the rage after all. I didn't hate him. I was only afraid of what he might do to me before he had taken me to my girl.

He uttered no sound when I whipped him, not the smallest murmur of surprise or pain, but when he turned into the wheel and released the clutch, I heard him making a noise deep in his throat. I thought at first that he was weeping with the sting of the wounds which I could see clearly, painted in a quantity of blood which poured down the trough of his neck on to his collar. But, as we drove along a little way, I suddenly realised that he wasn't weeping but laughing.

He drove well, ignoring the mess of blood entirely. The car turned into the main road and left Redburn in the direction of the Carsehorn boundary. When we stopped at traffic lights I dropped the pistol below the level of the seat and tried to look unconcernedly at the drivers to the right and left of us. Skinner too was unconcerned, making no demonstration

whatsoever, his attention on the amber signal waiting to pro-
ject the car forward again as if he was as anxious now to get
to the place where Irene lay, as I was myself. He took me out
by the Carsehorn Road. I thought we were going through the
town itself, but he cut off sharply down the back way past
the waterworks and came out at the Willmington fly-over,
branching off at the roundabout on to a road I didn't know.

"Where are we?" I asked him.

He licked some of the blood from his lips before he spoke.
"By-passin' Arrowmill," he said. "D'you want me t'stop?"

"No," I said. "I thought you understood where I want you
to take me."

"That's where we're goin'," he said. "Frig-all good it'll do
you."

I did not reply. I did not ask him the reason, but he told
me. It was his method of revenging himself on me for striking
him, I suppose. Justifiable within the letter of his own personal law, done without strain or effort, to crush the
last penny's worth of pleasure out of the situation.

"You'll know when we get near," he continued. "You'll
smell it. I mean, the bird's been dead for over a week, an'
she's bound t'be gettin' a bit gamey by this time."

I still gave him no answer. I held myself deep in the corner
of the rear seat and waited for him to go on.

"Pity it's so friggin' dark," he said. "Y'could see all the local
hot-spots otherwise. Just up here a shade an' we'll be passin'
the rustic glade where Booth an' his merry men found the
corpse of the Calder girl. Harriet. Did you read about her then,
last Autumn?" He waited. "No. Y'should read things like that
when the papers are good enough t'report on them. Very
educational reading it makes. All about how he got'r alone in
the wood and what he done to her. Highly enlightenin', ol'
man." He waited again. "Harriet. Ay, she was the goods. How
d'your sort put it—jolly vivacious, an' all that. A teazer
though. A teazer any way y'look at it."

"Did you kill her?" I asked.

"But compared with *some*," he went on comfortably, "*some* I could mention, poor bitch Harriet was nothin'. Yeah, I've got a good eye for the gals, okay. There was this one, not so long ago either, I'm told she was a humdinger. Like dippin' it in honey, but . . ."

"Shut your mouth, Skinner," I said. I knew full well I couldn't stop him. I daren't strike him again because he had taken the car to speed. I had to listen to him talk, try to blot out his words, to absorb myself in the rushing darkness above the hedges.

"But she was a snottery kid, all the same. Wasn't goin' t'admit that she was big enough and handsome enough t'take it all. A thing like that ought t'be left for others with more experience t'judge. An' she was ready, I'm tellin' you, ready an' able. Up to the hilt."

He gestured obscenely with his left hand, laughing again, and observing me occasionally in the tilted mirror to make sure I hadn't missed the implication.

"But then you wouldn't know, would you?" he said. "Fuzzy as a darkie's head an' never been kissed. Surprise. Surprise."

"How far now?" I asked, my voice thin.

"Not aw-fully far," he replied. "Not aw-fully far now, really. Are y'bored? She was. Bored stiff. This girl I heard about."

I could not let him defeat me now, because I knew he was taking me to her. There was no logical explanation for my certainty but I knew it just the same. It seemed to be the only suitable climax. Even he, I was sure, could think of no other thing satisfying enough to inflict upon me but to show me where she lay, knowing as he did the method of her death and the posture of her body.

I asked him outright, "What was this girl's name?"

"Buggered if I can remember it now," he said. "I'm sure

it was mentioned t'me. Why? Are y'interested? It's a bit late now, though, i'n't it. She wouldn't be much of a joy-giver now, even for an' old fogey like yourself."

"Probably not," I said. "I'd like you to try and recall her name, though. Just out of interest."

"Name some?" he said. "Go ahead, name some names."

"Barbara," I said.

"Nope."

"Marjory," I said.

"Wasn't that."

"Jean?"

"Keep going, mister," he said.

"Irene?" I said.

"Ay," he said. "Now that's more likely. Maybe that was the name, right enough. Irene. I think that was the name I heard right enough. Would it be Irene?"

"It might have been," I told him.

He began to slow the car down, gradually, peering out of the window in search of some landmark or other. Then abruptly he applied the brakes.

"We'll find out if I'm right. Soon now. Very soon now," he said.

I hesitated until he turned off the engine, then I hoisted myself out of the car. I was shivering, and yet perspiration had stuck my shirt to my back. The air was bitterly cold and the hedgerows and the arc of the fields beyond them very perfectly discernible, laden with thin snow set in ribbed patterns and dwindling furrows into the sky. The sky itself had a strangely luminous quality though there was no visible moon. The darkness, which had appeared so total and ultimate from the interior of the car receded, or at least diminished. Covering him with the pistol as adequately as I was able, I requested him to leave the car. I wasn't broken enough to disregard the loneliness of the place and desperation had not reduced my caution. That he would strike sooner or later, and strike for the death, I had no doubt at all. He clambered out of the car and stood facing me, one hand on the wing. He glanced down and patted the metal vigorously until it rang dully under his palm.

"Nice bit of machinery," he said affably. "Got a car m'self, y'know. Transport comes in very handy at times—y'know what I mean?"

"Where to?" I said.

"There's a path hereabouts," he replied, turning. "We take that."

"Walk ahead of me please," I said.

He twisted the collar of his coat high and pushed his gloves down over his fingers, then with a brief pause to collect his bearings he stepped on to the footpath at the side of the road and began walking along it away from the car. I kept on the opposite side of the road from him, and half a dozen paces behind him. The metal of the pistol ached against my naked fingers and I changed the weapon from hand to hand frequently.

We must have walked for fully two hundred yards before we reached the entrance to a narrow lane, of the kind that usually lead to farmhouses. He peered down it in an exaggerated fashion, lifting his hand to cover his eyes as if we walked in brilliant sunlight and not the night.

"This'll be it then," he said. "All ready."

"Walk in the centre of the road," I told him. "And I'll follow behind you."

"Bloody cold, i'n't it?" he said.

"Move," I said.

He started off suddenly, with enormous strides, his arms swinging. I had almost to trot to keep up with him. The silence was so utter, hemmed in by the frozen snow and the evening's fall of frost, that our footsteps had an explosive quality and even our breathing was not dissimilar to distant gunfire.

After perhaps fifteen minutes of fast walking, I heard the
steady trundling sound of water falling.

"Where are we?" I called to him.

"Coming down t'the river," he said, without stopping.

The lane which had run almost die-straight, began to dip
down now, in a long curve, and below me I could discern
through the black tracery of winter trees the deeper darkness
of the river in the glen. At some considerable distance on my
left a short row of street lights showed high enough to in-
dicate a viaduct. I rather thought we might be in the vicinity
of Pickering. My mouth and cheeks were drawn and wooden
with the cold and I had great difficulty in articulating properly when I called to him to slow down.

At the foot of the hill the lane debouched quite abruptly
on to the river bank, running directly out over the jet-black
water by means of a narrow single-span iron bridge. The con-
stant hollow tumbling of a waterfall was perfectly audible
now, rising up from downstream. As we crossed over the
single-span I could feel the vibration of the water transmitted
through the planking. At the nether end of the bridge Skinner
stopped, cupped his hands and blew into them, then with
vigour slapped his arms back and forth in the butcher-boy hug.

"You picked a hell of a bloody night for this caper," he
said with irritation.

"I didn't pick it," I said. "You did. Remember."

"Did I now," he said. He glanced at me. "Maybe I did.
Ay, maybe I did."

"Where is she?" I asked him.

"Down here," he said, jerking his thumb downstream.

I was five yards from him and I took the opportunity to
shift my attention for an instant. The bulk of the old building which appeared to hang out over the water was effectively
screened by a dense tangle of bushes. Only the few rigid lines
of its architecture which jutted beyond the ragged branches
told me that a building was there at all.

"In there?" I said.

"That's it, ol' man. The last resting place," he said. "What're y'goin' t'do now; blast me?"

"Take me in," I told him. "Show me."

"Ay, so y'want the works, d'you?" he said, sighing. "The whole bloody cabaret."

Without further prompting he padded down the tow-path towards the house. As we approached, I could see that it had been in service as a mill at one time, a paper-mill in actual fact. The brick façade was sugared with frost and the windows stared out of the white grime gauntly. A small undefined yard in front of it retained the paving stones and they too were smooth and white and slippery. Three steps led up to a door-less entrance. A fragile-looking catwalk, circled by a hand-rail, ran round the outside of the building meeting the steps at a shattered concrete platform. He walked over the paving and up the steps.

"The muff's in here," he said. "Comin'?"

I followed him into the building.

The place, in spite of the cold, smelled of filth and decay. I heard vermin scratching desperately in a prolonged escape as we entered. There was sufficient light from the window holes for me to watch Skinner moving surely but like a shadow, across the big room.

"Got a torch?" he asked.

"No."

"I'll strike a match: okay?" he said. "It's upstairs."

The flame bloomed yellow, showing me his face with the blood glistening on it and his teeth as he smiled. The wooden stairs went up close to the wall, the railings broken, hanging by twisted posts, in the darkest quarter of the building. He went up quickly, holding the match until it went out. I paused at the foot of the case until he struck another, then I climbed up towards him. He went on again in darkness, while I held back, listening to him and to the sound of his tread on the flooring above me. The faint spectral flicker of light against the wall on the level above me led me to the place. The message ground out in my brain said that he would attack me as I came abreast of him, so I crouched low into the darkness ready for him, but he had gone across the room, much smaller than the floor below, and was standing against the wall. The whole side of the place had crumbled away and the light, or at least the slight illumination, from the world outside shed itself through the broken wing with sufficient brightness for me to be able to see him well.

It looked like a wall, flat, blank, the bricks in regular arrangement. He stood by it, the fingers of his left hand spread, the tip only of each finger touching it. I stood quietly at the top of the staircase, watching him. He stared at the brickwork for some minutes, then, brushing the dust from his hands fastidiously, said, "She's in there, ol' man. Bricked up."

"I don't believe you," I said.

"True enough," he said. "Snug as a bug."

"No," I said.

"Look for yourself then," he said.

"No," I said. "You show me."

He shrugged, and said, "Okay: might take some time though. Took . . . my friend a good couple'f hours to fit'r in."

"Show me," I told him.

Carefully he began to remove bricks from the upper part of the wall. They had been fitted with considerable patience, but were nevertheless loose. As soon as he had taken away three or four, placing them quietly on the floor at his feet, the outline of the recess emerged, a chimney-place or a vent for machinery. He had not lied or deceived me. I realised that I was standing not ten feet from my girl. I realised that he was going to touch her again, without evidence of the slightest loathing, compunction or remorse. I realised it meant nothing to him at all. Nothing. I watched him easing out the bricks and piling them on the floor. I watched the wall vanish section by section until I caught the soft paleness within. He laid his forearm across the remaining structure at the height of his chest and reached through the wide slot he had already made. His hand found what it sought. He drew back again, jerked and stood aside. A shower of bricks crashed to the planking. I closed my eyes.

"There's your whorin' daughter, Pettigrew," he said.

The pale thing had fallen half out, lolling grotesquely forward, arms dangling, head and hair dangling too. Before I could move, he had taken a handful of its hair and drawn the head back, so that I could see its face. Its mouth hung open and the tongue lolled out, and the eyes stared directly at me. I saw that it was her. A tie was knotted round her throat, embedded in the skin.

I rushed at him, to wrest her from him. I think at the time I was afraid he was hurting her. It's very indistinct. I came running to her and he let her go. The remaining bricks collapsed across me as I caught at her. She toppled into my arms, her face touching mine, thrust into mine as in a kiss. My hands felt the bitter coldness of her bosom as I dragged her to me. I was screaming and crying, when Skinner struck me down.

I fell across the rubble, clutching my daughter, thrusting now. I realised at once what had happened. He had obviously intended to kill me with the brick, but some part of my girl's body had taken the brunt of the blow. The pain was above my ear, stinging me into a hideous rage. This whole sequence of events has no coherent meaning. It is all assumption, blurred, wiped together just as my emotions were indistinguishable, the terror from the hatred, the wrath from the sorrow, the urge to survive from the longing to die. By this time I'd dropped the pistol, and the next clear picture I have, as I fought my way to my knees again, is of the barrel of the gun thrust close to my face, and the sound of Skinner swearing obscenely and with a barely human ferocity. Then he tried to cudgel me with the pistol, but I took it on the arm. Then I was leaping towards the opening. Then he caught my arm and together we pitched backwards out of the room on to the catwalk. I think he was trying to find a grip on my throat, but I had my hands on his face, my fingers clawed deep into his eye-pits. Then he was gone for an instant, and I shouted to him to discover where he was, for to have him gone, the contact broken at that point, struck me as being more terrifying than anything else. The fist, or the brick, or it may have been the butt of my pistol smashed into my face, and everything receded, sucking away into emptiness. I had sufficient intelligence working secretly for me, even as I relinquished my hold on consciousness, to screw my body away. I picked out the impression of ease, the sensual joy of flight, the air cleaving between my spread fingers and flowing over my outstretched arms. Even after I struck the water I experienced no agony; not even the cold seemed capable of worming through to my senses. The current of the icy river, like the air itself, imparted only a magnificent sense of freedom. I kept my arms out and drank water and air, and blood from my broken nose, and hung poised between dying and living, while the strong pull of the current carried me with it. A period of total unconsciousness must have occurred on impact, for I don't recall having been under water at any time, nor do I recall the duration of the drift downstream, but it couldn't have been long or the weight of my clothing would have pulled me under to drown. When I opened my eyes I was lying on an oval of frozen mud. I knew enough to tell the water from the land. There was pain then, and sickness from the blood in my throat, and I could not breathe. But my body had taken over. I realised immediately that all I had to do was find someone. I had to keep going long enough to find someone. There was then, in sequence, the ebb and flow of agony as I got out of the mud and on to the snow. It was crisp and yielding with grasses bowed beneath it, and the harsh bark of tree roots under my hands. I may have crammed my head into the snow itself, deliberately, in the hope of clearing it, for I have the recollection of a short spell of lucidity in which I was actually walking upright like a man and the trees had fallen back from me. But however it happened I reached the steps at the foot of the viaduct where the woman and the man found me. I heard later that she was a prostitute of sorts, but when I finally met her, much later on, I found her very nice, and quite respectable. The man, and not unwisely, having phoned the police, just vanished into thin air. Perhaps he had a reputation to uphold.

14

Joseph

SHE SITS up in bed holding the blankets round her shoulders. I can just see her face and the white of her nightgown and no more in the pickle of light that sneaks through the curtains.

"Joseph," she says. "What is it?"

"The bastardin' bogies again," I says.

And she says, "Is Arnold in?"

I fetch a look up the street. It's not half the bogies: half a hundred of the bitches, with a fleet of cars like the bloody Eighth Army, lined up on both sides of the street. Wouldn't surprise me to hear the tear-gas bombs whistling through the windows.

"Is Arnold in, Joe?" she says again, at my ear now.

"How the hell should I know?" I says.

I try to stop her seeing out of the window, by dropping the curtain again. The linoleum's like walking on a frozen pond. I don't know whether to dress now, or not. The alarm clock says it's only half-two in the bloody morning. Them an' their bloody night-sweeps. I start to put on my cardigan, then my dressing-gown while they're pounding away at the downstairs door fit to bust. I sit on the warm bed to get on my stockings and slippers. No sense in me freezing to death. Then she comes back in.

She says, "He's not in his room. The bed's still made."

272

"That's fine," I says.

Rosemary comes in in her dressing-gown, the pink legs of her pyjamas showing below, above the slippers she got for Xmas.

"It's the police again," Nora says to her.

"Bastards," I says.

"You go back to your bed," Nora says to Rosemary.

Rosemary says, "Arnold's not in his room."

"I know," Nora says.

I say, "I know. I know. What's all this moanin' about Arno for?"

Nora grabs my arm as I start out on to the landing.

"Do you know where he is?"

"No, dammit, woman. I don't know where he is," I tells her.

I go down the stairs fast, before the bastards land up in the lobby in a shower of splinters. They must be about fifty strong, bobbies and dicks and pussies and all. And they've got enough paddy-wagons there to ride the whole street to jail in state. Send out the riot-squad, it's old Joe Skinner you're dealing with. Get him out his bed every damn' night, wear him down to a frazzle for the want o' sleep. That's the policy is it. Where the frig is Arno? What the devil's he been at now? What? A herd of blue animals come to tear the boy to bits as if he was a fox or a mad dog. The whole way: it'll be the whole way now.

"Well?" I says.

They're ranked up in twos. Booth and another one, Paige I reckon, knocking each other off the top step, then Muirhead and another one trying to see over the heads, then uniforms and the sergeant, right down to the gate. Donaldson hanging out his window over the way, bawling his tonsils to shreds, demanding to know what in Gawd's name all the racket's about.

Booth shoves me out the road, damn near slamming me through the hallstand, and him and a bobby's away upstairs before I can draw breath, while the rest come pouring over the stoup like rats before a hose. Nora and Rosemary crush against the banister, watching, big-eyed, like two weans, as if they'd never seen them glorious forces of law and order at their bloody ploys before.

"Wait a minute. Just hold your horses," I shout. "I want to see a warrant."

The fat sergeant moseys out of the living-room and says, "You'll see more than a warrant, Skinner, before you're done." My whole house is clattering and rampaging with them. I manage to slam the door. Booth comes downstairs again at a rattling trot and fetches up in front of me.

"Where is he, Joe?" he says.

"Who?"

"Your lovely boy," he says.

Paige stands behind him, the way they have, like they was cut out of two pieces of plywood and glued together. Paige says, "We've a warrant for him, Skinner. It's no good bitching about it."

I hear Nora sobbing as she comes downstairs, and the girl not far off it, saying, over and over again, "Oh, Mam, never mind, Mam. Oh, Mam. Oh, Mam, never mind."

"Are y'happy now?" I says. "Are y'bloody happy now? Upsettin' my wife."

Booth ignores me, turning, looking up past Paige, while Nora and Rose stop on the middle of the stairs and stare down the way at them. There's a uniform in the kitchen, clashing through the cupboards, and uniforms out the back too. I can hear the back door opening and closing. Booth says to Nora, "I'm sorry for this, Mrs. Skinner, but I've got to get Arnold."

"We don't know where he is," I shout. "And even if we did ..."

He puts his foot on the runner, "Can you tell us, Mrs. Skinner?" he says in his greasy voice.

"She can tell you nothin'. I'm the head of this house. If you've any questions, address them to me."

"Shut up, you," Paige says.

Booth's back is square to me now, and he goes up another couple of steps and puts his damn hand on my wife's arm, the bastard. I can just see his big black hunchy back and it's that I go for. Might, it's all them buggers know. Might, and scared women and girls in their own homes at night. I grab him round the neck with my arms, and by the Holy Jesus it feels good to have my hands on one of his kind. His big arse squinches under my knee when I haul him over. His hands go beating at the walls and knocks my pictures off, bringing them down on his head. When I start to lose my balance I fling him in front of me, and so I land on him at Paige's feet with an ouff that'll make sure he has sore guts for a week. This is Joe Skinner, you bastard.

I tell him, "Leave my family alone, you bastard." The hands close on my shoulders, pinning my arms, but I'll get a hack at his head before I'm through.

Somebody puts on the hall light just as they lift me off my feet and hold me out. I'm looking right into the bulb. What's the use of fighting them, they'll only get you in the long run anyhow. Booth though. I'd kick him to death, if I could get at him again. Twisting my arms and legs off, they are, enjoying it. Booth's head fills over the light bulb. I hears Muirhead saying, "Are you all right, Bob?" and Booth saying, while he stares down at me as if I was something he'd stepped on in a sewer, "I'll live."

"More's the friggin' pity," I says.

"What'll we do with him then?" one of the uniforms says.

Paige says, "Sling him in the wagon and take him down to Carsehorn."

Booth says, watching down at me all the time, "No, wait. Put him upstairs and leave a man with him. You."

They start to carry me upstairs between them, like a side
of beef. I just let go, limp. I hear Rose asking me, "Are you all
right, Da?" and I tells her I'm all right. The roof changes,
comes nearer, then they hoicks me to my feet and march me
into Arno's bedroom. The light goes on. One of the uniforms
waits behind, closing the door. He stands in front of the door
with his hands behind his back looking at me hard. I draw
myself together and tie the cord of my dressing-gown. The big
bugger keeps looking at me. I sit myself down on the bed. It's
cold up here.

"Can I light the fire?" I says.

He nods. I switch the switch and the heat starts along the
top bar, worming its way down 'til the three are alight. The
heat fans out at me. I'm shaking like a jelly and there's a big
piece of pain at the back of my head. There is hardly anything
in the room at all that would tell you Arno lived here. Just
his suit hanging up on its hanger on the outside of the cupboard door, and a stack of his paperbacks in a shoe-box beside
the dresser. Some of his ties on the rack and his cuff-links on
the Blackpool Tower ashtray on the mantel, and a hundred
box of fags.

"Can I have a fag, then?" I says.

The copper nods again, watching me all the time I take one
and light it off the bars. I'm sitting in his room, smoking his
cigarettes, and I don't know where he is even, or even where
they'll take him if they ever lay hands on him. This is more
than you bargain for: this. The whole way, maybe. But he's
a bright spark. They'll need to be up early to stick it on him,
connive among themselves as they like. There's no flies on
our Arno.

"What's it for then?" I says to the copper.

"What?" he says.

"What's the warrant for him for?" I says.

The copper says, "They'll have you for assaulting an
officer, I can tell you that."

"Never mind me," I says. "What do they think they have on the boy?"

He pulls in his chin, and brings his hands from behind his back, folding his arms, a big slow bear of a man.

"Murder," he says. "Can't do any harm t'tell you now."

"Who's he supposed to have done in?" I says, just for the sake of conversation.

"Quite a few," the copper says. "Quite a few."

"You'll never make it stick," I says. "You'll never make none of it stick."

"I reckon we will," he says. "Still, it'll be for a jury to decide."

"They'll never make it stick," I tells him again.

The whole way out, and the whole way back. Here I am sitting in his room, smoking his fags, and there's men downstairs come to take him away to hang. They'll never hang him. Arno won't let them hang him. I know Arno. He'll show them all yet who's the best of the bunch.

15

Rosemary

W E C A M E down together after a while, for neither of us could sleep. Mam lay beside me, her knees drawn up and her whole body huddled into a foetal position. She rocked herself slightly back and forth against the pillow, as if to comfort herself. I know that children deprived of affection do the same sort of thing, and monkeys too. But I was helpless. I could not tend to her properly either, because of him: thinking of him running and running; thinking when I shut my eyes tightly of his feet striking the cobbles in an alley, or crashing through the snow's smooth surface in some enormous field. It was the sort of nightmare from which I couldn't wake, or couldn't exchange for anything better than the thought of all the poor people involved with us. Three worlds were with me in the one room in the darkness. I couldn't stop them pressing on me and crushing me as under a tremendous sort of weight, and my Mam shaking beside me. I could do nothing for her, because of the other people involved with us. They seemed to stop me even putting my arm around her, my own mother. They seemed to be mad at her too, as if it was all her fault that he had ever been born to do what he did to them. A child too, like one of the children in my own class: just a wee girl, not even because he couldn't stop himself, because his sex is too strong for him, but because he wanted to. He does evil, spreads wickedness after him, acting against the teach-

ings of the Church. If he had followed the Church he might
have come all right, for there's deep-seated things in the
Church that can cure. My brother running and running away
from what he deserves, while I lie beside my Mam in my Da's
place running and running too. I heard my Mam say, "What'll
they do to him? What'll they do to him?" I turned my head
away from her and looked towards the window. They were
outside, waiting for him. If I could only have told him to go
away, not to come home ever again. But that's what the
trouble is now: he can't go anywhere without coming back
here. He can't fly away from them all, because it's not in him
to admit that he's ill. I don't know why he did it. Da knows.
Da knew why all along. And he realised before any of us,
when it was happening and what would be the outcome. He
had no occasion to be shocked when they came for Arno. He
made them take him away from us. We no longer had anything to say to him. It was my Da and my brother. He wanted
to be waiting for his son, not there at home but at the police
station at Carsehorn, as if he could only shout now, "Here
I am, because I knew too." I wanted so badly to pray, but
who would listen to a prayer for the soul of a man who had
struck down and robbed of life in lust. To shoot a child in
the face because he wanted to: not because he was afraid.
He had never been afraid in all his long life. I loved him when
I didn't know any better. I loved him, until I discovered,
until it was made known to me the hard way, that he wasn't
like the rest of us.

We came down together after a while.

I put on the kettle in the kitchen and went in to join Mam
in the living-room. She was seated by the embers of the fire
in the darkness, not rocking herself but sitting straight up
with her hands in her lap. It was not until I switched on the
lamp that I saw what she was staring at. He was lying in my
Da's chair, awake, watching. In his hand, laid against his
chest, was a bottle of wine from the cupboard. His face was

dirty and there was dried blood all down it. His clothes were torn and covered in mud and dirt. He didn't look like my brother at all.

"Do they know you're here, son?" Mam said.

Arnold tipped the wine bottle against his lips and shook his head. He sighed, then grinned at her.

"Nobody stops me coming home to see m'old Mam."

"What do you want, Arnold?" Mam asked him.

He struggled up from his lying position, grasping the bottle in two hands. He continued to smile all the time.

"What did I want? Now old yin what sort'f a question's that t'ask me, after me nickin' past half the bloody busies in Scotland t'get in."

"What is it you want, Arnold?" she repeated.

"Christ, what else d'I want but t'see you and Da and Sis here, before I scram."

"Da's been taken away," I said.

He nodded. "I thought they might pull that one."

"He hit one of the policemen," I said.

"Break his bloody back, I hope," my brother said.

"You're all dirty," Mam said.

"Yeah, well, you know, I had t'do a bit of skulkin'."

"Tell me the truth, son," Mam said.

"My God, Mam, I'm tellin' you the truth."

We spoke low, while outside the policemen waited. I wondered if they knew he was here. I wonder if they had compassion for us. Arnold hadn't any doubts about that at all. It was all very simple for him. He had invented such a web of lies and deceptions that he thrived on them now. He must have welcomed the simplicity of it all.

"They're here for you, y'know," Mam said.

"You're tellin' me," Arnold said. "They've got it in bad for me. But I'm not worried. There's time yet awhile. When I'm ready, that'll be time enough."

He drank more of the wine. The room, cold, was full of the sharp sweet smell of the stuff. He was almost too tired to hold the mouth of the bottle to his lips and some of the liquid had spilled on his clothes. There was the sour stench of sweat off him too.

"Tell me the truth, Arnold, just this once," Mam said.

"Ach, give me peace," he said. "You never believe it when I tell you the bloody truth, so why should you believe me now. It's a bit late in the day."

"Did you ... kill them people?" Mam said. She hadn't moved. Not even her hands in her lap moved.

"What people?" Arnold asked. He sank back in the chair again, drinking.

"Those girls, and those old women in the shop and ..."

"Whoa now, Nora," he said. "D'you think I did?"

"I'm not sure," Mam said. "I want you t'tell me, Arno."

"Well, the busies think I did, an' that's all that matters now."

"Where were you tonight?" I said.

"Hiding out," he said. "What d'you want me t'do? Chuck m'hand in?"

"Yes," I said.

"T'hell with that," he said. "Booth'll make bloody sure I never sniff a fair trial. I'm goin' out the way I come, an' I'll be out of this friggin' country before tomorrow night. I've got friends, y'know. I've got friends that'll stand by me in m'time of need. I thought ..."

"You thought we would," I said.

"Not you, y'stuck-up bitch," he said. "You're just worried about yourself. You don't give a monkey if your brother gets planted or not. I've met dames like you before now, and they made me sick. Sick."

"What happened to you tonight?" I said.

"If y'must know," he said "I got chased by a man."

Mam put her hand to her mouth quickly as if to stop herself speaking. Arnold was too far gone to notice anything. He was alone then in the only place in the world he had never been alone before in his life.

"A damn' nut. He thought it was me, just like Booth and the bogies. This bastard thought it was me. But I changed his mind for him."

"Did you kill him too?" I said. "Did you kill him too just as you killed that wee girl and those others?"

"Now hold on you," Arnold said. "Even if you are my bloody sister I'm not standin' any snash from you."

"It doesn't matter now," Mam said. "They've taken your father away."

"He'll be all right. They've nothin' much on him. Any decent springer'll get him out."

"Is that all that counts, son?" Mam said, "Gettin' away?"

"That's life, i'n't it, after all," he said. "Who made the rules. Them. They made the rules. I don't like rules. I never did. You know that fine."

"Rules," Mam said. "Y'can't expect the rules to work now."

"That's right," he said. "Rules is gone by the board."

"Why didn't you just run away tonight," I said. "What did you come back here for at all?"

"I told you . . ." he said, then, he stopped, rubbing his face with his hand. "I don't know why, Christ. I don't know why."

"Arnold," Mam said. She got to her feet, big and heavy inside the white nightgown. "Give me a drink of that stuff."

"What?" he said. Mam nodded at the bottle in his hand.

"To keep the awful cold out," she said, half-smiling at him, soft-voiced.

He reached up and put the wine bottle in her hand. She touched the top to her mouth and drank like a man, holding her head back, then she took the bottle away from her mouth and with all her might hurled it through the window-pane into the garden.

16

Muirhead

SHE TOUCHED her mouth where the cheap wine and the vomit had mingled and coursed down her cheeks to stain the yolk collar of her nightgown. All my hatred was refuted in the moment of that act, by the way in which she touched her lips as if suggesting silence, a loving and reverent silence. She drew her hand down, still not watching any of us but him, while Booth's voice, warm and muscular in its enthusiasm, told him his rights as a citizen. Then I suddenly ceased to be affected by any of it: the moment of triumph or of truth. I lost it. It slipped away from me when I looked at the woman, and at the girl and at Booth. And even Skinner with his mouth twitching back from his teeth. Even Skinner; because I still retained the image of him as he had been when we burst into the house—his body cradled in the big woman's arms and his face contorted with an anguish that had no roots in anything we knew of him. He held the woman to him and her fat white hand rose and fell softly over his head, to soothe and comfort him. And even after when he twisted away from her, renouncing her to our faces, he could only curse us— blithely, not even doing us the honour of steeling himself to bravado, or of needing a vestige of will-power to gain again the rock-hard conviction of his own inviolability. Truly he believes we still can't harm him.

284

I'm too old to disassociate myself from this, to cover up as well as Booth or Paige or Strachan can. Even McAlister there has the self-satisfied demeanour of the vindicated to protect him. And I can't. I really can't. The flesh of my arm crawls as Skinner's cuff brushes my wrist. He is sitting forward, his elbows on his knees. I don't look at him—imperturbability comes easy on the outside. I'm trying not to remember any of it, the women, or the child, or Pettigrew's face. Christ, to complete the irony, this will be my final accolade. The Skinner Case. The woman touched her lips as if the wine burned. . . .

His eyes watch flickering as the first light begins to come up behind the trees to the east, over Holmhill. We pass places of mutual interest: places he knows well, places I know well —a lane's end, the ridge of firs at the angle of the estate, a dense growth of evergreen swallowing the fine stone gate-posts at the church: the pubs and the shops and the houses. Houses full of people who will soon all know his name, and my name too perhaps, but who will only remember him. People lying hidden in warm beds behind those many windows, husbands and wives together limb to limb, children in cots in quiet dark rooms under the night-watch of battered dolls and teddy-bears. Clean people whom neither of us will never know exist. He stares at it all going past, his head raised now, shoulders coming back, his eyes dark and full of hunger as we prowl on steadily into the town.

Everything sinks slowly down into the half-light and cold early-morning silence. Everything numb and frozen, like the guts of a decrepit, frightened old man. An old man, I am, on the way out. Left to trail all this as my last uncherishable fragment of glory. He stirs again beside me. In a little while he'll talk, cooking his perverted lies in braggart and evasion, spinning out over the months through all due process of law his foul defeat, reducing it at last, in time, to an arid pattern of ritual justice. Squirming, snapping at life, his mouth and throat working on the words, masking his hate, up to the very

instant when the judge pronounces doom. Right to the instant
in which the hood blinds him and chokes him and shuts off
his voice.

I see the angle of his face with the light on it now, and I
feel him shift his weight against me, thigh to thigh. Touching me with his elbow, he says, "Hey, Mister Muirhead."

"What?"

"Y'wouldn't happen t'have a smoke, would you?" he says.

Right to the moment when the boards tilt and shoot him
into total darkness, some part of him too will go on snapping and squirming for life. Jesus Christ: perhaps like Booth
and every other man, I only long to pull the lever of the trap
myself.

"Here," I say, and give him the bloody cigarette.

NEIL GUNN 1891 – 1973
THE SCOTTISH COLLECTION

THE LOST CHART
A cold war thriller set in the Scottish city of Glasgow shortly after the Second World War, '*the Lost Chart*' moves on two distinct planes — the physical and the metaphysical.

THE LOST GLEN
The famous novel on the decline of Highland ways and values in the 1920s.

THE OTHER LANDSCAPE
'*The Other Landscape*' returns to the familiar setting of the Highlands but with a new element of dark humour.

THE SILVER BOUGH
Archaeologist Simon Grant comes to the Highlands to investigate an ancient cairn. A stranger in a strange part of the country, he finds that there are barriers to understanding between him and the people of the community.

SECOND SIGHT
The setting is a Highland shooting lodge, whose occupants are depicted in stark contrast to the local people. A violent death is foreseen. But whose? How? When? The drama is played out against a background of strange mists and elemental landscapes.

OFF IN A BOAT
'*Off in a Boat*' logs the adventures of a man, who at a critical point of his life, throws caution to the wind, and with his wife as Crew, navigates his way round the West Coast of Scotland.
Whilst Gunn masters the art of sailing and anchorage, the Crew explores the possibilities of the camera.

Other titles in the SCOTTISH COLLECTION

THE BRAVE WHITE FLAG *James Allan Ford*

THE LAST SUMMER *Iain Crichton Smith*

THE SCOTTISH COLLECTION OF VERSE
VOL 1 to 1800 *Ed Eileen Dunlop & Antony Kamm*

THE FIRST HUNDRED THOUSAND *Ian Hay*

DUST ON THE PAW *Robin Jenkins*

THE MERRY MUSE *Eric Linklater*

MAGNUS *George Mackay Brown*

THE BULL CALVES *Naomi Mitchison*

EARLY IN ORCADIA *Naomi Mitchison*

THE CHINA RUN *Neil Paterson*

WHERE THE SEA BREAKS *John Prebble*

A GREEN TREE IN GEDDE *Alan Sharp*

TIME WILL KNIT *Fred Urquhart*

WALK DON'T WALK *Gordon Williams*

SCOTTISH BIOGRAPHIES

BURRELL: PORTRAIT OF A COLLECTOR *Richard Marks*

AS IT WAS (Autobiography) *Naomi Mitchison*